Ravens

by

T S James & Martin D Smith

Copyright © 2024 T S James

ISBN: 978-1-917425-45-2

All rights reserved, including the right to reproduce this book, or portions thereof in any form. No part of this text may be reproduced, transmitted, downloaded, decompiled, reverse engineered, or stored, in any form or introduced into any information storage and retrieval system, in any form or by any means, whether electronic or mechanical without the express written permission of the author.

Acknowledgements

First and foremost, we wish to extend our deepest gratitude to our endlessly supportive wives, Linda & Jo. Your unwavering encouragement and love have been our inspiration throughout this journey. Your enthusiasm as both our foremost advocates and most astute critics has been indispensable.

Martin AKA 'Red Pen.' Your help in this, our first collaboration has been invaluable and has helped shape this book enormously.

Additionally, I must express my sincere appreciation to Publish Nation. Their expertise and help in bringing this book to fruition, has been a thoroughly enjoyable experience.

Other books available:

Shamera - (Gold Award) 1st book in the Trilogy
A Christmas to Remember
Confessions of a Male Nurse

Prologue

One year ago, my reality shattered.

I'm a journalist who once believed in the sanctity of evidence and the clarity of reason. My life was anchored in facts and scepticism, my mind a fortress against the inexplicable. But everything changed when tragedy struck close to home. My sister's death caused my mother immense grief. It was so deep that she turned to numerous people who claimed be able to connect the living and the dead for comfort. The result was her being swindled by countless frauds who exploited her pain, draining her finances and giving nothing in return. All I could do was watch her struggle against the tide of deceit. I was helpless to break the situation she was in, and it ignited a fierce resolve in me. I now spend my free time uncovering the truth about these so-called mediums, exposing charlatans who prey on the vulnerable.

One day I received an unusual request. A local group of ghost hunters had the idea that my sceptical approach would lend weight to their claims. They asked me to join them in their investigation into the rumours of strange happenings at Ravenswood Asylum. This decrepit building, long abandoned and steeped in grim legends, was said to be a nexus of eerie occurrences. Curiosity drove my desire to expose their fabrications, which drove me to accept their invitation. Armed with my critical mind and a notebook, I ventured with them into the heart of the unknown.

Ravenswood Asylum stood as a monument to decay and despair. Its rotting walls and forsaken halls held remnants of a past mired in suffering, places where light had long ceased to penetrate. As the ghost hunters started their investigation little did they know that something had been awakened, something beyond their comprehension, a force that fed on fear and sadness. With each step I took into the asylum's darkness, distinguishing reality from nightmare became more difficult. What started as another opportunity for me to debunk ghost stories rapidly transformed into a harrowing battle for survival. I faced horrors that defied logic, where the difference between the living and the dead became alarmingly unclear. In those grim corridors, where every shadow seemed to writhe with hidden menace, the challenge was no longer about proving or disproving myths. It was a fight against an ancient evil, a force that seemed determined to consume us all. Each moment drew me closer to the edge of my sanity as the cost of escaping the asylum grew ever higher. Would I emerge from Ravenswood Asylum with my sanity intact, or would I fall prey to the darkness that waited inside? This is the story of my descent into the unimaginable, a journey that tested my limits of disbelief and plunged me into the heart of terror.

Chapter 1

Prepare yourself for an extraordinary journey that began one year ago today. A tale of both scepticism and belief that combined science and the supernatural. My journey into the heart of Ravenswood Asylum challenged everything I thought I knew and has left me forever changed.

My name is Steve, a journalist by trade and a cynic by heart. My scepticism wasn't rooted in ignorance but forged from my rather practical mind that sought to find physical evidence rather than relying on hearsay and out-of-focus photographs. Following the death of my sister, my mother was conned out of many thousands of pounds trying to contact her in the afterlife. That experience drove me to spend every spare moment since then debunking ghostly happenings and exposing charlatans posing as mediums. This solidified my belief in the tangible, observable world we all inhabit. However, my latest investigation was about to challenge everything I thought I knew. Curiosity, mingled with my innate scepticism, led me to accept an invitation from a local ghost-hunting team. They believed my viewpoint would lend credibility to one of their investigations. It made me the ideal candidate to join them and observe everything that happens in their exploration of the Ravenswood Asylum for the Clinically Insane.

As we approached the asylum, the crunch of gravel underneath our wheels seemed to add to the eeriness of the decrepit building before us. We parked under a large, gnarled tree. Its branches stretched out over us like a giant skeletal hand, casting elongated shadows which danced eerily in the moonlight. Climbing out of our vehicles, a sense of unease ran through us as we stood looking up at the Asylum. The clouds parted revealing a moon which hung like a ghostly lantern in the night sky. The foreboding structure of Ravenswood Asylum loomed from the darkness, its silhouette etched with a history of horror. As the wind howled, a sinister rustling amongst the trees whispered tales of the madness once confined within these crumbling walls.

And so, there I was a sceptic among believers, poised to enter the halls of the notorious asylum. The building, shrouded in a history filled with darkness and despair, stood before us as a testament to the suffering endured by its former inhabitants. Stories told of strange happenings within its walls, souls condemned, trapped, and unable to find peace in the afterlife.

As the evening's darkness crept in around us, we circled the old asylum. The silence in the grounds was punctuated only by an owl hooting somewhere close by. Making our way around the decrepit building, attempting to acquaint ourselves with its oppressive aura, I felt an undeniable sense of dread crawl over me, goosebumps appearing on my skin despite any rational explanations.

The asylum now silhouetted against the dusky sky, a monolith of despair. Its crumbling brickwork and ivy-entwined walls seemed to pulsate with an eerie life of their own. Every instinct screamed at me to flee, yet I was rooted, captivated by the dark allure of the building which once contained the tormented minds and bodies of the clinically insane. I can't explain why this feeling came over me. Ghosts don't exist. We approached the dilapidated structure, the moon, casting a haunting glow on the building's facade, its broken windows like empty eye sockets staring back at us.

"You ready for this, Steve?" asked Mark, the team's leader. A man whose belief in the paranormal was as unwavering as my own disbelief.

"I suppose," I replied, my voice unexpectedly betraying a hint of apprehension. It wasn't fear of ghosts that unsettled me, but the thought of what human minds could conjure in the absence of light and reason.

Approaching the heavy wooden front door, Fiona placed a trembling hand on it and pushed, it opened, its rusty hinges groaning in protest, a corridor swallowed by shadows lay ahead. We flicked on our torches; the beams slicing through the darkness as a sudden gust of wind blew through the decrepit doorway. Dust danced in the air, hitting our lungs and forcing us to cough as we squinted through the haze. The scent of decay and mould clung to everything, a testament to many, many years of neglect.

As we crossed the threshold, the air felt colder. The shift in temperature seems to whisper of the unseen. Our footsteps echoed through the deserted corridors, a haunting drumbeat playing on my nerves. "The energy here is overwhelming," Fiona, the team's medium, muttered, her voice trembling slightly. "They're aware of our presence."

I wanted to dismiss her words, to rely on the logical explanations which always grounded me. Yet, as we delved deeper into the asylum, my belief was challenged by shadows which seemed to move of their own accord, and unexplained noises filling the empty spaces with dread.

Venturing further inside, the air grew even colder; the beam of our torches danced across peeling paint and discarded furniture, left from a bygone era.

"This place is a goldmine of activity," intimated Fiona, her voice barely above a breath. "The spirits here seem restless tonight."

I rolled my eyes in the darkness, it made no sense but I couldn't shake the feeling that something unseen was watching, waiting, its stare intensely fixed on my every action. With each reluctant step I took, a cold shiver ran down my spine as if I was crossing a line into the realm of the unknown. The air was stale and the building itself seemed to pulse with a life of its own, a life wrought from many years of anguish and despair. As we delved deeper, the darkness seemed to be absorbing everything from our torch beams to our very essences.

What secrets did this place hold?

As the door creaked shut behind us, it felt as though our fate was being sealed. It then occurred to me the night had only just begun, and my scepticism was about to be tested by those silhouettes dancing just beyond the reach of our torches.

Stepping cautiously into the dim corridor, our senses were amplified, ears straining for noises that sounded like voices of the past, eyes darting to catch every fleeting shadow. We made our way to the Nurses station, where Tom pointed to the spot where a teenage girl's life tragically ended. "This is where they found her body," he announced, his voice carrying a gravity chilling me to the bone. "Some say it was misadventure; others say murder."

The surrounding air seemed thick as if it had absorbed the sorrow and madness that had once lived within these walls. Despite my scepticism, I couldn't deny the eerie mood which hung over us, a feeling of being watched, of whispers just beyond the edge of our hearing. The night stretched out before us, filled with the threat of unseen horrors and unexplained phenomena.

Fiona's gaze fixated on the upper floor balcony, her voice trembling slightly in the vast space of the asylum. "Do any of you see that?" she said in a hushed tone, pointing upwards, her finger trembling. "It's a face." Her eyes widened with excitement as she stared at the apparition none of us could see. "It looked like a pale woman in white was staring at me," she murmured.

My heart settled when Fiona finally turned away, dismissing the vision as a trick of the light. She'd been looking into a reflection in another room's mirror, which explained why the rest of us hadn't seen anything. A collective sigh of relief brushed through us all. We continued our cautious exploration, examining each darkened corner and hidden crevice before advancing further into the asylum's depths.

Tom and his crew had been granted exclusive access to explore the mysterious, and reputedly haunted corridors of the asylum.

Curiosity piqued, I asked Tom, "What drew you to this place? What's the story here?"

Tom's face was a mask of serious contemplation as he recounted tales as chilling as the very air around us.

"Strange occurrences, inexplicable events," he began. "Doors slamming shut, footsteps echoing in empty halls, faces glimpsed momentarily, then vanishing. People have even claimed a sense of being followed by an unseen presence, hearing ghostly voices murmuring either, 'help!' or 'get out!'."

I shook my head, a wry smile of scepticism on my face. "Surely that's just someone's overactive imagination at play?"

Tom nodded. "Perhaps, but hopefully tonight might change your mind. Now, let's get set up, shall we?" he urged.

Fiona and Tom sprang into action, positioning cameras and sensors throughout the building. They were methodical, each move calculated and precise. Their equipment was state-of-the-art, designed to detect even the faintest anomalies. Despite my scepticism, I found myself drawn into their world. My curiosity increased by the prospect of uncovering something truly inexplicable.

As the night unfolded, a sense of expectancy hung in the air. Fiona and Tom, both seasoned in their field, moved with a quiet confidence. They reported witnessing unexplainable events which fuelled their determination to find the truth.

"Fiona, how did you find yourself in the field of ghost hunting?" I asked, as we waited for something to happen.

She recounted the tale of their beginnings, a call from a desperate couple plagued by what they believed to be spirits. "We spent two nights in their home but found nothing," Fiona said, a touch of regret in her voice. "Not every investigation yields results, but we keep searching."

Tom joined us, his presence solid and reassuring. "Stay vigilant tonight," he advised. "You may be a sceptic now, but who knows? By morning, you might just be a believer."

As Fiona set up a REM POD on the Nurses station, my curiosity got the better of me. "What does that do?" I asked, my voice betraying a hint of genuine interest.

Fiona calmly explained,

"The REM POD's antenna detects energy disturbances in the electrical field which trigger it to alert us to possible contact with spirits. It signals any contact with flashing lights and an audible alarm. Any entity or object with its electromagnetic field can cause a disruption which would be detected by the REM POD. We theorise the energy lingering after death is akin to the energy we possess while alive. To set it off manually, you must come very close to the aerial or touch it, thus disrupting the electromagnetic field. Walking around or waving your hand near it won't activate the alarm."

Fiona demonstrated by gracefully waving her hand close to the aerial and banging the top of the desk. No lights flashed; no alarm sounded. I mimicked her action, attempting to trigger the alarm, I did indeed need to physically touch it which then caused the lights to erupt in a dance of colours, and the alarm to sound.

She offered a knowing smile before continuing. "To avoid accidentally setting off the REM POD, we need to be mindful of our mobile phones and walkie-talkies. These devices can trigger it too. This is one of the favoured tools among paranormal investigators, it can be placed in a separate area from the investigators. The REM POD then alerts them with an audio signal when it has been activated. This allows the investigators to take readings elsewhere in the building without needing to be physically present in the same room as the device."

Mark and Janet, two other members of the ghost-hunting team, headed back to the van, which was to act as their command centre. There were cameras and recording equipment in there enabling them to watch us closely and alert us to things we might have missed. Fiona, Tom and I, along with Carl, another of the teams mediums, remained to begin the hunt for the supernatural. An eager anticipation bubbled inside me as I watched Tom extract more equipment from a large silver case.

"What's first on the agenda?" I inquired.

"We're starting with EVP recorders, Electronic Voice Phenomena. These are unexplained voices captured on our audio recording devices," Tom replied, his voice steady and reassuring.

"But couldn't the recorders just be picking up interference from local radio bands or static?" I queried, my scepticism peeking through.

"That's always a possibility," Tom conceded. "However, we meticulously analyse each recording to eliminate such interference. When we pose questions, we hope to receive intelligent, complex responses. Sometimes the answers we receive are so precise, they can only be attributed to spirits intelligently answering back."

Before proceeding further, I felt the need to clarify my position. "I must apologise for any of my questions which might seem sceptical or dismissive. Please understand, it's not my intention to offend or disrespect. As a sceptic, I can only trust what I witness first-hand and, in that way, conclude it was not being faked."

Tom's response came with a warm, reassuring smile. "That's absolutely fine. We're used to such inquiries from non-believers. It's your prerogative to question our findings, and it's our objective to hopefully provide you with incontrovertible evidence. Rest assured, nothing here has been, or will be, manipulated. Every sound, motion, and occurrence are being documented in the command centre. Besides Janet and Mark, who are outside, we're alone here. Carl will later attempt to demonstrate his ability to communicate with the spirits." Tom's assurance was a testament to the seriousness and dedication with which they approached their craft, setting the stage for a night of exploration.

"Alright, I'm prepared whenever you are," I said, my voice uncontrollably laced with tension.

Tom activated the voice recorder and positioned it carefully on the tabletop. "Is there anyone here who wishes to communicate with us tonight?" he inquired, his voice steady in the enveloping silence, "Can you tell us why you remain here?" After a moment's pause, he switched off the recorder and played back the audio. We leaned in as one, a collective breath held, only to be greeted by the disappointing crackle of static.

Undeterred, Tom repeated the two questions, his voice resonating in the darkness. Again, the response was nothing but the eerie hiss of static.

Carl, with his eyes closed and head tilted, whispered, "I'm sensing nothing in this area. Perhaps we should venture to the first floor."

"Why the first floor?" I asked, my interest rising.

"People have reported hearing unexplained voices there. Some have even said they have experienced being forcefully pushed against the walls," Carl explained.

We reached the staircase, its form looming ominously from the gloom. Step by step, we ascended, our senses heightened, straining to catch any sound or movement. Reaching the top, Fiona grasped Carl's arm.

"Look, down the corridor," she said urgently, pointing towards a room on the right, "I just saw a shadow figure slip into that room."

Fuelled by her observation, we hastened down the corridor, our night vision cameras scanning the darkness. As we neared the room, the door abruptly slammed shut, stopping me in my tracks, my heart started racing wildly. Disbelief etched on my face, as I watched Tom courageously open the door. I approached and peered in. "Who's in here?" I asked, my voice echoing in the quiet room.

I entered the room, my gaze darting around, searching for any hint of a crew member or an explanation. Our torches cut through the gloom, revealing a room cluttered with debris and decay. The walls were stripped bare, the damp had claimed the old paint. There was no place for anyone to hide, no alternative exits. The windows were barred and sealed shut; the wind was not the culprit here. How had the door slammed?

Carl stepped into the centre of the room, his expression grave. "There is an angry presence here," he announced, scanning the space as if seeing beyond the visible. "It doesn't want us here."

Fiona, ever the professional, took out her own voice recorder. "Is anyone here with us? ... Do you wish for us to leave?" The air turned frigid, the temperature dropping rapidly.

Fiona played back the recording. Her voice echoed eerily in the room, a disruption in the dark void. "Is anyone else here with us?" She replayed the segment, our anticipation palpable. Suddenly, a hoarse, raspy affirmation broke through the static, 'YES!' It was unmistakable. She replayed it, and again the same 'YES!' resonated.

Fiona was unable to conceal her excitement. "This is amazing. We've never had responses this quick or this clear before."

But my scepticism, as always, planted a seed of doubt in my mind. Could this have been pre-recorded? I needed to be sure.

"May I try?" I asked, the rational part of me seeking to debunk any trickery. "It would help eliminate the possibility of any pre-recorded responses." My suggestion was met with nods of agreement as we all stood enveloped in the chilling mystery of the room, each of us pondering the reality of what we might be facing.

"Here, have a go," Fiona offered, her voice tinged with a hint of mystery. "Press here to record and here to stop."

"Thank you." I took the recorder with a slight tremor in my hands, mustering as much courage as I could, I attempted to stop my voice wavering and spoke into the device. "Is there anyone in this room who does not want us here?" I paused, allowing the silence to fill the space before stopping the recording and handing it back to Fiona.

We huddled together, listening intently to the playback. My voice echoed in the room, "Is there anyone in this room who does not want us here?" Then, amidst the hiss of static, a loud, raspy voice shattered the silence, 'GET OUT!' A chill coursed through my body, goosebumps erupting along my neck and arms. At that same moment, the door slammed shut behind us with an ominous thud.

"Whoa! What the..." I rushed to the door, and straight away my palms became slick with sweat. Grabbing the handle, I tugged desperately at the door, only to find it immovable. Tom joined me, his attempts equally futile. A strange, muffled cry echoed from the other side, causing us to recoil. The door shook violently in its frame, its creaks resonating through the room like a scene from a gothic horror movie.

Carls' voice broke the eerie stillness, "She killed herself. She hung herself in this room. I don't know who she was but I can feel her presence."

As abruptly as it began, the rattling of the door stopped. Tom cautiously opened the door revealing a silent, empty corridor.

My heart pounded against my ribcage. "Incredible! How on earth did you orchestrate this? That was impressive. You certainly had me going there." I gasped, half in disbelief, half in awe.

Tom's face was ashen, his eyes wide with genuine shock. "I swear... we didn't stage any of this. It's all real."

He grabbed his walkie-talkie. "Tom to command centre... anything on the first-floor cameras? We're heading back. We need to examine any recordings."

We regrouped at the command centre where Mark and Janet had been reviewing the footage. They played back the moment the door slammed; the sound echoing through the speakers. The video showed us heading towards the room, and a short time later a dark silhouette fleeting across the screen just before the door slammed shut for the second time. No one seemed to tamper with the door as the corridor appeared deserted.

My gaze fixated on the screen. "You mean this actually happened? It's a genuine supernatural event?"

Excitement rippled through Fiona, Tom, and Carl as they pored over the footage again, searching for any discrepancies. They turned to each other, all slapping high fives with shouts of "Yes!"

Tom turned to me. "So, what do you think now?"

I hesitated, my scepticism at war with what I just witnessed. "I'm... I'm not sure how you did that. But it was certainly impressive."

Tom's smile was confident, reassuring. "You really are a sceptic. I promise you; we didn't fabricate this."

"And the voice?" I asked.

"That wasn't us, either," Fiona affirmed, her face beaming with delight.

As I watched, Carl became captivated by the audio, his attention fixated on the headphones, his eyes widened. "Whoa! Everyone, listen to this."

He passed the headphones to Tom. "Check this out, mate."

I stood there, a part of me still rationalising the recent events, while another part of me was teetering on the brink of belief. The night was still young and already the asylum was unveiling its haunting secrets. What else lay in wait in those shadowed halls and desolate rooms? Only the night would tell.

Tom settled the headphones over his ears and nodded excitedly. He heard sounds, disembodied sounds, coming from the corridor, particularly a soft voice which happened right before the doors started rattling violently. As the clip concluded, he turned to me with an urgency knitting his brow. "Steve, listen to this."

I took the headphones, and closed my eyes, immersing myself in the auditory world of the spectral recording. Moments later, my eyes flew open, a look of disbelief etching my features. Not fully comprehending what I was listening to, I passed the headphones to Fiona.

"Did you hear that?" Tom's tense whisper cutting through the atmosphere.

I nodded, my voice barely audible. "It was like a voice pleading, 'Let me in.'"

Tom's excitement was infectious. "It's genuine, I promise you."

Janet, her curiosity piqued, fished her mobile out of her pocket to check the time. "It's still early. Let's continue. We can't stop now. This place has to be the best place we have ever researched. There's got to be so much more for us to uncover. This could put us up there with the best."

Despite my initial scepticism, I couldn't deny the unexplained phenomena we'd encountered. My logical mind was battling with what my eyes and ears had just witnessed. This cannot be real. I had to figure out how they, or someone else, was manipulating the situation. Carl, however, leaned back, a grin spreading across his face, relishing the thrill of the hunt which drove his passion for the paranormal.

"Right, everyone, you heard Janet, let's get back to it," Tom declared, stepping out of the van. "We've got more evidence to gather."

Back in the building, the aged floorboards groaning under our feet, we could hear what sounded like their mournful cries echoing like forlorn wails of the long departed, woven into the very fabric of the asylums' abandoned halls. It was as if it was mocking our mortal fears with subdued, ethereal laughter.

Fiona halted abruptly; her posture tensed. I sensed her apprehension, imagining she'd glimpsed something sinister lurking in the dark. The group gathered closer, peering into the darkness where Fiona was pointing. It was a rat, scuttling across the room from out of the shadows, prompting a wave of relieved laughter.

The group settled into the next phase of their investigation, their equipment at the ready to receive any ghostly signals.

"Let's try the spirit box next," Fiona suggested, as we made our way upstairs.

Tom nodded, his determination to uncover the supernatural was evident. Meanwhile, I was still grappling with my scepticism. "What exactly is a spirit box?" I asked.

Tom explained, "It's a device used to communicate with spirits.

"When you communicate with a spirit, they can't articulate like a living person," Tom explained. "Spirits use the energy of various radio frequencies to make their presence known. The Spirit Box scans through AM and FM channels, attempting to capture any spectral voices."

As the spirit box crackled to life, scanning through frequencies, we listened intently, waiting for a voice from the other side to break through the static. Anticipation charged the air as each member of the team was poised on the edge of discovery, collectively holding their breath in suspense.

"So there's a chance we're just picking up a local radio station's broadcast, then?" I interjected, my scepticism rising again.

Tom shook his head, a hint of a smile playing on his lips. "Not exactly. The theory that spirits can use radio waves to communicate, though not entirely proven, is widely accepted among investigators. The Spirit Box is programmed to cycle rapidly through the frequencies. This reduces the likelihood of coincidental broadcast voices. If we hear a consistent voice across multiple channels, it's a strong indication of a spiritual presence."

"Hmm, I remain unconvinced. Any device capable of receiving external signals is subject to misinterpretation." I argued, my arms crossed, subconsciously taking a defensive stance.

"We're meticulous in our approach," Tom assured. "We carefully examine and filter all pieces of evidence, and just like you, we don't accept things at face value. Although, I admit we do get excited when things happen, a lot of our evidence we debunk when we sit and examine it properly."

The spirit box unleashed a torrent of hissing white noise into the room. Fiona and Tom took turns asking questions. Occasionally, a fragmented sound, possibly a word, pierced through the static. usually incoherent utterances. Carl's gaze intensified as he looked down the corridor. "There's a strong entity here, lurking just out of sight. Keep the questions going, let's see if we can get it to engage with us," he urged.

"Fine, I'll give it a go. What is my name?" I asked, a tremor in my voice betraying my apprehension.

My heart stalled as a distinctly masculine voice replied, "Steve." It was as clear as day. I continued, feeling an odd sense of connection. "What is your name?"

Silence followed, so I repeated, "What is your name?"

This time, a faint, childlike voice whispered, 'Susan.'

Surprised at hearing a child's voice, I asked, "How old are you, Susan?"

"Eight," replied the voice instantly.

Carl nodded at me encouragingly. "Carry on." His hands waving, motivating me to continue.

My face contorted with thought as I asked, "Why are you here?"

A soft, forlorn voice answered, "Afraid."

"What are you afraid of?" I pressed.

"Him," came the cryptic response.

Tom was visibly animated. "Fantastic, keep it up."

"Who frightens you? Does he have a name?" My voice shook slightly as I posed the question. The room was tense with anticipation, the spirit box humming with static. The voice had disappeared.

"Are you convinced yet?" Fiona inquired. A twinkle of excitement in her eyes.

I hesitated. "It is an intriguing experience, sure, but these voices could be interference or external influences on the equipment."

"I assure you; we don't manipulate anything. What we're all hearing is as authentic as it gets," Tom said earnestly, still trying to convince me.

"I wasn't accusing you," I clarified. "I'm just wary of the technology's vulnerabilities."

Fiona nodded understandingly. "That's fair."

"This is an entirely new experience for me. I admitted. What about all of you?"

"We've had our share of encounters," Fiona replied. "But every investigation is unique. This one, so far, is the best we have ever had. Intelligent answers to our questions. Doors slamming shut in our presence. It's fantastic."

Tom looked at me. His face betrayed an ominous thought. "How about a sensory deprivation session?" he suggested. "As the response with the spirit box was so good, I feel the spirits are eager to communicate with you."

Fiona looked at me. "It might heighten your experience."

"What's involved?" I inquired, curiosity taking hold, despite my reservations.

"As the sceptic, we'd sit you in a room alone and blindfolded. Headphones are connected to the spirit box. This isolates you from our questions and any external noise. I won't lie, it's intense. People often report feeling a presence or even physical contact during the session," Tom detailed.

"Alright, I'm game. Let's see what happens," I consented, a mixture of apprehension and intrigue coursing through me.

"Excellent! Let's get everything set up. Fiona, will you assist Carl, please? I need to fetch some more batteries from the van."

I offered to go fetch them while they set the apparatus up. I hurried out to the van, returning swiftly with a handful of AA batteries. The four of us stood on the first floor outside the room where the door had previously slammed shut and rattled violently within its frame. As I stood in the ominous space of the corridor, I couldn't help but wonder what awaited us over the next few hours. Would this experience sway my scepticism, or would it reinforce my disbelief? Only time would tell. I realised I was no longer certain of what I might or might not believe.

Chapter 2

From the darkened corridor in the forsaken asylum. I cautiously moved towards the threshold of the experiment room, hesitating with each step. A shudder of dread crawled along my spine, a testament to the internal conflict gnawing at my very core. Here I was, Steve, the confirmed sceptic, ensnared by an uncharacteristic yet instinctive fear.

Two monitors had been set up in the room, bathing it in an eerie glow. Amidst the chaos of wires, I could see the silhouettes of Carl and Fiona. They were engrossed, their attention tethered to the flickering screens. With each step further into the room, I felt as though I was delving deeper into my own trepidation, betraying the primal urge to turn and flee from the horrors this place spoke of, I continued towards them.

"Steve, are you ready for it? This could be sensational," Carl's voice, a source of normality in the gloom, momentarily grounded me. Yet, that feeling was fleeting.

"I... yes, I'm here," I stammered, my voice getting caught in my throat, betraying the sense of doubt and fear growing within me. How could I, a man who prided himself on his rational mind and sceptical heart, find himself so ensnared by the palpable dread which this cursed place exuded? The old floorboards moaned and creaked beneath my feet, the eerie sound like a foreboding groan of doom. A sense of unease twisted inside me. Why was I so apprehensive? Surely, ghosts were just figments of the imagination, right? Was it merely the fear of the unknown?

Standing in the room's dark interior, a chill engulfed me again. Invisible tendrils of ice seemed to wrap themselves around my bones. I hesitated once more, caught between the instinct to flee and the commitment to proceed, finally, I sat on the chair Carl and Fiona had prepared. It felt more like an electric chair with me its next victim rather than a simple piece of furniture. I held out my hand, it started, quivering, my sweaty palm betraying my overwhelming apprehension. My chest felt like it was going to explode with each heartbeat, like a drum of impending destruction. A chilling sensation drove at my core, sending shivers down my spine. I scoffed to myself at the ludicrous fear, reminding myself again that ghosts were merely figments of overactive imaginations.

"All set?" Carl's voice broke through the tension.

I nodded, even though a part of me was telling me not to do this.

"Close your eyes," Fiona's voice commanded softly, yet it resonated like the chime of a death toll in my subconscious. I took a measured breath and shut my eyes, plunging into the pitch-black domain of my dread. I reminded myself I was a sceptic, but I could not seem to shake my primeval fears. Fiona placed the blindfold on me, before placing the headphones over my ears. I found a peculiar tranquillity amidst the white noise. A deceptive calm washed over me. This wasn't too bad after all.

Fiona's next touch jolted me back to reality. As she removed the headphones and blindfold, I encountered the emotionless stare of the video camera and the other recording devices which now appeared to me as tools of interrogation instead of research.

"How did it feel? Comfortable?"

"It's strangely unsettling, and calming at the same time," I said, caught up in the weird feeling of it all.

"Excellent," Fiona beamed, her enthusiasm shining through. "When you're ready, I'll activate the video recorder. Now it's time to delve deeper into the spectral abyss. I'll be in the room and ask questions. You won't hear my voice; the white noise will drown it out. I need you to say out loud anything you hear coming through the white noise. Whatever it is you hear, just say it out loud, repeat exactly what you hear. No matter how bizarre it may sound, your job is to recall what you hear, not to make sense of it. That will come later."

Everyone but Fiona left the room. I was now feeling vulnerable, very vulnerable. With a slight tremble in my hand, I gave Fiona the thumbs-up, setting in motion events which could unravel the very fabric of my perception of reality. A multitude of wires and equipment surrounded me. However, it was the mysterious ghostly potential which filled the room with electric energy and made me feel uneasy as I got ready to go again.

"Are you comfortable?" Fiona asked. She knew 'comfort' was far from what anyone would feel in this room.

"As much as one can be in a situation like this," I replied, my voice shaking ever so slightly as I replaced the blindfold.

Fiona flipped open a well-worn journal filled with documented happenings and questions. "All right, I'll start asking questions now. Remember, say out loud anything you hear."

With a final nod, I replaced the headphones. My heart leapt into my throat. I felt isolated, disconnected from reality. Fiona began her questioning. I strained to hear her words, but couldn't, they were muffled and inaudible through the white noise. The session had begun, and with it, a chilling journey into the unknown.

Beside FionaFiona was a digital recorder, catching every nuance, hoping to capture any voices inaudible to human ears.

"Is anyone present in this room with us?" Through the relentless static buzz filling my ears, a faint voice emerged, drowning in the continuous drone of white noise. "So cold," said an ethereal voice floating through the air.

"I heard something say, 'So cold.' It was more of a whisper," I said, my own voice barely above the hiss of the static.

"Why are you here?" Fiona continued, her tone imbued with a cautious respect for the unseen presence we were attempting to communicate with.

The static in my headphones quivered, as if the airwaves themselves were trembling with the anticipation of any contact. Then, clearer than before, a voice emerged, laden with an agony seemingly beyond earthly comprehension. "Trapped," it wailed, echoing through my very soul.

My skin erupted in goose bumps. "Trapped," I repeated, my voice carrying a shiver I could not control.

"Do you have a message for us?" her eyes wide with hope and anticipation.

The response which followed was a chilling blend of a sob and a scream, so twisted in its tonality it seemed to defy the natural laws of sound. "LEAVE!" it shrieked, "GET... OUT...

NOW!" The voice's unearthly tone penetrated my ears, burrowing into my psyche with genuine terror.

I ripped the headphones off. "It said, Leave! Get out now!" The words spilled out in a rush. The veneer of scepticism which had once shielded me was now shattered. My eyes were widening with a terror that was all-consuming.

Fiona inhaled a short sharp breath, her expression a complex mix of concern and an insatiable hunger for the unknown. "It seems we've made contact," she acknowledged, the weight of countless unanswered questions heavy in her thoughts. "It's all good. Now, please replace your blindfold and headphones. We must continue." She said, reassuring me, "We've opened doors. We must allow them to come through. The investigation must carry on."

With a fearful heart and a mind now teeming with dread, I again replaced the blindfold and headphones. The darkness enveloped me once more. The white noise resumed its insidious broadcast, and I braced myself for whatever might come next in this chilling communion with the unknown.

I shivered, my mind recalling the last echo of that unearthly demand. "Leave! Get out now!" I couldn't shake it off; it clung to me like a cold shroud. My hands were clammy as I plunged myself back into the pitch-black void. The darkness wasn't just around me; it felt as though it seeped inside me, filling every crevice of my being with a foreboding chill.

"Are you alright to continue?" Fiona's voice was loud and broke through the static, her tone threaded with concern, her lips close to the right side of the headphones.

I nodded. "I think so," I replied, my voice betraying the unease that had taken root within me. "Yes, I'm okay to continue," I said trying to sound convincing.

Fiona resumed the session, her presence somehow comforting despite the growing tension. The white noise from the headphones became a backdrop to my accelerated heartbeat, each pulse a reminder of the surreal situation I had found myself in.

"Can you tell us your name?" Fiona continued, her question hanging like a challenge to the unseen.

Silence followed, then a faint voice, fragmented and incoherent, filtered through the static. I strained to listen, there was a noise. "Elizabeth, it sounded like Elizabeth," I said. A voice from another time, another existence.

"Elizabeth, are you trapped?" Fiona's voice resonated with a mix of authority and empathy.

The response was silence, followed by a sudden surge in the static that made me jump in my seat, a crackling that felt aggressive. It seemed to grow louder until, "No escape," A voice replied, each word a drop of ice-cold water running down my spine. "It said 'No escape'," I repeated to Fiona.

"Why is there no escape?" Fiona probed further, her dedication unwavering despite the ominous atmosphere.

Not words, but sounds, sounds of desperation and fear, filled the headphones. My stomach twisted into knots at the guttural moan, a sound of eternal suffering and torment.

The temperature in the room seemed to drop rapidly, the cold seeping into my bones. As I listened intently to the white noise filling my ears, I heard a voice come through clearly, "Cold... so very cold..." A voice whimpering, its sorrow cutting through the static like a knife.

The experiment continued. Each question asked unravelling more of the tragic tapestry that was Elizabeth's story. She spoke of loneliness, of endless wandering in a place where time had ceased to exist. With each sob and scream, her words became more heart-wrenching.

As we progressed, I began to notice a change in the atmosphere. The air felt heavier, charged with an energy which was both terrifying and electrifying. It appeared as if the veil between our world and the next had thinned, allowing emotions, memories, sounds, and perhaps even more to seep through.

"Elizabeth, are you alone here?" Fiona asked.

The response was a silence, then a cacophony of voices, all speaking at once, a discordant symphony of the damned. "Many... so many voices." I relayed to Fiona, "I cannot make out what they are saying. They are speaking all at once."

Their voices overlapping, and intertwining in a desperate chorus, wanting to be heard. I flinched, the intensity of the experience becoming too much to bear. My breathing was coming in quick gasps, each one a fight against the rising panic. But I was determined to see this through, to understand the forces we were dealing with.

"Who are the others?" Fiona's voice was steady, her aim was to understand the situation.

I repeated their lament, "Lost... we are all lost..." the voices had replied. A hint of despair echoed the sentiments of countless souls.

As the session continued, each revelation was more harrowing than the last. The voices spoke of past tragedies, of sorrow bound to the decaying walls of the asylum, of spirits unable to move on. The atmosphere was thick with the weight of their untold stories, each demanding to be heard. After what seemed like an eternity, Fiona signalled the end of the session by touching my knee. I removed the headphones and blindfold, the room around me swimming back into focus. My body felt heavy, as if I was carrying the weight of Elizabeth's sorrow.

"How did it feel?" Fiona asked, her eyes searching mine for any sign of what I'd experienced.

"Overwhelming," I admitted, the word barely encapsulating the depth of what I'd felt. "It was like touching another realm, another reality."

Carl entered the room. "We've made significant contact," he said, a note of satisfaction in his voice. "This could be the breakthrough we are looking for in understanding the afterlife."

As I stood up, the room spun, a reminder of the intense spiritual energy I'd just engaged with. The experiment had ended but the experience had shaken my scepticism to its core. The voices, the cries, the laments of despair, they were all imprinted on my mind, a stark reminder of the mysteries that lay just beyond our understanding.

I sat down again. "Carl, what tales can you tell me about this place?" I asked trying to take my mind off what had just happened.

"The tales of Ravenswood's Asylum are not just stories," Carl said. "It was a place of unimaginable horrors, masquerading as a sanctuary for the mind. They built this place to house the Clinically Insane here, on the outskirts of Stonebridge, in the late 19th century. It was supposed to be a beacon of progressive psychiatric treatment, or so the founders claimed. In reality, it became purgatory for those who were unfortunate enough to pass through its iron gates. Dr Ravenswood, a man whose ambition was eclipsed only by his cruelty, owned the building which gave him free reign to do as he liked. His obsession with the human mind led him to conduct experiments, blurring the boundaries between treatment and torture. He subjected patients to ice baths, electroshock therapy, lobotomies, and a host of other treatments, all without their consent or any justifiable reason. The corridors of Ravenswood regularly echoed with the screams of the tormented, a macabre symphony playing endlessly, both day and night."

"As the inhumanity of Ravenswood's practices grew, so did the asylum's reputation. Families stopped sending their loved ones, and the funding dried up," Fiona added, her voice a sombre melody in the darkness. "But the doctor refused to abandon his life's work, delving deeper into madness until one fateful night."

Carl stepped back in, continuing the story. "The incident which led to the asylum's closure remained shrouded in mystery. A fire broke out, consuming much of the upper east wing, when they finally extinguished the flames, they found Dr Ravenswood among the casualties. His body was charred beyond recognition, clasped in his arms were the scorched remnants of his research notes. The firemen told stories of shadows moving through the smoke and of screams that weren't human.

The asylum stood desolate after that fateful night, left to rot and decay, becoming a monument to the horrors that occurred within its walls. They say the souls of those who suffered here are now trapped, reliving their torment forever. Dr Ravenswood, some believe, never left. They say he roams the halls, continuing his vile experiments on the spectral inhabitants." Carl concluded.

I shuddered. This was supposed to be a sanctuary, a place of safety. How could a doctor become so evil? I struggled to comprehend the suffering which took place here. We packed up the equipment from the first floor and went downstairs, each of us lost in our own thoughts. The investigation had finished for the night, but the journey into the unknown had only just begun. What other secrets lay hidden within the walls of this old asylum? What other voices were waiting to be heard? Only time, and hopefully tomorrow night's exploration, would tell.

Under the cloak of night, the haunted walls of the dilapidated building seemed to reverberate with the echoes of its sinister past. Carl's breath appeared before him in the freezing air. Each puff of breath served as a reminder of the growing fear now occupying the once magnificent hallway. Carl and his team worked their way through the labyrinth like corridors, their cameras and sensors hungry for any sign of confirmation of the afterlife.

The night had seen a tumultuous symphony of inexplicable sounds, voices, and fleeting shadows. Slamming doors and soul-searching moments sowing seeds of terror in all our minds. As the dawn approached, a sense of relief settled over the group. We knew our vigil had reached its end, for now at least.

"Alright, that's it, we're done for tonight." Tom said. The team nodded.

As we gathered the last of the equipment, the place grew colder, a subtle but unmistakable change. I paused, my eyes scanning the shadows. "Did you feel that?" I asked.

The others stopped. "What is it?" asked Fiona. Then, as if in response to her question, a distant door slammed with a thunderous boom, sending a shockwave through the silence. We exchanged glances, each of our faces etched with the same unspoken thought. We would be coming back tomorrow night to continue the investigation.

Drawing a deep, steadying breath, I led us away from the building. The complex mix of relief at escaping the night's harrowing sights and the inner turmoil of evidence clashing with my scepticism was, to put it mildly, deeply frustrating. We emerged into the early morning, the waning moon a sliver of silver against the black sky, casting an otherworldly glow on the forsaken building.

Reaching the van, parked under the branches of the ancient oak, the sudden vibration of Carl's phone interrupted his thoughts. A glowing notification signalled a message from Ron, the asylum's new owner. He read the text out loud to us. His fatigue disappearing in a surge of curiosity. "Good evening, Carl. I trust the manor was communicative tonight?" the message read.

Despite his cold, numb fingers, he typed a response to Ron describing the night's intriguing events. "The evidence must undergo a comprehensive investigation. We need to establish conclusively its authenticity." The screen showed Ron was typing back, the quick reply, a confirmation of his impatience. "Splendid! I am eager to receive your findings. How does 1pm outside the asylum suit you for a catch-up and to do the interview?" Carl typed his reply, confirming the time and agreeing to the interview.

As I looked back at the building, it looked no less formidable in the light of day. Its darkened windows were like eyes keeping watch over us. As we left Ravenswood asylum behind, it stood silent and imposing, a timeless sentinel awaiting our next visit. We still had not revealed the full story it had to tell. The drive back was a silent one, each team member lost in their own thoughts, the events of the investigation lingering in their minds.

Exhausted, I fell into bed and surrendered to the call of sleep. Time to get up came all too soon. We would have to drive back to the asylum, where the interview with the new owner awaited. As we arrived, I noticed Ron was already there, waiting. Carl brought the new owner over to meet me. "Steve, this is Ron Williams, the new owner of this property. Ron, meet our resident sceptic, Steve."

Ron extended his hand. "So, you're the sceptic?" he inquired, his voice carrying a note of curiosity.

Taken aback by the firmness of his handshake, I managed a smile tinged with discomfort. "Yes, the team thought it prudent to include me, to scrutinise their findings through an unbiased lens."

Ron's eyebrow's raised. "But doesn't being a sceptic imply a certain... reluctance to believe, to have a closed mind?"

My reply was measured, my tone steady despite the stifling atmosphere of the old building. "Being a sceptic means seeking the truth and questioning until the evidence paints a clear picture. I'm here to dissect the supernatural manifestations, to hold each claim against the harsh light of scrutiny."

Ron nodded approvingly. "That's a philosophy I can respect. Carl mentioned you're keen on interviewing me about my plans for the building, especially concerning the ghost hunters?"

"Yes," I confirmed. "A brief interview in front of the building would be ideal."

"Lead the way," Ron consented with a gesture of his hand.

Outside, under the shadow of the imposing Victorian edifice, I prepared for the interview. Tom, who had set my camera up, adjusted the angle to get the best view of the asylum.

"It's ready," Tom announced, stepping back to survey the scene. "If you two can stand here, I'll hit the record button."

I turned to Ron and started the interview with a brief introduction of us both, and then proceeded with my questions. "This building, with its history, is now under your care. Rumour, has it you plan to renovate it and open the doors to those intrigued by its history and alleged hauntings?"

Ron's eyes reflected a flicker of the building's dark past. "Indeed. I aim to restore it to its former glory and, yes, permit ghost hunters to explore its depths. It's important to preserve such places, not just for their historical value but for the stories they hold. And, of course, the lessons we can learn from the past."

My gaze hardened. "And the stories here are grim and horrific, aren't they? This was once a mental asylum for the clinically insane, a term from an era which was decidedly less enlightened. A phrase we no longer use, a lesson learnt, as you put it. It was supposed to be a place of safety for the infirm, yet it has a horrific past."

Ron sighed; a sound swallowed by the building's depressing atmosphere. "Yes, in Victorian times, such places were more like prisons than hospitals. The Asylum was notorious for its deplorable conditions, overcrowding, understaffing, and abysmal treatments were regrettably the norm. Patients at the asylum were treated in a way that stripped them of their dignity and humanity. They endured barbaric 'treatments' which caused both physical and psychological scars. They were subjected to a medical examination, which was most often invasive and humiliating, and after the examination, they were assigned to a ward," he paused for a moment taking a breath. "The wards, designed to accommodate up to ten patients, were often overcrowded, housing as many as thirty at a time. Some patients ended up sleeping on straw mattresses on the floor and the whole place lacked basic hygiene facilities. The staff would use straitjackets or other methods of restraint to control patients who were deemed dangerous or violent. This often lead to physical harm which worsened their mental health. Treatments for supposed mental illnesses were often primitive, experimental and mostly ineffective. Practices, I am glad to say, we have learnt from, and no longer use."

I nodded, my face a mask of professional detachment. "It's a sombre legacy, one filled with suffering and unanswered cries for help. What do you say to those who fear you're disturbing and profiting from a site filled with so much pain?"

Ron looked back at the building, its windows like dark, hollow eyes. "I say it's crucial we remember and learn from these dark chapters. Not to sensationalise, but to acknowledge and ensure such atrocities are never repeated. The past, however grim, must be acknowledged and learnt from."

"Why would one invest in such a morose piece of history?"

Ron's eyes turned toward the remnants of the building. "We must not obliterate history, however harrowing, however upsetting," he began, his voice a low and measured. "It can serve as a grim reminder, a beacon for change. And yes, there's a spectral fascination to these halls that calls to me."

My expression tightened. "Some might argue you're profiteering from past agonies."

Ron's gaze didn't waver. "A fair point. But consider this; the revenue generated here will be used to fuel efforts to eradicate current suffering in similar institutions worldwide. The strict restraints, isolation as punishment, cold water therapy, and electric shock therapy. These aren't relics of a bygone era, but present-day nightmares in some countries around the world."

I nodded, the gravity of the subject etching lines on my face. "Thank you for your candour. It's a commendable venture, and hopefully, it will cast a light on those dark corners of the world still lurking in the shadows of the past."

Ron paused, his eyes surveying the decrepit facade of the building. "Furthermore," he continued. "We honour the memories of those who once roamed the corridors of this building by welcoming those who tread lightly between the realms of the living and the dead. We believe in the possibility of giving peace, allowing unsettled spirits to find solace in our acknowledgement of their suffering."

His words seemed to hang in the air. A breeze, carrying with it echoes of despair and madness blew past us. I shivered, feeling the penetrating gaze of the asylum's ghostly inhabitants upon us. Tom, busy with his equipment, glanced up, his face screwed up in concentration and eyes squinting. "Did you hear that?" he asked. "It's like... like someone's crying."

Ron's expression remained unchanged, but his voice softened. "The walls have absorbed much anguish. On still nights, people say you can still hear the cries and whispers of the dead. It's a stark reminder of the human cost of ignorance and cruelty."

Resolved to maintain my composure, I pressed on. "So, you plan to preserve as much of the original structure as possible?" I said trying to steer the conversation back to less spectral matters.

As we conversed, the sun reached its peak, casting a stark, bright glare against the asylum's facade. The atmosphere seemed to lighten with the afternoon heat. Aware of the relentless advance of time. I concluded the interview. "Thank you, Ron, for this insightful and, frankly, haunting discussion. Your vision for Ravenswood Asylum is as ambitious as it is noble."

Ron nodded, his figure outlined against the bright sky. "It's a responsibility I don't take lightly. We owe it to the past, the present, and the future to remember and to learn."

Tom stopped the camera rolling, and the interview was over. Ron turned to me. "A word to the wise, Steve. From what I have heard and witnessed, spirits can go all out to convince those who doubt their presence."

I wiped my brow and turned to face Ron. "That's quite a statement, Ron. Are you suggesting the building is truly haunted?" A hint of sarcasm barely hidden in my question.

Ron leaned in closer, his voice dropping to a serious tone. "I've seen things Steve. Heard things. This place... it changes when the night comes. I've heard footsteps when no one's there, seen lights flicker without cause, and the cold... sometimes it's like winter's breath in the heat of summer. And … What about your experience being locked in the room, the door rattling in its frame? I heard about it. Surely it must have you questioning your beliefs?"

My scepticism flickered across my face. "Surely there's a rational explanation? Old buildings have quirks, after all."

Ron chuckled cynically. "You think I haven't considered that? But tell me, how do you rationalise a whisper in your ear when you're the only soul around? Or the feeling of being watched from empty rooms?"

I shifted uncomfortably. "I can't say I have all the answers. But it's hard to swallow, you know?"

"I understand," Ron replied. "I was like you once. But this building... it has a way of making believers out of the staunchest sceptics. Just be careful. If you come back tonight, respect the place. Don't provoke what you don't understand. It doesn't like it."

"What do you mean?"

Ron shrugged. "Simply telling you to be careful."

I nodded. The weight of Ron's words surprisingly settled heavily upon me. "I'll keep it in mind. Thanks for the heads-up."

We stood in silence for a moment; the asylum towering behind us, as if listening to our conversation. Finally, I broke the silence. "Have you ever tried to communicate with these spirits? Find out what they want?"

Ron's eyes darkened. "Some things are better left alone. I let the ghost hunters do their thing, but me? I now keep my distance. If you stir the pot, you might not like what bubbles up."

Ron had been very cryptic and slightly evasive with his answers. I wondered if he had something to do with the strange occurrences. "Alright, Ron thank you for your time, I appreciate the honesty. And the warning of course."

Chapter 3

Later that day, we returned to Ravenswood Asylum. The sun hung low on the horizon; its rays cast long shadows, stretching across the decrepit grounds like grasping fingers. The ghost hunters were setting up an array of equipment for the second night of their investigation. Amidst them, I adjusted my video camera, its familiar weight a comforting presence against the growing unease in my chest. Though a sceptic, I couldn't shake off last night's experience. My mind was whirling with questions. Was all this real? Did Ron have a hand in their construction? Or had it all been a set-up by these local ghost hunters?

Fiona approached, her gaze falling upon my carefully prepared gear. "I see you have brought some of your own equipment," she remarked, her voice laced with a curious undertone.

"I mean no offence," I replied, carefully adjusting my camera's settings. "But by bringing my own equipment I can be certain there's nothing pre-recorded or any kind of foul play involved. It's crucial for verifying any supernatural occurrences we might capture." My voice remained calm and assured. My words carried the weight of my scepticism, which in the past served as a barrier I had diligently kept between myself and the unknown. Yet, I confess, the events of last night have shaken the very foundations of that barrier.

Fiona's smile broadened, understanding and perhaps a hint of challenge sparkling in her eyes. "No offence taken. I do hope you get some evidence on your own equipment. That way, you can't say it isn't real, and you can hang up your scepticism badge." Her words were an invitation to the dance of belief and disbelief that we were both a part of. As the daylight waned, the team gathered in the grand but crumbling entrance hall of the asylum. The air was again thick with dust, and the intense history of suffering seemed to permeate every crevice of the building. We stood in a semi-circle, our faces illuminated by the soft glow emanating from the flickering screens of the thermal cameras.

Tom, the tech-savvy member of our group, stood fussing over an array of monitors and cables. He was meticulously calibrating the sensitive equipment used to capture any minor irregularities. His occasional muttering of curses and random shouts of joy helped balance out the tense atmosphere during our preparations. As the final streaks of sunlight disappeared, plunging the building into twilight, our collective breath was held in anticipation of the evening's events. The large dusty hall darkened once again, its windows staring, as if challenging our intrusion. A cold draft squeezed through the broken panes, caressing the nape of my neck with what felt like a sentient touch. Goosebumps ran down my arms. I reassured myself that it was merely from the draft of cold air.

Carl laid out the plans for the evening. We would explore the various hotspots of paranormal activity that had been previously reported to occur within the asylum's walls. Fiona, with her claimed sensitivity to the otherworldly, leading one team. myself with the other team, holding my video camera, ready to document every moment. Our footsteps echoed through the deserted corridors as we explored deeper into the building. The beam of my torch cut through the darkness, showing peeling paint, rusted bed frames, and other remnants of a bygone era. The air was musty with the scent of decay and the unspoken horrors that once occurred in these forsaken rooms.

We reached the room believed to be the epicentre of the asylum's hauntings, a place where the veil between worlds was supposedly at its thinnest. The door creaked ominously as Tom pushed it open, revealing a chamber shrouded in shadows. The remnants of a once-padded cell were clear at the far end of the room, the walls scarred by the desperate clawing of long-departed inmates, and more recently of rodents looking for nesting material. We began setting up our equipment, with digital displays and blinking lights, my heart began racing in anticipation of what we were about to undertake. The air grew colder, a chill seeped into my bones, I couldn't shake the feeling of once again being watched by unseen eyes. Time stretched and distorted as we waited in silence, our breath forming ghostly wisps in the frigid air. Every creak and groan of the old building sent a jolt of adrenaline coursing through my veins. I kept my camera trained on the darkest corners of the room, half-expecting some twisted spectre to materialise within the viewfinder.

A low moan reverberated through the room, a sound so forlorn and filled with anguish that it rooted me to the spot. Tom gasped, his eyes widened as he turned in a slow circle, his senses reaching out into the oppressive darkness. "It's here."

His voice was barely audible over the pounding of my heart. The team instinctively moved closer together, a wordless pact of solidarity against the unseen force that seemed to be enveloping us. The temperature in the room dropped further, our breaths vaguely visible as puffs of mist in our torchlight. A sense of anticipation and fear mingled in the air, a heady concoction that threatened to overwhelm my senses.

There was a mysterious and sorrowful presence that wanted to pull me in, encouraging me to abandon scepticism and delve deeper into the unknown. But I held firm, the grip on my camera tightening, a lifeline to the tangible, rational world I was determined to cling to. The low moan ebbed away leaving behind a silence that seemed to fill our ears. The darkness was thick, a deep velvet that consumed the light of our torches. Rotting straitjackets and rusted chains were scattered across the floor. Around us, the walls echoed the silent screams of countless lost souls. The room felt like it was closing in on us. There was a strong sense of foreboding in the air, so intense you could virtually touch it. The remnants around us bore witness to the room's suffering. With every breath, a chill ran down my spine, as if the shadows themselves were whispering, telling of the horrors of the past. These were the secrets never meant to be uncovered. The silent screams of those lost souls appeared to merge with the darkness, creating an atmosphere so thick with sorrow, it was as though their stories were woven into the very fabric of the room.

My breathing was quick and short, my usual confidence now overshadowed by an unexplainable tension. "I... I can't catch my breath," I whispered, the words barely escaping my lips. "Did you hear that?" I said, my voice trembling like a frightened child's. The question was rhetorical; we all heard the mournful cries of the tormented spirits of the past. A shiver ran down my spine. The primal fear of the unknown taking hold once more. I wanted to dismiss it as the wind, the building settling, or anything that would provide a logical explanation. But the dread curling ever tighter around my stomach told me it was neither. The rest of the team also stood rooted to the spot, their faces void of emotion under the low glow of the equipment. The air was thick, like the charged calm before a storm set to erupt. A faint scratching sound began, like nails on the chalkboard of the damned, it grew louder and insistent. It emanated from the far corner of the room. I panned my camera towards the sound, my hands steady despite the fear that threatened to overwhelm me. The viewfinder showed nothing, yet the scratching continued, a relentless sound that seemed to claw at my nerves.

"Steve," Tom said, his voice breaking the silence. "Look at the wall."

I turned to look where he was pointing out. My breath caught in my throat. The barren, peeling plaster had started to writhe and pulsate, as if some abomination was striving to break free from its confines. I looked on, petrified and unable to think clearly. Words appeared, etching deeply into the deteriorated plaster created by an unseen, malicious power.

"HELP US!" the wall screamed in silent agony, the letters jagged and frantic, etching a display of pure terror. A gasp, strangled and disbelieving, rose from our team, the reality of the situation striking us with the weight of a tombstone. This was no mere trick of the light, no figment of my over-stimulated imagination. The feeling of reality was heavy, just like the fear making me feel trapped and terrified. It felt like something unspeakable was lurking just beyond our reach.

"Can you see that?" whispered Carl, his voice a trembling thread of sound in the domineering silence that choked the room.

I could only nod, my eyes fixed on the hellish inscription, as a cold realisation settled in my heart. We were not alone. The air seemed thick with the scent of decay and old secrets, the walls themselves bearing witness to an ancient horror that now turned its gaze towards us. The room felt smaller, the shadows deeper, and in that moment, we understood the true nature of terror, not as an abstract concept, but as a living, breathing entity. The darkness pushed in on us from all sides, as though to consume us. The weight of countless anguished souls bore down upon us, their pain and despair a tangible force that begged for our help while threatening to drive us into madness.

I fought against the panic that clawed at my mind, my professional curiosity attempting to do battle with a deep-seated urge to flee. "I need to document this," I said, my voice a hoarse whisper. "We need evidence... I need evidence."

Even as I spoke, I knew that no amount of evidence would truly capture the terror of that moment. The haunted asylum was coming alive around us. Its stories of pain and horror manifesting in ways we could never have imagined.

We stayed in that room for what seemed like an eternity. Every sound and shadow screamed of years of suffering. Eventually, the overwhelming sensations eased, as if the spirits had made their point and were retreating into the shadows once again. We looked at each other silently, each of us lost in our thoughts and our fears.

As we left the room and entered the long corridor we had walked through earlier, an unearthly screech echoed through the building, stopping everyone in their tracks. The ashen faces of Fiona's team greeted us as we met in the corridor. We stood motionless in a silence that felt more oppressive than that unearthly screech. Their eyes betrayed an unspoken dread, mirrored by the terror in our own eyes and etched into our souls. What made that sound? We were there to investigate, but I had no desire to encounter whatever caused that noise. We all made our way to the common area, a space where once the mentally ill, the desolate and the deranged might have mingled, now a temporary sanctuary for us, the living.

No one spoke. The anticipation of it happening again held everyone's voice. Our glances at each other were solemn, an acknowledgement of the shared ordeal. Fiona, her face serious, spoke first, her voice a low whisper. "This place, it holds more than just the echoes of the past. It's like they're reaching out, desperate to be heard, to be freed from their perpetual torment.

This is both scary and amazing. We've had nothing as strong as this before."

Carl nodded. "This is serious. I think we could be way out of our depth here."

His words were ponderous, like a ghostly shroud enveloping us. We knew then what we sought was no longer a mere thrill or a tantalising piece of evidence. We were becoming part of the story, actors in a tragedy, the origin of which began long ago. With a collective resolve, we ventured further into the asylum. If the spirits sought either release or recognition, we would try to be their conduit. The decision was not made lightly. Each step we took was laden with the weight of a thousand sombre tales.

Our exploration took us down decrepit hallways, through wards where the air was so thick you could cut it with a knife. The walls seemed to whisper, voices of the past seeping through the peeling paint and rusted metal. We set our equipment in the central hall on the second floor, a place where the energy seemed most concentrated, most active. As the night wore on, the phenomena intensified. Shadows danced at the edge of our vision, elusive yet without doubt, present. The temperature fluctuated wildly, waves of cold followed by warm, oppressive, feelings of doom, as if we were at the mercy of unseen forces.

Then, amidst the discord of unexplained noises and shadows, a figure appeared. It was a blur at first, a distortion in the air. But, as we watched rooted to the spot in a mixture of fear and fascination, it took form. A woman, her face twisted in an eternal scream, her hands reaching out to us, pleading. The encounter was brief, a moment stretching into infinity before she vanished abruptly. The room fell silent; the tension dissipating like mist at dawn.

We were left with nothing but the haunting images of her agony and a lingering sense of sorrow that clung to our skin.

"Did everyone see that?" my voice quivered. "Please tell me we all saw that."

A stunned silence filled the room. Everyone trying to come to terms with what we witnessed.

"We have to help them," Fiona whispered. Her voice was a choking sob of empathy for the tortured souls.

But how do you help the dead? This question haunting me more than any apparition. Tension and trepidation filled the room as Fiona's suggestion hung heavily in the air. I hesitated, the rational part of my mind screaming against the folly of engaging with the unknown. Yet, the haunting plea of the spectral woman tugged at the edges of my resolve. Tom, ever the pragmatist, started to set up a spirit box, its static-filled broadcast filling the room with an eerie symphony of crackling sounds. Fiona closed her eyes, her lips moving in silent preparation. The rest of us stood in a tight circle, a band of modern-day necromancers summoning the courage to delve deeper into the abyss.

"We need another video camera setting up. I think there is a one downstairs." Said Tom. "We should cover as many angles as possible."

Before anyone replied, the spirit box crackled and hissed, a cacophony of noises that seemed like the chaotic murmuring of a crowd. Then, amongst the discord, a voice emerged. It was clear and unmistakable. "Help us... please, help us," it moaned, the plea dripping with a desperate mixture of sorrow and rage.

We all froze, the blood in our veins ran ice cold. Fiona's eyes snapped open, her gaze intense and focused. "Who are you?" she asked, her voice steady but her hands trembling.

The box crackled again; the voice returning stronger this time. "Tormented," it whispered. "Trapped."

An icy chill ran down my spine, the revelation hitting me like a physical blow. These spirits, these echoes of the past, were not just remnants of history, they were sentient, aware of their eternal imprisonment within the decaying walls. Carl stepped forward, his recorder in hand, capturing every syllable of the ghostly communication. "What can we do to help you?" he asked, his voice a blend of fear and determination.

The answer was a long time coming; the static ebbing and flowing like the tide. Then, an unfamiliar voice, a child's voice, high and clear, yet desperately sad. "Free...us."

The simple plea was more heart-wrenching than any of the horrors we'd witnessed that night. A sigh rippled through our group. Fear and resolve settling in our hearts, creating a whirling mixture of emotions. We now knew our investigation had become something more, a mission to bring peace to the restless souls trapped in an endless loop of torment. The night grew darker, enveloping everything with its heavy cloak and absorbing the hopelessness and sorrow that seeped from the walls. The silence became suffocating, broken only by the faint sound of melancholic whispers echoing in the air. In every corner, the scent of dampness filled the air, intertwining with the musty and desolate atmosphere. It felt as though the very essence of despair lingered here, casting a sombre feeling to the scene. We continued our attempts to communicate, the spirit box a bridge between worlds. Each voice that emerged told a story of pain and fear, a fragment of a life tragically cut short.

As the night wore on, the atmosphere in the asylum became more oppressive, as if the air itself were reluctant to move, burdened by untold sorrows. The shadows seemed to stretch and twist, forming shapes that defied the logic of the light cast from our torches. The walls whispered with the voices of the lost, their words intertwining with the static from the spirit box in a haunting chorus. I felt a prickle of fear dance down my spine, my heart racing with a mix of dread and determination. Beside me, Fiona's face was pale; her eyes reflected the flicker of our torchlight. Her mediumship abilities drawing the spirits ever closer. Her recorder carefully capturing every sound, every ethereal whisper, collecting more proof of the afterlife.

The corridor's temperature plummeted, the cold becoming so intense it seemed to cut straight through us. The static from the spirit box climbed to an ear-piercing screech, causing us all to flinch. Then, abruptly, it stopped. Leaving a silence so complete, it hummed in our ears. Out of the silence, a loud bang echoed through the corridors. It reverberated off the crumbling walls and along the endless corridors. A series of bumps and scrapes followed it as if something was being dragged across the floor directly above us. We exchanged glances, the unspoken question clear in our eyes. Should we investigate? The mission to communicate with the spirits and record proof was turning into something far more harrowing. But, the drive to discover what was really happening, to help these trapped spirits, pushed us onward.

Gripping our equipment like shields, we moved as one towards the staircase, each step creaking ominously under our weight. The sounds emanating from the floor above continued, growing louder as we ascended. The third floor was in worse condition than the second, the walls here scarred by fire and the floor littered with even more unrecognisable debris. The noise led us to what once had been a patient's room. Hanging off its hinges, the door was barely attached. It swung gently to and fro as if moved by an unseen hand. Taking a deep breath, I pushed it open revealing a scene that would stay with me, it would haunt me forever.

In the centre of the room lay the body of Tom.

His form contorted in a macabre display, his eyes distended with an indescribable expression of stark terror. Bloodied footprints encircled him, tracing a path on the floor, leading to the broken window at the far end of the room. How he got to the room first, none of us could fathom. Yet, here he was before us, lying in this ghastly pose. Fiona screamed. She hid her eyes from the awful sight and burst out crying, "What is happening?" she shouted.

"Look at his face," said Carl, "is he dead?" his voice quivered with a mixture of dread and disbelief. "It's like he seen the devil himself."

We edged closer, every step hesitant, as if the room might betray our presence to something we didn't want to find us. The air emanated with an unspoken terror, the scent of blood mingling with a pungent, metallic odour that exuded from the walls themselves. The glass window, once a barrier to the outside world, now lay in jagged pieces, scattered across the floor. It was evidence of the violence that occurred here. The shards glinted ominously in the dim light.

"Did something come in... or did something get out?" whispered Carl, his eyes not leaving the grotesque spectacle of Tom's final moments.

None dared answer, for in our hearts we now knew Ravenswood Asylum held secrets far older and more malevolent than any of us could have imagined. We stood there, united in our silence, each lost in our thoughts of fear and revulsion, realising the horror which had befallen Tom might be just the beginning. The shock of the sight had us all rooted to the spot. Fiona let out another strangled cry, her hand covering her mouth. Carl stared at Tom's body, he dropped his video recorder, the sound of its impact was inconsequential compared to the thundering of our hearts. I panicked, my mind finally giving in to the fear I felt. "We need to get out! We need to call the police." I gasped, my voice choking with fear. The urgency to flee, to escape this nightmarish place, surged within me. An unholy scream came from the corridor, panic now set in. But even as I spoke, I felt it might not be that simple. The asylum had us in its grasp, and it wasn't ready to let go.

We hastened our retreat from the room, leaving behind the body of our friend, the gravity of the situation gripping us in a state of shock. As we stumbled back towards the staircase, the building came alive around us. Doors slammed shut. Laughter echoed through the halls, a cruel, mocking laughter that seemed to chase us. As we descended to the first floor, a piercing scream shattered the air, cutting through us. Fiona let out her own scream, her body rigid with terror. It was a primal sound, laced with unadulterated terror, reverberating off the decayed walls. Fiona's legs gave way beneath her, and she crumpled to the ground, her body writhing as if in the grips of an unseen tormentor. Her eyes, wide and unseeing, rolled back into her head, exposing the whites in a grotesque display. Her mouth was agape, contorted in an endless silent scream as if she were trying to expel the core of her fear. Carl and I rushed to her side, our fear momentarily forgotten in the face of her distress.

As her convulsions subsided, she lay there, a broken figure, her chest heaving with each laboured breath, her eyes fluttering shut. The silence that followed was more terrifying than her screams. An expectant quiet that seemed to press down upon us, reminding us that whatever caused this was still present, still watching. We were left in a state of heightened alertness, each sound, each shadow making us jump, our nerves stretched taut. In the chaos, the forgotten spirit box burst into life. Its static-filled voice pierced through the air, saying, "Too late... too late..." It could have been a statement or a warning. The surrounding atmosphere was charged, the air thick with malevolence. We were not alone, and whatever accompanied us was not merely a remnant of the past, it was here now, active, angry, and all too aware of our presence.

Trapped in a nightmare, the asylum was a maze from which there was no waking. Each corridor twisted back on itself, each room a new tale of horror. The spirits, once pleading, now seemed to revel in our terror, their cries turning from sobs of despair to shrieks of laughter and delight.

From out of the shadows, a figure came towards us. We stood frozen to the spot. It was Tom. "What happened? I heard the screams." Carl cried out at seeing him. "But ... You... You were..." he stammered.

A chill clawed its way down my spine, freezing and sharp. What on earth was unfolding around me? Confusion clouded my thoughts, a thick mist I couldn't see through. I'd been hurled into a situation so terrifying; it shook the core of what I thought I knew. Fear gripped me, an icy hand around my heart. These noises, these events, I'd convinced myself they were just tales, figments of overactive imaginations. Yet here I am, face-to-face with a reality so bizarre, so unnerving, that it was changing my view of the world. Had my eyes been closed all this time? How had I never stumbled upon shadowed corners of existence like this before? The realisation dawned on me, awkward and unwelcome. Ignorance had been my shield, now I was stripped of it, I stood vulnerable and exposed to the unknown.

"I was what Carl? I went downstairs to the Nurses station to set up a camera."

Carl walked over and poked Tom in the chest with his finger.

"Ouch! What did you do that for?" Tom asked, staring at Carl.

"We saw your body. You were dead."

"Dead? What do you mean, I was dead?"

The confusion swirled around us like a fog, thickening with every passing second. Carl's face was a picture of pure disbelief, his finger still hovering in front of Tom's chest. Fiona, still on the floor, her convulsions now eased, looked up with wide, terrified eyes and screamed again. Her gaze flitted between Tom and Carl, her breaths shallow and rapid. "What is going on?"

"I... No... WE! saw you," Carl stammered, his words tumbling over one another. "In a room upstairs... your body, twisted and covered in blood. It was you, Tom!"

Tom's face paled, his brow furrowing in confusion and fear. "But I've been downstairs, setting up another camera, I told you we needed another video camera. When no one replied, I went to set one up."

The air felt dense, each word was a struggle against the darkness that seemed to close in around us. The noise that once filled the halls had been swallowed up by a silence so deep it felt as though the very building was holding its breath, its attention fixed on us with a spiteful curiosity. The overwhelming quiet heightened our sense of isolation, wrapping us in a cloak of unease. I tried to rally my thoughts, the logical part of my mind grappling with the scenario before us. "We need to look... to confirm," I said. My voice was a lot steadier than I was. "If what we saw wasn't Tom, then what, or who, was it?"

Together, with a shared but reluctant agreement, we headed back to the room where the body was discovered. The walk there felt like a march towards our deepest fears, every step weighed down by the terror of what might greet us upon arrival. It was as if the hallways lengthened, stretching endlessly before us. This wasn't just a physical journey back to a scene of horror; it was a descent into the unknown, each of us grappling with the chilling expectation of what lay ahead. As we approached the room, the door was as we left it, ajar, foreboding. With a deep breath, I pushed it wide open; the others flanking me, united against the unknown. No one was in the room. The body was gone, there was no blood, there was no trace of the gruesome scene we had witnessed just moments earlier. The only evidence that anything transpired there was the glass on the floor and a lingering sense of unease that hung in the air like a second skin.

"How...?" Fiona's voice trailed off, her gaze sweeping the room in a desperate attempt to make sense of the impossible.

"It's a trick," Tom said, his voice laced with conviction. "This asylum, these spirits... they're playing with us."

Fiona grabbed Carl by the arm. "I don't like this anymore. This is now too dark, it's evil, and we are not equipped for this. I think we need to leave. They want us to leave!" The panic was clear in her voice.

The realisation was clear; we were pawns in a macabre game orchestrated by the unseen inhabitants of the asylum. The spirits, once thought to be helpless victims of circumstance, now seemed to be hate filled entities. It seemed they could manipulate reality at their whim. The weight of the situation settled on us. The night was far from over, the hours until dawn stretched out like a lifetime. Carl stepped forward. "We need to regroup, to plan our next move. No one has been hurt, hopefully, we can keep it that way and perhaps we can still help these trapped spirits."

The mission to help the spirits had taken a sinister turn, and now it was our own safety that was in jeopardy. We retreated to the relative safety of the common area, our makeshift base within the asylum. The equipment lay scattered, forgotten in the chaos. The spirit box, still crackling with static, served as a grim reminder of the voices that led us to this point. "We can't just walk away," I found myself saying, the words leaving a bitter taste in my mouth. From doubter to believer, I had come full circle. "Not without figuring out what's going on, not without trying to put an end to it." It was a strange feeling, this pull between the urge to flee and the need to stay, to dive deeper into the mystery. Fear twisted inside me, yet there was an undeniable draw towards helping those innocent trapped spirits find peace. It was a conflict of emotions, a battle between self-preservation and a newfound sense of responsibility.

The others nodded, their faces grim, but with a common resolve to continue, to face whatever horrors awaited us. This was not born out of a desire for adventure or acclaim, but out of necessity. We were in too deep, the asylum's grip too tight to break free without answers. As we formulated a plan between us; the building creaked and groaned, a symphony of despair and warning. An unmistakable anger was exuded by the restless spirits. The message was obvious; the horror that awaited us was beyond anything we could have imagined. We were in the heart of the darkness, the eye of a storm of spectral rage and sorrow. And as the minutes ticked by, each moment stretching into eternity, here in the common area we prepared ourselves for the next phase of our ordeal.

Chapter 4

In the dim light from our torches, the common area looked less like a sanctuary and more like a deathly trap. The shadows thrown by our lights seemed to twist and writhe on the walls. The silence was uneasy, only broken by distant, inexplicable sounds, sounds that echoed through the empty halls. The occasional bump, a distant whisper, a soft mocking laugh all adding to my uneasy feeling. "We need a plan," I said, breaking the tense silence. "We need to understand what's happening here and how to stop it."

Carl nodded, his expression serious. "So, you are a believer at last."

"It would appear so. There's no way all this could be faked." I replied, a hint of resignation in my voice.

The walls of the decrepit building seemed to close in on us, the peeling paint resembling decaying skin. Shadows danced in the flickering light of our torches, as if mocking our frail attempts at courage. The smell of mould and something far worse, the stench of long-forgotten tragedies surrounded us.

A blood curdling scream punctured the silence, causing everyone to jump. The sound was raw, filled with such terror it chilled us to our very bones. It was a stark reminder of the evil presence controlling the asylum, a sinister presence which claimed many souls.

"We need to focus on finding the source," Carl said, his voice steadier now. "The heart of this darkness. Maybe it's a cursed object or some unholy ritual gone wrong. Whatever it is, it's anchoring the evil here. We have to tread carefully. This place isn't just haunted; it's a focal point of psychic trauma. Every step we take, every corner we turn, could bring us face to face with something dangerous, something unspeakable."

Fiona, her voice still quivering from her earlier ordeal, spoke up. "I think... Yes it is… it's feeding off our fear. We need to stay calm, and rational. Fear, our fear, that's what gives it power."

Fiona's suggestion seemed impossible, 'stay calm' that would be a daunting task in a place designed to instil terror. Yet, it was a lifeline, a sliver of control in the uncontrollable.

"We need to stick together," I suggested. "No one should go anywhere alone. We need to set up cameras. We can keep watch in shifts. We need to stay alert."

"Ghosts or spirits rarely threaten or set out to harm the living. They normally reach out, sometimes wanting help to cross over into the light. There is something else at work here." Carl informed me.

The group nodded their agreement, each of us understanding the importance of unity in the face of such an unknowable threat. We gathered our scattered equipment, setting up a perimeter of cameras and sensors around the common area. The spirit box continued to crackle and hiss, a reminder there was an invisible presence surrounding us.

As we worked, it felt like the asylum was watching us, its silence overbearing, and its darkness complete. The sense of being observed, of possibly being hunted, felt real. I couldn't shake the feeling that the building itself was alive, the very walls permeated with the pain and rage of its past inhabitants.

Then, as if to affirm my fears, a sudden chill swept through the room. The temperature dropped, our breath fogging in the air once again. A soft, sorrowful wail echoed down the corridor; a sound so full of despair it was physical in its intensity.

The equipment flickered and buzzed; the screens filled with static, as if something was interfering with the signal. Then as suddenly as it began, the chill passed, the temperature returning to normal; the equipment stabilised.

"What was that?" whispered Tom, his voice barely audible over the sound of our rapid, shallow breaths.

"A warning," said Fiona, her eyes wide. "A warning of what's coming. I still think we should leave. We can come back with more equipment, with people who have more experience than we have, even a priest if we have to."

Carl placed a comforting hand on her shoulder. "You said we have to keep calm. Right now, we are safe. We've just never experienced this level of activity before. If it gets worse or we become threatened, we can call it a night. Don't forget Janet and Mark are watching on the screen in the van."

"But we've not been able to get them on the walkie-talkies."

"It's probably the thick walls of this building, or maybe a glitch in the system. It's happened before." Carl said, trying to comfort her.

We settled into an uneasy vigil, our eyes constantly scanning the gloom, our ears straining to pick up any sound above the whisper of our own breathing. The night stretched out before us, each minute stretching into an eternity of tension and fear.

A sudden movement caught my eye. The camera, set up to monitor the corridor, was showing an image of a dark figure moving towards us. It was hazy, indistinct, but undeniably human-shaped.

"Something's coming," I whispered, warning the others.

We watched in frozen anticipation as the figure drew closer, its movements jerky and unnatural. As it stepped into the light of the common area, its features became clearer, eliciting an uncontrollable gasp of horror from us all.

Tom backed off, "What the…" Fiona let out an ear-piercing scream, startling Tom as he fell over a cable and ended up sitting uncomfortably on the floor.

It was something wearing Tom's face. His features twisted into a grotesque parody of a smile, the eyes empty and black. It moved towards us with a slow, deliberate pace, each step echoing ominously in the silent room.

The real Tom scrambled to his feet, his expression one of sheer terror. "That's not me," he stammered. "I don't know what it is, but it's not me! Keep it away!"

The terror in his voice was like nothing I had ever experienced. The apparition didn't speak, its smile never wavering. It reached out with one hand, its fingers elongated and twisted. We scrambled backwards; our backs were now against the wall. Fear stole my voice as I tried to shout. The thing still wearing Tom's face advanced closer, a living nightmare, a sign of more terrible things yet to happen. Or was this the end?

As the moonlight seeped through the bars of the broken windows, we knew we had nowhere to run. The night was far from over. We were trapped in a place where the boundaries between life and death, sanity and madness were blurred beyond recognition. And as we faced the twisted image of our friend, we understood the asylum was only just starting to reveal its true power. Dawn was hours away and we faced a chasm of fear and uncertainty.

The room was alive with our fear. The grotesque figure with Tom's face continued its slow, deliberate advance, its hollow gaze seemed to pierce right through us. We were cornered, the walls of the room we once considered our sanctuary, now feeling like the closing sides of a tomb.

"Back off!" Carl shouted, his voice hoarse with terror. He brandished a piece of broken chair like a makeshift weapon, but the entity merely tilted its head, considering him with an eerie detachment.

"Carl, don't!" I hissed, grabbing his arm. "It's not human. You can't fight it like one."

But even as I spoke, the apparition halted its advance, tilting its head to one side. Then, with an abruptness that sent a shiver down my spine, it simply vanished, leaving behind a cold spot and an echoing silence.

We stood there for a moment, breathing hard, our minds racing to make sense of what happened. Fiona sank to the floor, her body trembling uncontrollably. "It's another warning," she whispered, "A warning of something worse to come. We need to leave… now!"

The real Tom, his face as pale as death, looked at each one of us in turn, his eyes glazed with disbelief. "What's happening here?" he stammered. "What was that thing?"

"We don't know," Carl admitted, feeling a sense of despair wash over him. "But it's clear something in this asylum doesn't want us here. We're playing by its rules now, and it's a game it means us to lose."

The need to act, to do something, was overwhelming. "I agree Fiona, we should leave," I said, as I helped her to her feet. "Get out in the open, hopefully, leave this thing behind."

Everyone agreed it was time to get out, to leave this spectral nightmare behind. As we moved through the corridors, our torches cast long, dancing silhouettes that seemed to mock our plight. The asylum was a maze, a warren of despair, twisting and turning upon itself in seemingly impossible ways. It, or something, was playing with our minds. We went down to the Nurses station. There had been less activity there, maybe we would be safer. When we reached it, Fiona made her way to the front door. She tried to open it, but it held fast. Locked by an invisible force. She made her way back, tears falling from her eyes, "It won't open... the door... it... won't let us open it."

The sense of entrapment thickened the surrounding air, a manifestation of despair surrounding the once mundane Nurses' station transformed it into an eerie scene. Remnants of old medical charts and scattered papers were a grim reminder of the frenetic activity which once took place here.

"We need to think," I urged, my voice low, trying to instil a sense of calm. "There's got to be another way out, maybe a window, a service door, anything."

Fiona wiped away her tears, fear being replaced by a fierce determination. "We can't give up. We can't let this place beat us."

The front door creaked open, Janet, and Mark entered the building. Carl looked at them with surprise at their appearance, he shouted, "Stop! Don't come any further! Get out! Get help!"

Too late, the door slammed shut behind them. Janet tried to open the door. But it was stuck tight, as though someone had locked and bolted it shut again. Janet's hands trembled as she rattled the doorknob, her efforts futile against the unseen force holding it closed. "It won't move!" she cried, her voice edged with panic.

Mark's face paled as he backed away from the door, his eyes scanning the dimly lit hallway. "What's happening?" he muttered, more to himself than anyone else.

Carl, gathering his wits, stepped forward, his expression grim. "This is no ordinary building," he explained, his voice low and steady. "It's a trap, a prison for the spirits haunting it, and now, it seems, for us too."

Mark looked towards Carl, "What do you mean it's a trap?" He turned back towards the front door. Mark tried in desperation to open it, pounding on the door with despair, his fists echoing off the stout wood like a morbid drumbeat. The finality of the door's closure seemed to suck the air from the room, leaving us all gasping in the tightening grip of the asylum.

"Why didn't you stay outside?" I asked, trying to mask the rising panic in my voice. "We told you both, no matter what, don't enter!" said Carl.

Janet, on edge and stressed, said nervously, "We thought there was a problem with your equipment. The screens stopped working and showed only static interference, so we decided to come and find you." Her voice faded as she realised the seriousness of the situation.

Carl leaned against a wall; his face looked sombre. "Tell me you've seen the stuff we've been dealing with, right?" he asked. "You've got everything recorded, haven't you?"

Mark shook his head. "No, nothing, we saw nothing. As Janet said, the equipment stopped working; we have been trying to rectify it. We agreed it must be a fault with the equipment in here. That's why we came in."

As he spoke, the reality of the situation settled deeper. We were not merely investigators or thrill-seekers now; we were captives, bound together in a shared nightmare not sure when or if it would end. The asylum's past, a history of tragedy and horror, was unfolding before us, each new revelation a thread in an ever-tightening noose of despair.

The place grew colder again, its oppressive atmosphere more suffocating. Noises echoed down the halls, the voices of those who had passed over, weaving a chorus of misery and warning. Shadows still flickered at the edge of our vision, always just out of sight, always watching.

The laughter started again. It echoed down the halls, a sound both childlike and yet utterly devoid of innocence. It was joined by other sounds, the clank of chains, the thud of unseen feet, the wailing of voices long silenced. The building was alive with the tormented spirits of its past, and they were closing in.

A young girl's voice, ethereal and sorrowful, echoed down the dank corridors, winding its way into our souls. "Help me!" she implored; the simple plea laden with untold years of suffering. "We need to help her." cried Fiona.

Everyone looked at each other as the child cried out again. In silent agreement we followed the sound, our footsteps hesitant yet determined, leading us deeper into the asylum. The voice guided us to a dilapidated ward. The walls, once decorated with drawings were now peeling along with the old, damp plaster. A stark reminder of the innocent lives corrupted within these cursed walls. We agreed it must have once been the children's ward. Faded murals on what was left of the walls, once meant to be comforting, now looked sinister in the flickering light. As we looked around the room, the door slammed shut behind us, the sound final and foreboding. Before we could react, the temperature plummeted, it was icy cold. Here, the laughter and cries of children once filled the building, now replaced by a domineering silence.

"What is it with the cold air and the slamming doors?" I shouted, "Enough is enough! You wanted us to leave, then let us leave!"

Fiona placed her hand reassuringly on my shoulder, "Steve, it's alright. It, or they, are just trying to unnerve us."

"It's doing a good job." I thought to myself. My heart felt as though it was trying to beat its way out of my chest.

"Where are you?" Fiona called out, her voice quivering with a mix of fear and compassion. "We're here to help you."

A shadow moved in the corner of the room, small and frail, trembling with each sob. As my torch beam settled on the figure, it revealed a young girl, her dress tattered, her eyes hollow pools of darkness. She looked up, her gaze piercing through the gloom, her mouth moving in a silent scream.

"Can't leave... won't let us leave," she wailed, her voice a chilling caress in our ears.

"Who won't let you leave?" Carl asked, his voice steady but his eyes betraying his terror.

"The doctor," she replied, her voice dropping to a fearful murmur. "Still here... always here..."

The revelation sent a shiver down my spine. A doctor, a figure of authority and trust, was now a twisted spectre of torment. The asylum's history was rife with tales of cruel, unorthodox treatments, and it seemed the orchestrator of these horrors was still very much present, his malevolent spirit ensnaring the souls of his former patients.

Fiona glanced towards me. We exchanged a look, a silent agreement passing between us. We had to find this entity, confront it, and free these trapped spirits from their perpetual nightmare. But as we prepared to delve further into the mystery, children's laughter started again, this time closer, more menacing.

From the darkness, figures emerged. More children, their eyes hollow, their mouths open in muted cries of terror. They danced around us, their movement's fluid, like a grotesque parody of ballet.

"We mean you no harm," I said, trying to keep my voice steady despite the pounding of my heart trying to escape my chest. "We're here to help you."

But the ghostly children paid no heed. They drew closer, their hands reaching out to us, their touch ice-cold as they brushed past us. Fiona began to chant. Her words were a mix of prayer and plea, but it was clear we were outmatched. Our presence was an affront to the suffering permeating every brick and beam of the building.

And then, a deep guttural groan emanated from the other side of the door. As suddenly as the children appeared, they vanished, leaving us alone in the icy cold of the ward. The depressing atmosphere lingered, a reminder of the entities watching us, now unseen, but I had the feeling they were still here.

"We can't stay here," Carl muttered, his face filled with fear. "We have to keep moving."

"We need to help them. We have to help them." Fiona pleaded, her voice steady despite the tears glistening in her eyes. "They're trapped here, bound by whatever holds this asylum in its grip."

"We will help them, I promise. We'll find a way to free them." Carl reassured Fiona.

The door swung open. We took our chance and raced out of the room. Disoriented, we raced down the corridor, away from the stairs. We turned a corner, there was an open door to our left, we hurried into the room. It was a small chapel. Rows of chairs were upturned and scattered across the floor. In front of us was the altar; in front of the altar was a figure, standing with its back to us. To our left and right, ghostly figures started to manifest, standing, watching. The door closed slowly but firmly behind us, creaking on its old iron hinges.

"Not again." I muttered, "What is it with these doors?"

We were all rooted to the spot as the figure at the altar turned and moved towards us. Its movements were slow and deliberate. I couldn't shake the feeling we were far from understanding the true depth of the thing holding this asylum in its clutches. As the figure drew closer, its form becoming clearer with each torturous step, I realised our night of horror was far from over. The figure stopped. It spoke in what can only be described as a loud gasp, "Help us, free us."

"How? How do we free you?" begged Carl.

"It wants your souls as it took ours." It gasped.

As soon as the figure stopped speaking, it along with the ghostly apparitions vanished.

"Who... or what was it?" I asked, no longer trying to hide the fear in my voice.

Fiona shook her head as her gaze fell to the floor. "It has to be evil... it cannot be anything less."

Words stuck in my throat as I tried to speak, but fear prevented me from getting them out. I stamped my foot hard on the floor, trying to regain my composure. "How do we fight evil? Do we have any Holy Water or crucifixes? Please tell me we at least have a bible."

Tom looked at me and inhaled deeply, his voice soft and apologetic, "We came here looking for ghosts. We have had minor success in the past recording voices, the occasional door closing by itself, mainly EVPs. We've never come across anything evil, or a haunting on this scale, ever! We are totally unprepared."

"This is a chapel or prayer room, isn't it? There must be something here." I said, clutching at straws.

Carl agreed, suggesting we explore the room. The moon's weak rays struggled through the stained-glass windows, casting ethereal shadows across the floor. Our gaze settled on the small, neglected altar at the front. It was covered in a layer of dust, and adorned with a small crucifix, a weathered Bible, and a rosary. They seemed like relics of hope in a place swallowed by a dark shadow.

"Why are these still here?" Tom's voice cut through the silence, tinged with curiosity. "You'd think they'd be long gone by now."

"Perhaps these belonged to the spirits lingering here. Maybe the figure who spoke to us put them here, he was standing at the altar when we came in," said Fiona, her fingers hesitantly brushing the rosary beads. "These are symbols of comfort; maybe they'll offer us some protection in this darkness."

We formed a circle around the altar, clutching each other's hands in a symbol of faith. I have never been religious, but at that moment, I was willing to believe in anything which might offer us some hope.

"Let us pray," Fiona said, her voice stronger now, commanding. And so, we did, our words a mix of different prayers and pleas united, with a single purpose. As we prayed, the temperature in the room began to rise, the harsh cold retreating as if pushed back by our collective will. The darkness seemed to recoil, the gloom at the edges of the room drawing back.

Without warning, a violent force shook the chapel. The stained-glass windows shattered, sending a cascade of coloured shards raining down upon us. Then a howl, a sound so full of rage and despair it seemed to come from the very depths of hell.

We crouched low, covering our heads, the religious artefacts clutched tightly in our hands. When the chaos subsided, we looked up to find the chapel transformed. The darkness was back, the moon now hidden behind a menacing black cloud.

"It's angry," Fiona said, her voice trembling. "We've challenged it, and it's shown us its power."

But even as she spoke, I could feel a shift in the atmosphere. The evil that pervaded the asylum was still present, but it was no longer all-encompassing. I got the feeling we had made a dent in the darkness, however small.

"We need to keep going," I said, standing up, and brushing glass from my clothes. "We've hurt it, whatever it is. Stopping now is not an option."

The others nodded, a new determination in their eyes. We were all fighters, rebels in a war against an unseen, unknown enemy. As we left the chapel, our spirits were lifted slightly. The asylum seemed quieter now. The atmosphere had lifted just enough to allow us to breathe.

But, as we navigated the twisting corridors, we knew the respite may only be brief. The dark entity holding the spirits captive, would not give up easily. It was a force of pure evil. As we moved deeper into the heart of the nightmare, we prepared ourselves for what was to come. Each step took us further into the unknown. Each breath could be our last, but we were determined to fight, to free the captive spirits, and ourselves from the asylum.

The uneasy darkness seemed to mock us with false promises of safety. Each creak and groan of the asylum was a reminder we held no dominion here. We moved carefully through the halls as quietly as we could, our bodies alive with adrenaline and fear.

In our search for a way out we stumbled upon the asylum's library, a room we hadn't encountered before. The room was a confusion of books and papers, reminders of the forgotten studies and diagnoses that had happened here. The smell of mould and decay was overpowering, but it was the silence which unnerved us the most, a dense, expectant hush that seemed to hold its breath.

"Look at this," Fiona said, her voice trembling as she picked up a yellowed paper. It was a doctor's notes, detailing experimental treatments that had gone horribly wrong. As she read aloud, the words painted a picture of tragedy and cruelty, of patients subjected to inhumane experiments leaving them broken, or worse.

The history of the asylum was unfolding before us, each document, each room revealing more of the story. It was a tale of immense suffering and pain, of a place where the line between treatment and torture had been irrevocably blurred.

"We still need to find the source," I said, my resolve hardening. "There's something here, something that's holding them all here. We need to find it and end it." I could not believe these words were leaving my mouth. I had started the night a confirmed sceptic, now I felt like a full-blown ghost hunter. It was surreal.

"The answer could be here," said Carl, closing his eyes and cocking his head slightly to the right. "Was this all caused by an experimental treatment? I feel this place may hold the clue."

Agreeing, we continued our exploration, delving deeper into the documentation in the library. As we looked at the papers, a sudden blinding white light made us close our eyes tightly.

When we opened our eyes and readjusted to the light, we found ourselves in a treatment room. It was lined with white glistening tiles, the starkness of the room was a shock to the senses after the darkness of the corridors and the library. Instruments of dubious medical purpose lay scattered across a metal table, their surfaces stained with the passage of time. In the centre stood an archaic electric chair, its straps frayed and worn. A silent testament to the torturous treatments inflicted upon the unsuspecting and the unwilling.

Our hearts were pounding in our chests, the sudden transition disorientating and terrifying. "How did we get here?" Janet whispered; her voice filled with fear.

"It must be the asylum... playing tricks, shifting reality," I replied, my gaze fixed on the ominous chair. "It's not just the spirits that are trapped. The very essence of the place is tainted, twisted by the atrocities committed within these walls."

Carl approached the chair cautiously, his hand hovering inches from the backrest. "This is it," he said, his voice barely above a whisper. "This is where it happened... where they tried to cure madness with madness."

We gathered around him, a morbid curiosity drawing us closer. The room felt charged, heavy with echoes of screams and the despair of broken minds. Fiona reached out, her fingers tracing the contours of the chair, her face pale and drawn.

"We need to understand," she said, her voice firm despite the tremor that ran through it. "We need to understand and to put an end to this."

"What is there to understand? They were tortured." Tom said, an edge to his voice.

Janet looked puzzled, her brows furrowed in thought. "I didn't think the Victorians had electricity."

Calming down, Tom put a comforting arm around her shoulders, "Yes, the late Victorian era had electricity. It was a new marvel. Many cranks back then thought of cruel ways to use it to cure people's illnesses."

The door to another treatment room creaked open, revealing a sight stopping us in our tracks. A spectral figure lay strapped to the treatment table, its form shimmering and indistinct. We realised it was one of the patients. They were reliving their torment repeatedly. The spirit's eyes met ours, a plea for release written on its face. As we watched, rooted to the spot, the apparition faded away, leaving a cruel sadness settling in our hearts.

The realisation was a ponderous one. The asylum was a prison, not just of walls and bars, but of pain and despair. And we were caught in its grip, witnesses to the suffering which permeated every inch of the place.

We spent what felt like hours in these rooms, pouring over the documents, piecing together the grim history of the asylum. The experimental treatments, the unqualified staff, the overcrowded wards. It was a recipe for disaster, a disaster that had played out in the most horrific of ways.

As we read, the pieces began to fall into place. The entity haunting the asylum, the 'dark one' as the spirits called it, was a creation of the horrors which occurred here. It appeared to be a mix of the torturous doctor, and something born of the pain, the fear, and the rage of countless tormented souls. A hostile force that had grown in power and malevolence with each passing year.

In another blinding flash of white light, we were transported from the treatment room back into the library. The atmosphere of the asylum seemed to close in around us once more. I looked around the room, then at the others. "What just happened? Was that really possible?" My voice echoed around the dusty room, a stark contrast to the sterile horror of the treatment room we'd just vacated.

Carl rubbed his eyes, as though he could dispel the visions that haunted us. Janet shivered, drawing her arms around herself as if to ward off a chill that was more spiritual than physical.

"But the flash of light. The treatment room," she said, her voice trembling. "It was like being thrust through time."

Fiona, ever the pragmatist, was pacing, her steps measured, but her brow furrowed in thought. "We need a plan," she declared. "This 'dark one' the spirits speak of, it's the key to everything. We need to confront it, to understand it if we're ever going to break free from this... this nightmare."

The experimental treatments carried out here were nothing more than torture masquerading as a cure and had left a scar on the very soul of this place. It was a scar time could not heal. It was as if the very walls were closing in, eager to claim us as its next victims.

Chapter 5

As the group discussed their next move, each creak and whisper increased the feeling that unseen eyes were watching their every move. The weight of their experiences, the horrors they witnessed, fractured the once solid unity of the team. Cracks were appearing in their once-committed resolve. The team now wanted to move in different directions. Janet, Mark, and Tom wanting to find a way out, but Carl was insistent, his voice betraying a hint of the fear which gnawed at his resolve, "We've come too far to back down now," he stated, "we owe it to those spirits trapped here, as well as to ourselves."

Janet's nerves had been frayed to breaking point, she shook her head vehemently. "No. We... I... need to find a way out. This place... it's too much. We're not equipped to deal with this level of malevolence."

The argument escalated, voices raised in fear and frustration, until we could no longer move forward as a single group. Janet's voice trembled as she confronted Carl. Her torchlight casting long, wavering shadows on the decaying walls of the asylum corridor.

"Carl, we need to move, now!" Janet's eyes were wide with fear, her breathing was quick and shallow. "This place... it's a death trap, you know we're not equipped to deal with this, whatever this is!"

Carl his face set in a grim determination, shook his head. "Janet, I understand your fear but think about it. They can't leave," he said, gesturing around the room, "and even if all of us could get out, what happens to the spirits trapped here? They're bound by something otherworldly, and we might be their only chance of salvation."

Janet paced back and forth, wringing her hands. "But our lives are at risk! Every moment we spend here, we're playing into its hands. I've seen enough horror movies to know how this ends if we don't get out."

"Horror movies aren't real life." Carl countered, his voice calm but firm. "Yes, there's potential danger, but there's also a chance to make things right. We have a responsibility, not just to ourselves, but to those who suffered and are still suffering here."

Janet stopped pacing, her gaze meeting Carl's. "Responsibility? Carl, we're not real ghostbusters or exorcists. We're in way over our heads!"

Carl stepped closer, placing a reassuring hand on her shoulder. "Maybe so, but we've learned so much already. I don't think we should turn our backs on this now."

Janet's eyes glistened with unshed tears, the burden of their decision pressing down on her shoulders. "But what about us Carl? What about us? What if we don't make it out?"

Carl sighed, "I can't guarantee our safety, Janet. But I can't leave knowing I could have at least tried to help these poor souls. If you want to leave, I won't stop you. We can split into two groups, one to find a way out, the other to continue investigating."

Janet bit her lip. The internal struggle was written on her face. "And if we split up, we're more vulnerable. This place... it's like it's alive, and like Fiona said, it's like it's feeding off our fear."

"I know," Carl admitted. "But together or apart, were facing danger either way. At least this way, we can choose to face it on our own terms."

Janet nodded slowly, her mind made up. "Okay. We split up. But Carl, promise me this, if it gets too dangerous, you'll get out. Don't be a martyr."

Carl nodded, a solemn promise in his eyes. "I promise. And you be careful too. If you do find a way out, bring back help."

With a sorrowful heart, Janet agreed. A hasty meeting was convened. A plan was laid out, two paths forged in the darkness of uncertainty. With heavy hearts, we split into two teams, Carl, Fiona, and myself determined to delve deeper into the asylum, while Janet, Tom, and Mark resolved to find an escape. As we parted ways, tension filled the room, each member acutely aware of the risks and the slim hope that drove them onwards.

The asylum loomed around us, its history a shadow which stretched long and dark, a mystery deep and all-consuming. Ahead lay terror, tragedy, and the faintest glimmer of redemption. The darkness closed in as we continued down our separate paths. It served as a reminder, in Ravenswood Asylum, nothing was certain, and everything came at a cost.

Carl, Fiona and myself, fuelled by a desperate need to understand and end the nightmare, moved through the dark corridors of the Victorian building. At the heart of this forsaken place, amidst corridors choked with the whispers of the past, lay the main administrative room. A windowless chamber where daylight had never reached. Its door, once a barrier to the secrets held within, now hung loosely on its hinges. It was an eerie unspoken invitation into the gloom. As we crossed the threshold, the dust of forgotten decades and the scent of decay assaulted our senses. The room, stripped of its former purpose, was a hollow shell, its walls lined with empty shelves and cabinets which had once bristled with the records of sorrow and madness now stood empty. A large, broken, dust-covered desk sat at the centre, a remnant of a bygone era. There was no light in the room other than the light from our torches. Silence ruled this sanctum, a silence so profound it seemed to scream. It was punctuated by the occasional drip of water echoing like footsteps in the void. This forgotten chamber, seemed to hold a mirror to our souls, reflecting the personal horrors we carried within ourselves.

The room shimmered, and suddenly, I found myself not in the decaying room at the centre of the asylum, but in my childhood home, the scene of my own personal tragedy. A harrowing memory started to unfold, as vivid as if it was happening right now. It surged through me with merciless clarity. Fire, its voracious flames ravenously engulfing my home. It was unyielding, I could sense the searing heat, the acrid smoke assaulting my eyes and choking my breath, the fear, raw and unstoppable, taking over my very being.

"Emily!" My voice emerged as a hoarse, strangled cry; my single word swallowed by the roar of the inferno. My younger sister, her face contorted with fear, was trapped within this diabolical scene, her fate shrouded in the flames and smoke, her voice a haunting cry within the relentless crackling of the fire. The blaze danced with a timeless grace, casting a lurid glow that painted the night in shades of red and orange. Each crackle, each pop of the timbers was like the sinister laughter of a cruel spectre, rejoicing in the destruction. The heat was like a living thing, a beast clawing at my flesh, seeking to devour me and everything else in its path. "Emily! I have to find her!" My voice sounded distant, as though separated from me, it was a desperate, trembling plea.

My world seemed to narrow down to the singular focus of rescuing Emily, each moment stretching into an eternity filled with dread and despair. The air was filled with the acrid tang of destruction. Each breath was a battle, every step a defiance against the seemingly insurmountable dread threatening to consume me. I could feel the intense horror of the situation. I was overwhelmed by fear and helplessness as I struggled to push through the suffocating tendrils of the fire. "Carl's hand gripped my shoulder, pulling me back to a grim reality just as horror-filled as my visions from the past."

"Steve, you need to focus. Whatever you're seeing, it's not real. It's the asylum playing with your mind."

His words were a lifeline, pulling me back from the brink of madness. I blinked several times, as though washing the smoke out of my eyes. The horrific vision dissipated but left a residue of soot-like despair clinging to my soul. I was back in the dank and virtually empty room. The distant echo of the asylum's sad history whispering around us, but the horror of the fire lingered, a phantom pain that refused to be ignored.

"We have to move," I said, my voice barely a whisper, the memory of the fire still seared into my mind. "We can't let this place break us."

As we moved into an adjacent room each shadow seemed to dance with hidden intent, each whisper a reminder of the countless lives that had been broken within these walls. Then without warning, the door slammed shut behind us, the sound echoing in our ears like a death knell. We spun around, only to find the way we came blocked, the door immovable, its surface cold, damp, unyielding.

"This place is changing," Fiona said, her voice a mix of fear and awe, her eyes wide, staring around the room, "It's like it's reshaping itself around us, playing with our minds, trapping us here."

"It is playing with our minds Fiona. This is not reality." Carl tried to reassure us.

I tried to force the door, but it held firm. The light from our torches appeared to dim, the shadows on the walls creating a macabre dance. The stench of decay, sickly and sweet assaulted our senses with each breath. Our fear pressed in on our chests, tightening like vices. We were in a living nightmare, and through it all, the memory of the fire haunted me, a relentless spectre flickering at the edge of my consciousness. Emily's face, etched with fear, was a constant reminder of the guilt and pain I carried with me every day. The haunting memory of that fateful night, when everything was forever altered, remained with me, unhealed, a wound, a deep scar etched upon my soul. The asylum, with its eerie presence, seemed determined to reopen that wound.

Fiona's sharp intake of breath broke my thoughts, her features twisting into an expression of utter horror. It was as if she was no longer confined within the asylum's bleak walls but had been transported just as I had been.

She was in her past, in a terrible and painful memory, she was teetering on the precipice of a raging river. Her brother, fighting against the torrential current of a fast-moving river was holding onto a small branch of the tree growing on the edge of the river. He extended an arm desperately towards her, his pleas for rescue echoed in her mind, lodging firmly in her heart. "Please, someone, help him!" Fiona's voice broken, shattered, her outstretched hands grasping at the cruel illusion of her brother. The river's roar was deafening, a wild cacophony of rage and urgency, its turbulent water was relentless. Her eyes, wide and glistening with unshed tears mirrored the acute agony of the past replaying before her.

I reached for her, my hands clamping onto her shoulders to wrench her from the claws of her torturous vision. "Fiona! It's not real. You're here, with me, in the asylum. This is just what it did to me, it's a cruel trick of the mind," I implored, my tone a mixture of sternness and compassion. Fiona gasping with fear, her body quaking as if the raging waters themselves enveloped her. "But I can see him! There, in the water! I couldn't reach him back then, and I'm powerless now!" Her words were punctuated by sobs, each one a droplet in the torrent of her enduring guilt and sorrow. She watched as his grip failed and he was washed away.

I held her in a firm embrace, a bastion against the tempestuous sea of her grief, whispering words of comfort, bringing her back to reality. Gradually, the relentless clamour of the river ebbed away from her mind, and the spectral image of her brother disappeared, fading into a dark void. The chill of the indifferent walls of the asylum encased her once more, a grim reminder of the present. Yet, even as reality reasserted itself, the echoes of Fiona's tormented cries for her brother lingered in her thoughts. A haunting refrain of the heartache no walls could contain. We were silent for a moment, each of us grappling with the echoes of our past. The asylum was merciless, it preyed on our deepest regrets and fears, it was a predator of the psyche and it knew where to strike.

"We have to keep moving," I finally said, my voice low, "Or we could be lost to these visions forever."

Fiona nodded, wiping the tears from her cheeks, her expression hardening with a resolve born from the very depths of her grief. Carl tried the door once more, this time there was no resistance, it opened easily. Confused but relieved, we stepped into the corridor

"Let's go." Said Carl, "We have to end this for all the souls trapped here and for our own."

We continued our journey through the asylum, each step a defiance against the darkness which sought to consume us. Each corridor seemed to stretch on and on, endless tunnels of despair mocking our efforts. Slowly, one of the doors ahead of us creaked open, a sliver of light in the darkness, beckoning us. We approached cautiously, feeling countless unseen eyes watching us. Stepping into the room, a wave of oppressive energy washed over us with a palpable sense of malice.

"I feel we need to call out to the spirits. I don't know why... it's just a feeling." Fiona said. "Let's use this small table," She said blowing the dust from its surface.

We gathered around the table, our hands reaching out, finding each other in the gloom, a circle of unity, a barrier standing against the darkness wanting to divide and conquer.

Fiona closed her eyes and lifted her head towards the ceiling. "We call out to the spirits of this place," Fiona began, her voice steady and clear. "We acknowledge your pain, your suffering. Our purpose is to assist you in finding peace."

Her words echoed, not just in the room, but throughout the very fabric of the building, a call to arms for the souls lingering in the shadows. The temperature in the room dropped, an icy chill bearing down on us, a tangible manifestation of the countless tragedies that unfolded within these walls. Carl's face was etched with anguish as he was abruptly catapulted back into his own nightmare. He was standing on the merciless landscapes of Afghanistan, a stark contrast to the asylum's dim and ominous corridors. To him, the room was alive with the sound of gunfire and desperate shouts of war. The relentless spectre of chaos and unspeakable horrors encircled him, his muscles tensed, every fibre of his being reverting to the battle-hardened soldier within. His hands were frantically searching for the absent weapon, gritty desert winds battered his face, carrying the pungent stench of gunpowder and the cloying scent of fear. Instinctively, he flinched at the thunderous, rhythmic sound of helicopter blades menacingly overhead, its dark silhouette lit up by an enemy missile.

"Carl!... Carl! Are you alright?" My voice, desperate to bridge the chasm between reality and his memories, to cut through the maelstrom of his mind. "You're in the asylum, remember? Don't let this place unravel you!"

Around us, the asylum stood silent. An eerie mausoleum of forgotten souls. Yet for Carl, the echoes of distant battlefields continued to rage, a relentless storm only he could perceive. His battle was not with the here and now, but with the shadows of his mind, where wars of the past continued to haunt him. An eternal struggle between the world of grim reality and the unyielding nightmare of his memory.

For an excruciating moment, he was immobile, his eyes a reflection of his harrowing past, glazed over with the indelible imprint of war. Gradually, as if it was wading through the dense fog of battle, the sound of my voice seemed to reach him. He blinked rapidly, his frantic eyes softening as the cruel desert mirage ebbed away, yielding once again to the reality of the asylum. Gasping for breath, his chest rose and fell with the intensity of a man who'd just escaped the clutches of death. "I was there again, Steve," he gasped, his voice was hoarse, his eyes darting about, half-expecting an enemy to ambush his from the shadows. "I was back in the heat of combat. It all felt so real." His words hung with the weight of the unspoken horrors in his mind. Fiona placed a hand on his shoulder, steadying him.

"It's what this place does, Carl. It digs deep into our darkest memories and makes us live them again. But you're here, with us, now." Fiona, her face still pale from her own ordeal, added softly, "We've all seen our personal hells here. It wants to break us Carl. We can't let it."

Carl nodded slowly, his breathing gradually steadying. "You're right. We must push on. We can't let it use our fears against us."

Our visions had tormented us, pulling at the very fabric of our sanity. But somewhere, deep within my own nightmare, a part of me knew it hadn't been real, it was the asylum using our darkest fears against us. We clung to each other; our expressions haunted but resolute. a small island of sanity amid the madness.

"We can't let it win," I echoed, my voice hoarse. "Come on we need to start moving again."

Janet, Tom, and Mark's journey towards escape was no less harrowing. They had found themselves in the elderly patient's wards, the rooms a tortured catalogue of suffering. Each door they opened revealed fresh horrors, reminders of the pain that permeated every brick, every floorboard of the building. In one room, the apparition of an old woman confronted Mark, her face twisted in an eternal scream, her hands clawing at the straps which bound her to a rusted bed frame. In another, Janet had stumbled upon a solitary confinement cell, the scratchings from bloody fingers still visible on the walls. Tom entered a room only to be surrounded by ghostly patients, thin skeletal faces staring at him in silence. Their resolve faltered as their desire to flee battled with the despair threatening to drag them down, but they pushed on. They had to, driven by the primal instinct to survive and escape the hell the asylum had become.

Each moment of time that passed was an eternity of fear and uncertainty. Both groups, isolated in their own pockets of horror, continued their respective quests, each unaware of the other's plight. The asylum seemed to stretch on forever, as if it was an endless maze.

Dawn lingered a mere three hours away, but its tentative rays were a distant promise in the overbearing gloom. The entity, the malevolent force that had the asylum in its spectral grip, was marshalling its power. We, a ragtag band of the broken, bore the weight of being its only challengers. With each hesitant step, we delved into the belly of the beast, towards the pulsating core of the malignance that plagued us. The building itself seemed to throb with a sinister intent, its walls whispering of untold horrors, resolute in its resolve to not yield without first unleashing its fury.

"We can't falter now," I said, my voice a frail thread in the darkness.

Each shadow seemed to dance with the threat of unspeakable terror, every creak, every groan of the ageing structure a sign of the dread to come. Our breaths came in shallow, ragged gulps, each one burdened with what lay ahead. The darkness was not merely the absence of light but a living, breathing entity, cloaking everything in a shroud of despair.

Janet, Tom, and Mark moved cautiously through the darkened hallways of the asylum. "We've got to find a way out," Janet gasped, her voice panicked, barely above a whisper, as if afraid of awakening the dormant spirits hiding in the shadows.

Tom nodded, his face set in grim determination. "There has to be a service exit or a window we can break through. Anything to get out of this place."

The corridor stretched into a never-ending tunnel of darkness. Mark's voice broke the silence, his tone one of strained optimism. "Look, there's someone peering around a door up ahead. Maybe it leads outside."

They approached the door. It was partially open, the rotting wood, swollen from damp, preventing it from opening further. With a collective effort, they pushed it; the hinges groaning in protest as it opened. The room inside was bare, its windows barred; there was no other way in or out of the room. "What was it you saw Mark?" asked Janet.

"I'm not sure; it looked like someone peering out of the room looking at us."

An icy shiver ran down Tom's spine. "Well, there's no one here now, and we cannot get through those bars."

They moved to the room opposite, a small room; each wall had a narrow full-length mirror fixed to it. Every mirror facing another, mounted on opposing walls, creating an infinite reflection between them. The reflections cast back at them were distorted in ways which made their stomachs churn. It was as if the mirrors reflected their physical forms, but twisted and more sinister.

"Something's not right about this place," Mark said, his voice trembling slightly. "These mirrors... they're like eyes, watching us, and why are they placed like this?"

Janet approached one of the mirrors, its surface covered in a fine layer of dust. Her reflection gazed back at her, it was her, but it wasn't her. The eyes in her reflection appeared hollow, the mouth twisted. She reached out to wipe away the dust to gain a clearer view of her image. "Janet, don't!" Tom shouted, but it was too late. Janet's hand touched the mirror's surface, and in an instant, she was pulled through it, her body vanishing as if the mirror were a vertical pool of water. Tom and Mark rushed forward, but Janet was gone, her cries for help echoing faintly from within the mirror.

"Janet!" Mark shouted, his voice filled with panic. He reached out towards the mirror, but Tom pulled him back.

"Don't! It's some kind of portal... a gateway to another place, a place I don't think we want to enter."

They both stepped back, breaths taken with fear, they stared at the mirror. Janet's face appeared again, her features contorted in terror as she pounded on the glass from the other side, her fists creating no sound nor leaving any marks.

"We have to get her back," Tom said, his eyes wild with fear.

"We do, but how?" Mark asked, his voice filled with desperation. "We know nothing about this. Let's go and find the others."

They stood there, totally helpless as Janet's cries grew fainter, her image disappearing into the darkness beyond the mirror's surface. The room seemed to close in around them, the other mirrors reflecting their horrified faces back at them, a gallery of fear.

"We can't just leave her," Tom said, his voice breaking. "We have to bring her back."

Mark nodded. "We'll find a way. But we need help."

With the burden of sorrow in their hearts, they left the room; the door closing behind them with a definitive thud. The corridor again stretched out before them, a path of uncertainty and fear. But they pushed on, driven by the need to rescue Janet and to escape the nightmare which was Ravenswood Asylum. They moved through the darkened hallways, trying to find their way back to Carl and the others. Every shadow whispered of danger, and every creak sounded a warning.

The asylum was a labyrinth, its secrets hidden in the darkness, its horrors waiting just out of sight. They knew they couldn't give up, not when one of their own was lost in the grip of an otherworldly terror. Their search for the others continued, their torchlights flickering in the gloom. Shouting out, they hoped the others would hear them and come looking, "Help! Carl! Steve! Help!" Tom cried.

Their calls echoed down the corridors, the sound bouncing off the walls then fading, consumed by the silence. The asylum was absorbing their cries, its endless halls and closed doors seeming to mock their efforts.

"We need to stay focused," Mark said, trying but failing to keep the tremor out of his voice. "If we let fear take over, we're as good as lost."

They continued on, each turn and each doorway offering a glimmer of hope that was quickly snuffed out by another long stretch of hallway or a room leading nowhere. The building seemed to reshape itself around them, an ever-changing maze designed to disorient and terrify them. As they turned another corner, they found themselves entering what appeared to be an old medical treatment room. The examination bed was rusted, the mattress rotted away to practically nothing. In the dim light of their torches, they could see the walls were covered in scratches and writings. These were the desperate markings of those who were once confined here.

Tom immediately stopped, his light falling on a particular section of the wall. There, written repeatedly, was. 'EMILY HELP STEVE.'

"I think that was Steve's sister's name. I'm sure I heard him mention her." Mark whispered, the realisation hitting them like a physical blow.

"But… She can't have been a patient here."

The scratchings on the wall seemed to pulsate in the torchlight, as if imbued with the frenetic energy of its creator. "EMILY HELP STEVE," the words echoed through the room, a repetition inscribed by an unseen hand. It was then they heard it, a soft sobbing coming from the end of the ward. Cautiously, they made their way towards the sound, their hearts pounding in their chests. The sobbing grew louder as they approached until they were standing before a closed door. Together, they pushed it open.

Inside, they found nothing but an empty room, the sobbing now gone, silence filled the room. The sense of loss and longing was intense.

"We must be getting closer," Tom said, his voice a mix of fear and determination. "The asylum is reacting to us; it's trying to break us."

As they left the room; the door swung shut behind them, sending a shiver down their spines. They moved swiftly, continuing their search, calling out for their friends, desperate for any sign of life in the vast, dark silence of the asylum. The darkness pressed in from all sides threatening to crush them. They pushed on, their resolve fuelled by the need to rescue Janet and bring her back from whatever hell she had been taken to. Finally, after what seemed like an eternity, they heard a response. A distant shout, a voice they recognised, my voice.

"Over here!" I shouted, relief flooding my voice. "We're over here!"

They rushed towards my call, and there, at the end of yet another long corridor, we saw them, their faces etched with worry and exhaustion.

The two groups embraced, finding much-needed human connection amid the horror we found ourselves in. We huddled together, our voices hushed yet urgent, as we hastily traded stories. The chilling tale of Janet's inexplicable vanishing gave us the most concern.

"We need to find her," I said, my voice filled with a fierce determination. "And we need to end this. Together."

Gathering our courage, our fear tempered by a shared bond, no longer individuals caught in a nightmare; now a team, united once more, against the darkness, our set out with renewed purpose to confront the horror, save Janet, and release the trapped spirits at Ravenswood Asylum.

Chapter 6

Heading back through the corridors, our steps were hurried yet cautious. The path was lit by only the rapidly dimming light from our torches, the batteries running out. The silence was only interrupted by our breathing and the random eerie cries of the departed. As we progressed, the history of the place revealed more of itself, but in fragments, as though teasing us about its past. A bloodstained trolley here, the remains of a straight-jacket there, each piece a relic of anguish. We passed rooms which seemed to be alive with the residue of past horrors; the place was thick with the psychic remnants of screams and forlorn sobs.

"Keep your eyes peeled for the room of mirrors," Tom instructed, his voice a whisper. The method of Janet's disappearance pulling at each of us, a silent motivator driving us forward.

Carl, with a deep, steadying breath, closed his eyes for a moment, reaching out with his senses. "I can feel her... she's here, scared, disoriented, but still here. The mirror is... I don't know... it's more than a mirror. It's a threshold to somewhere else, twisted and dark. If we can't get her out, we'll lose her forever."

As we retraced the steps of Mark and Tom to the room of mirrors, the atmosphere turned into an icy embrace whispering of unseen terrors. The door, ominous and uninviting, stood before them, it was slightly ajar, a stark contrast to its firmly closed state when they left it. "This is it," Tom declared with a mix of resolve and apprehension, eyeing the door warily. "Be careful, it's open. Someone or something has been here."

"Or... is still here." Whispered Mark.

With trepidation, Carl entered the room. "It's all clear. The room is empty."

The rest of us entered, scrutinising the four mirrors, each surface warping and twisting reality into grotesque parodies of our bodies. Carl inched forward, his gaze locked onto the mirror which had claimed Janet. His expression one of grim determination. Mark raised a cautionary hand, pointing towards the dark yet reflective surface of the mirror. "That's the one. Be careful Carl, do not touch its surface! We don't want to lose you to its clutches too."

"Janet, can you hear me?" Carl's voice boomed, resonating with authority and a hint of desperate hope. "It's Carl. We've come to rescue you."

A whisper, as fragile as a cobweb, filtered through the hushed room. "Carl? I'm here... it's dark... So dark... I can't find my way out."

"Janet, look around. There must be something, a symbol, an artefact. See if there is anything that might serve as a clue to get you out of there," Carl implored, his face etched with fierce concentration.

The room tensed, every breath was being held, every heartbeat had paused as Carl maintained his tenuous link, a beacon of hope in the depressing gloom. Minutes stretched into what seemed like hours, each moment a drawn-out echo in the silence.

As Carl was trying to maintain contact with Janet, Tom, attempted to shed light on the mystery by directing his torch at the other mirrors in the room. Every mirror reflected the beam except one. One mirror devoured the light, like a gaping cavity of darkness. Suddenly, Janet's faint voice could be heard. "There's a mirror here... a light just shone through it."

Tom spun towards Carl, his voice tinged with urgency. "What's she saying? I can't quite hear her."

"She mentioned a mirror, light passing through it," Carl replied, his eyes never leaving the sinister mirror.

Tom approached the mirror, determination etching his face. "I'm going to try once more. Janet, if you see the light, call out to us!" He cast his torch beam towards the mirror again. As before, the light vanished into its depths.

Janet's voice, slightly stronger, filtered through. "I see it! A light... it's coming through a mirror here. It's shining through!" Her words, a beacon in the darkness, ignited a spark of hope. The room, thick with suspense, waited as Tom and Carl prepared to harness this newfound clue. It was a potential lifeline to save Janet from her dark prison.

"Good. Focus on that mirror, Janet. Try to connect with your reflection," Carl directed, his voice a guiding light through the darkness.

The spirit box crackled into life, all eyes focused on the white noise. "I haven't turned it on." Fiona said, clearly startled.

Something or someone was trying to come through. Ears strained at the white noise, then a girl's voice broke through and appeared to punctuate a partial message, "Go... through... the..."

"What did it say?" Mark Asked.

Fiona straining to hear more. "It sounded like 'go through the'."

Mark looked perplexed. "Go through the what?"

Janet struggled to breathe, gasping and trembling with each inhale, while an eerie silence surrounded her. Janet called out, her voice sounded faint, distant. "It's... it's so cold, unbearably cold. I, I don't know where I am. I'm scared." She stammered, her voice trembling with fear. "My reflection in this mirror... it's my face, but distorted. I'm terrified. Please, help me! Get me out of this nightmare!" Her plea laced with raw panic.

"Janet, listen to my voice," Fiona interjected, trying to pierce the veil of fear surrounding her. "You need to concentrate on the thought of being back here with us. Picture the room, picture us. Let that picture guide you back to us."

The silence that followed was suffocating. Each passing second felt like an eternity. We yearned for even the slightest hint, a flicker of movement which would signal Janet's imminent return.

Suddenly, the surface of the mirror rippled, a wave of energy shimmering on its surface. Janet's voice came through louder, but with a distinct undertone of tension. "There's something else here with me. It's trying to keep me in here."

Carl's face paled, his psychic senses attuned to the struggle unfolding in the realm beyond. "Fight it, Janet. You're stronger than it is."

The voice came through the spirit box again. It was clear and determined, "Go through... mirror... go through."

Carl was the first to react. "Janet, you must go through the other mirror! The one where you saw the light. Trust me! GO THROUGH THE MIRROR WITH THE LIGHT!" He shouted, Janet's faint voice came back. "I'm scared."
Carl tried to make a psychic connection with her. "Trust me Janet, go through the mirror."
We could only watch as the mirror's surface continued to undulate, an otherworldly battle reflected in its depths. Janet's reflection, a ghostly image superimposed on the swirling darkness, seemed to push against an unseen force.
Each passing moment felt like an eternity as the tension of anticipation built. Then, in a moment of sudden clarity, Janet's image sharpened. She was now standing out against the background as the dark presence receded into the periphery of the mirror.
"I think it's working," Janet gasped, her voice filled with a mix of exhaustion and hope. "I can feel myself getting closer to you."
"Keep going, Janet!" Tom urged, his hands balled into fists at his sides, as if ready to fight whatever was holding Janet. "We're right here, waiting for you!"
With one final push, a look of intense concentration etched on her spectral face, Janet lunged forward. The mirror's surface shattered, a cascade of shimmering fragments fell to the floor as she tumbled through.
We rushed forward, catching her as she fell, her body trembling from the ordeal. "You did it, Janet," Carl whispered, relief washing over his features. "You're back with us now."
Janet stood up and threw her arms around Carl. She clung to him tightly. Her breaths were ragged gasps as she adjusted to the reality of being back in the room. "It was so dark, so very dark, and icy cold in there. But I kept thinking of you all, of the world I belong to. And somehow, I got through the mirror."
The room fell quiet; the shattered pieces of mirror the only remnants of the struggle that had taken place. We knew our time in the asylum was far from over, the path ahead fraught with unknown dangers and more horrors to face, but for now, we took a moment to revel in our minor victory, the return of our friend from the clutches of an otherworldly prison.

Janet looked at each of us. "Now, can we get the hell out of here?" Tears welled up in her eyes.

"Absolutely, let's get out of this forsaken place," I agreed, my voice steady despite my intense fear. "We will return better prepared and confront this nightmare head-on."

The faint, eerie echoes of the asylum breaking the silence, reminded us our respite was only temporary. We each knew, in the recesses of our minds, the entity which haunted these halls was merely biding its time, lurking in the shadows.

As we navigated our way back to the Nurse's station on the ground floor, the asylum became charged with an unspoken foreboding. The dim corridors, lined with peeling paint and the echoes of long-forgotten despair, seemed to close in around us. A reminder of the horrors we had faced and those yet to come.

It was at the Nurse's station we first noticed a change in Tom. His footsteps became uneven, his gaze distant and glazed. Without warning, his body convulsed, like a puppet jerked by unseen strings. His eyes, once filled with determination, now flickered with an otherworldly darkness.

"Tom?" I called out, my voice tinged with alarm. "Tom, can you hear me?"

But the Tom who responded was not the friend we knew. His voice, once warm and familiar, now resonated with a chilling, guttural tone. "Tom is not here anymore," it sneered, its words slithering through the cold air.

Panic surged through me as I realised the entity had possessed him, twisting his form into a vessel for its own purposes. We stood frozen, unsure how to combat this new threat from within our own ranks.

A wave of panic crashed over the rest of us as we witnessed Tom's body contorting in a nightmarish fashion. His limbs started to bend in an unnatural and grotesque manner, the sickening sound of bones breaking and joints popping assaulting our ears. My skin crawled, I could virtually feel the agony and torment coursing through Tom's twisting body.

"Fight it Tom, fight it!" Carl shouted, advancing forward, his voice a blend of fear and defiance. "Don't let it control you!"

Yet, the entity within Tom only sneered, a sound that chilled us to our bones. "Futile," it hissed through Tom's lips, "He is mine now."

An evil laughter came from Tom echoing through the empty hallways of the asylum, advising us of our dire situation. Tom's once familiar form now stood before us, deformed and broken, a mere puppet of the dark force which had taken residence within him.

"We need to move now!" I urged, snapping out of the paralysing fear. "We can't stay here!"

Carl nodded. "Right. We need to find somewhere to hide, to plan our next move."

We backed away slowly, keeping our eyes fixed on Tom, whose twisted smile only grew wider. With a sudden burst of speed, we turned and ran, our footsteps echoing loudly in the unnerving stillness of the asylum. As we navigated the labyrinth of corridors, the atmosphere grew thicker, it was as if the very walls were alive and breathing with their own evil intentions. We blundered into a small room, its walls lined with decaying medical equipment. Quickly, we barricaded the door with an old metal cabinet, the sound of metal scraping against the floor, grating on our already frayed nerves.

"We need a plan," I said, trying to keep my voice steady. "We can't just run blindly around this hell-hole."

Fiona looked around the room frantically. "Are we all here?"

Janet nodded, "Yes, all but Tom." she panted.

Mark paced the room, his mind racing. "We need to expel that thing from Tom. But how? We don't even know what we're dealing with."

As we deliberated, the sound of footsteps approached, slow and deliberate. Tom... 'it'... was hunting us, its presence a suffocating force that seemed to seep through the very walls. The door rattled violently; the sound jarring us to our core. "Open up!" Tom's voice, twisted and distorted, called out mockingly from the other side of the door. "Let me in."

We held our breath, praying our makeshift barricade would hold. Outside it pounded on the door, the force of its blows causing the metal cabinet to shudder.

"Think, think," I muttered under my breath, my mind racing for a solution.

Carl's eyes widened. "The chapel! Maybe there's something there, Holy Water, anything that could help. Who's got the crucifix? Where's the bible?"

Fiona reached for her small backpack. "I've got both."

The worn-out door rattled again; its feeble protests told us it couldn't hold out much longer.

"We need to move this cabinet, turn off our torches." Said Carl. "When Tom ... when that thing enters the room, I'll throw this old jug into the far corner. Hopefully, it will move towards the noise, and then we run towards the chapel."

We eased the barricade from the door and took cover behind it. Our torches were switched off, and we waited in the darkness. Time seemed to stand still for a few agonising minutes. Our hearts pounded ferociously, echoing in our ears like drumbeats. Each throb amplifying the dread of the entity's imminent intrusion. The tension was real, every breath a struggle against the suffocating fear. The door rattled violently in its frame as it unleashed its fury, its relentless pounding raising our levels of fear to new heights. Suddenly, with a force that seemed to shake the very foundations of the building, the door burst open. A surge of terror gripped me, sending tremors through my body that I couldn't control.

In a desperate bid to distract the entity, Carl hurled the jug towards the far corner of the room. The sound of glass crashing against the floor reverberated through the room. For a split second, the entity's attention diverted towards the sound, giving us a glimmer of hope. It walked over to investigate the noise.

"Now!" Whispered Carl "Make our break for the chapel," Urgency lacing his voice.

With Fiona clutching the bible and crucifix tightly, we ran out of the room. The entity's malevolent laughter seeped through the walls, a chilling reminder of the danger lurking only feet away. We could hear what used to be Tom following us as we raced through the maze of hallways. The sound of its pursuit was relentless, a constant reminder of the nightmare we were trying to escape.

Reaching the chapel, we slammed the door closed behind us; the sound resonating through the desolate corridors. The chapel, once a place of solace and prayer, now lay in ruin, its pews overturned, and the altar desecrated.

"We need to find some Holy Water," Carl said, his eyes scanning the room.

As we rummaged through the debris, we could hear laughter echoing through the halls, getting closer and closer. "You cannot hide," it taunted.

Fiona placed the bible and crucifix on what remained of the altar, her hands trembling. "Hopefully, this should give us some protection."

Frantically we searched the chapel, and, in a small, dusty cupboard, we found a small vial of what we hoped was Holy Water, its contents still intact despite years of neglect. The enraged howls intensified, the sound of the entity's approach filling each of us with dread once again. Its presence was unmistakable, a sinister force charging the very air we breathed. The dark entity now residing within Tom's body, burst into the chapel. A shiver of fear collectively coursed through us.

"It's here," Fiona whispered, her voice barely audible over the pounding of our hearts.

We steadied ourselves, turning in unison to face the horror of its ghastly arrival. Tom stood there, his form twisted, and barely recognisable, a human body now being controlled by the dark will of the entity. Tom's eyes, once warm and familiar, burned with cruel fire, and his smile twisted into a grotesque parody of how Tom used to be.

Fiona held the bible and crucifix aloft, her voice steady as she recited the Lord's Prayer. Carl stepped forward, the vial of water in his hand. "In the name of all that is Holy, I command you to leave this place! Leave here! Exit our friend's body! Leave him alone!" Shouting he brandished the vial. "IN THE NAME OF ALL THAT IS HOLY, I COMMAND YOU TO LEAVE!"

Carl splashed some of the Holy Water at the body of Tom. The water sizzled upon contact, emitting a hiss like serpents coiling in the dark. Tom's twisted form merely juddered, a mockery of pain, as if the entity within scoffed at our feeble attempts. The room turned frigid, a cloak of dread enveloped us, as if the atmosphere conspired to suffocate our spirits. Silhouettes danced along the decrepit walls whispering secrets of their tragic histories, of lives cut short and souls ensnared by madness and despair.

Tom's voice, or rather, the sinister echo now resonating from his throat, filled the room with a chilling laugh. "Do you think your faith can save you here?" it taunted, its tone dripping with malice. It's control over Tom seemed complete, a puppeteer manipulating its marionette with grotesque precision.

Fiona's hands trembled, yet her resolve did not waver. Her voice rose above that of the entity. "Our faith is stronger than any evil who dares to confront us!" she proclaimed, her conviction piercing the shadowy veil.

I could see the strain on Carl's face. The muscles in his jaw tensed in determination. He was a man who had faced horrors before, but nothing of this power. We'd all heard stories of the asylum, of experiments breaching the boundary of ethics and humanity and of patients who were subjected to unspeakable torments. It was said the doctor in charge, a man of science corrupted by a thirst for knowledge beyond the moral compass, opened a doorway to something ancient and evil. And it was in this forsaken place. Amidst the echoes of screams, we now stood, confronting not just the entity possessing Tom, but the accumulated anguish of countless lost souls.

As we grappled with this terrifying development, the asylum seemed to respond, its walls groaning as if in pleasure at our plight.

Fiona held the bible and crucifix directly in front of the entity. "I command you to leave."

The entity recoiled momentarily, a hiss escaping its twisted lips. But it was only a brief respite. With a guttural snarl, it stepped towards Fiona, its gaze piercing through her defences.

"Run!" Carl bellowed, pulling Fiona back as the entity advanced.

We turned on our heels, fleeing the chapel in a panicked rush. The entity's laughter was the sound of madness, following us, stalking us through the dark corridors.

We struggled to breathe as we sprinted, the entity's presence somehow never far behind. The dimly lit hallways stretched out endlessly, a nightmarish maze with no escape.

"Here!" I yelled, spotting a heavy door. We burst through it, closing it quickly behind us. Carl and Fiona pushed an old desk against it, barricading us in, and the entity controlling Tom's body out.

The room was dark, save for the sliver of moonlight filtering through a cracked, dirty window. We crouched, our hearts hammering in our chests, as we listened to the sound of the entity's pursuit.

"We can't keep running," Janet whispered, her voice laced with fear. "It just keeps up with us. We need a better plan," Janet said, her eyes scanning the room for anything we could use as a weapon.

But what could we use against such a force? The entity was not just a physical presence; it was a manifestation of pure evil.

"What does it want?" I asked, trying to keep my voice steady. "Don't we need to understand why it's here?" As I spoke, a low growl came from the other side of the door.

Carl whispered, "We can't stay here," there was an urgency in his voice. "We need to move."

The growl intensified, the sound vibrating through the room. The door shook under the entity's assault.

"Look there," Fiona whispered urgently, gesturing towards a small service hatch. "It might lead to the basement."

With no time to spare, we ran over to the hatch. Our hands worked frantically to pry it open, once we succeeded it revealed a foreboding abyss beneath us. The space was narrow; a menacing shaft into the unknown, but it was our hope, our only hope. One by one, we lowered ourselves into the hatch. The descent was difficult, the walls of the shaft crumbling and dusty, cold and unyielding. Our movements were cautious and deliberate as we navigated the tight space. As we reached the bottom, our feet touched solid, hard ground. Around us lay the shadowy expanse of the asylum's underbelly, a new labyrinth of potential dangers and hidden horrors.

"Where now?" Mark asked, his voice barely above a whisper.

"We've got to find a way out," I replied. "There has to be another exit."

Moving cautiously, we navigated the cluttered basement. The silence was terrifying. A loud crash echoed through the space, freezing us to the spot, our hearts skipping a beat. Was the entity down here with us? We huddled together, moving as one through the darkness. The batteries in our torches were almost dead, their faint light our only guide in the gloom. Reaching a stairwell, a sense of dread washed over us. Knowing the entity was near, we climbed the stairs slowly, quietly, each step increasing our fear. Emerging onto the ground floor, we found ourselves in familiar corridors. But the entity's presence felt as though it were everywhere, a suffocating force threatening to overwhelm us.

"Come on, we need to keep moving," Carl urged, his voice strained.

We navigated our way towards the main front door, each step a gamble in the twisted game we were being forced to play. The entity was toying with us, its danger a constant threat at our heels.

Finally, we saw it, our exit, a glimmer of hope in the darkness. We raced towards it, our escape within reach. But, as we neared the front door, a chilling laugh echoed around us. Tom stood between us and our freedom; his twisted form more terrifying than ever.

"We can't give up," Carl said, his voice a rallying cry. "We have to fight."

I knew we had to get away. In sheer panic, I grabbed Fiona by the arm and dragged her away from the others. My heart pounded in my chest, adrenaline fuelling my desperate flight back to the stairwell. The entity's laughter echoed in my ears, a sinister backing track to our frantic escape.

"Steve, wait! We can't leave them." Fiona's voice trembled, but there was no time to slow down. The possessed husk of our friend was too close, the sound of his footsteps a relentless drumbeat of doom. "Where are we going?" Fiona gasped as I pulled her along,

"Anywhere but here," I muttered, though I knew it wasn't much of an answer. I glanced around, searching for any familiar landmarks, any sign that could lead us to safety. I saw the entrance to the basement and raced towards it.

I took the stairs two at a time, with Fiona right behind me as we plunged back into the cloying darkness of the basement.

The air grew colder, the walls sweating moisture that reflected what was left of our torchlight. Each step felt like a descent into another world, a place where light and hope were but distant memories. The asylum's history whispered around us, tales of madness, tales of despair, tales of lives snuffed out in the name of twisted science. I could almost hear the screams of those long gone, their agony seeping through the stone.

"Are we safe down here?" Fiona's voice quivered with fear.

I glanced back at her, seeing the terror etched on her face. "Safe? I don't know, I doubt it." I replied, failing to muster any semblance of confidence. "But at least we're out of sight, for now."

A sudden crash above us made us both jump. "Keep moving," I whispered, my voice barely audible over the pounding of my heart. The basement was black, not able to see a hand in front of my face, the dim light of my fading torch barely penetrating the gloom. My breath came in short gasps, each one tasting of dust and fear. As we fumbled through the debris, my eyes frantically searched for any hint of another exit. Then I saw it. What looked like an old coal hatch, partially hidden beneath a pile of rotting boxes and their forgotten contents. My heart leapt. This could be our way out. I lunged towards it, my hands frantically clawing away the obstacles barring our path. Fiona joined in quickly scooping up handfuls of debris, throwing it aside as quickly as she could. Working tirelessly, she aided in my frantic effort to clear the obstructed path. Her determined movements, mirroring my own, added to the sense of desperation as we both sought a way out.

The hatch was old, its metal rusted and sharp to the touch. I grasped the handle, my fingers tearing at the corroded metal. It didn't budge. Panic surged through me, we couldn't be trapped here, not now, not when freedom was so close. I kicked at the hatch, the sound of my desperate blow echoing through the silent basement. Again and again, I kicked it with all my might, each kick a desperate plea for escape.

"Come on Steve, get it open." Fiona pleaded.

Gathering all my strength, I hurled myself against the hatch. With a tortured cry of rusted metal and a desperate splintering of wood, it finally gave way, revealing the faintest hint of dawn's first light. We scrambled through the opening, the rough edges of the hatch tearing at our clothes and skin as we crawled up the old concrete coal shoot. At the top a wooden hatch blocked our exit. I pushed it hard, and to my surprise it gave way easily. Finally, we were out. Falling to the ground outside, the cool, fresh air was a stark contrast to the suffocating gloom of the asylum's interior. My lungs heaved, drawing in deep breaths of freedom.

Lying there, on the dew-drenched grass, we looked back at the imposing structure of the asylum. The sky was painted in an array of pinks and oranges, the first light of dawn breaking the night's hold and illuminating the building's facade, which stood as a silent sentinel to the horrors within. But we knew the entity was lurking in those shadows, waiting for its next victims. What of the others? Were they still alive? We needed to get help, and fast. The fight wasn't over; it was only just beginning. But for now, the two of us had survived and it was up to us to get help. Exhaustion and fear clung to me like a second skin as we stumbled away from the asylum, the dawn's light casting long, eerie shadows across the ground. The relief of our escape tempered by the knowledge our friends were still trapped inside. We had no idea what unimaginable horrors they could be suffering at the hands of that evil force.

"We have to get help," I gasped, my voice ragged with fatigue.

Fiona, her face pale and drawn, nodded in agreement. "Yes, the police, the fire brigade, anyone who will listen. They have to believe us."

We ran to the van; I picked my phone up, its screen a welcome glow in the dim light. My fingers trembled as I dialled the emergency services. "Hello? Yes, I need to report an... an incident. It's urgent, it's an emergency."

The operator's voice was calm, a stark contrast to the chaos we fled from. "Can you describe the nature of the incident?"

I struggled to find the words. How could I explain the unexplainable? "It's the old asylum on the hill. There's something... Something wrong there. People are trapped inside."

There was a pause on the other end of the line. "Are you reporting a fire? A break-in?"

"No, it's not like that," I said, frustration mounting. "There's something inside that building. Something evil. We barely escaped with our lives."

The operator's tone changed, scepticism creeping in. "Sir, are you sure you're not mistaken? The asylum has been abandoned for years."

I clenched my jaw, fighting back a surge of panic. "I'm not mistaken. Send someone now! Our friends could be dead!"

The line went silent for a moment. "Okay, sir. I'll send a unit to check it out. Stay where you are."

I ended the call with a hollow feeling in the pit of my stomach. Would they make it in time? Would they be able to do anything?

Fiona placed a hand on my shoulder, a silent show of support. "We've done what we can for now. Let's just hope they get here soon."

We moved away from the asylum, it unnerved us with its foreboding presence looming in the background. As we waited for the police to arrive, I couldn't help but wonder what fate may have befallen our friends. The idea of them isolated and terrified, enduring the torments of that sinister entity, was nearly too unbearable to contemplate. The first rays of sunlight breaking through the morning mist, cast the world in a new light. But the darkness of the night's events still lingered, a haunting reminder of the nightmare which had unfolded within those cursed walls. In the distance, we could hear the faint, yet reassuring sound of a police siren, a sign of help.

Chapter 7

As the police car drew near, we waved our arms wildly, desperate to catch their attention. Coming to a halt, four officers, their presence imposing and authoritative, emerged from the vehicle. The car's red and blue lights flashing in the early morning light, cast an eerie, otherworldly glow over the scene. The officers approached us, their steps measured and wary. The tallest one, who appeared to be in charge, spoke first, his voice deep and commanding. "What's the emergency here?"

My voice quivered, any attempt at calmness betrayed by the urgency lacing each word. "Inside that asylum there's a terror, far beyond any ordinary dangers. Our friends... they're trapped in there, ensnared by it."

Another of the officer's, her gaze sharp and discerning, eyed the crumbling building. "You're suggesting there's something dangerous in there, a ghost?" Scepticism was painted across her features as she surveyed the structure's forlorn appearance. Fiona's response came as a whisper laced with terror. "It's no mere ghost; it's an embodiment of evil. Our friends, they're... they're probably under its control now."

Doubt flickered between the officers; their disbelief was obvious. The senior among them addressed us with a resolve that seemed to dismiss the chilling reality we faced. "Your accounts first, please. The details might help us in finding your friends."

Fiona urgently pleaded, "Please, you must act now to rescue them!" Her fear was growing and her eyes filling with terror. As the male officers armed themselves with torches, the female officer, with notebook in hand, prepared to document our account. I jumped right into the story, telling about the things that happened to us that night in the asylum. Her incredulity was a tangible barrier, her pen pausing as she attempted to process our testimonies of the dark forces and spectral threats we had encountered. "And you expect us to mount a search based on tales of phantoms?" Her disbelief was a cold slap, dismissing the gravity of our fears.

"It's not merely a phantom, or ghost," I corrected her again, frustration seething within me. "This is a menace that defies your wildest fears, a darkness that devours light, hope, and sanity."

The conversation hung suspended in a moment of shared uncertainty. This building, now a monument to human suffering, harboured an evil that mocked our understanding of reality. We desperately pleaded for help, for immediate help, fearing for our friends' safety. The officers were understandably sceptical, following their professional instincts. This was a plea not just for rescue, but for acknowledgement of the darkness that can dwell in places forgotten by time and marred by tragedy. As the officers deliberated, the weight of our predicament settled heavily upon us. "Please, we are not making this up. Our friends are trapped in there with something evil. You must rescue them!" Fiona pleaded again, tears now rolling down her cheeks.

The three male officers reached the front door. "Alright, we'll do a sweep of the building. But for your safety, we'll need you to remain here."

We watched anxiously as they turned on their torches and radios. For a moment their figures were silhouetted against the building's imposing facade. Then they disappeared inside, and a sense of dread washed over me. Minutes ticked by. Fiona was pacing back and forth, wringing her hands. I stood there, frozen, staring at the building, waiting for any sign of movement, hoping for our friends, or the police to appear. A blood-curdling scream echoed from within the asylum, shattering the morning's fragile peace. Fiona gasped; her face drained of colour.

"They need help!" I shouted, as I started moving towards the building.

But the female officer, who had stayed behind, held up a hand. "Wait! You can't go back in there. It's too dangerous."

More screams followed, along with the sounds of chaos, loud bangs, shouts of confusion and screams of fear.

"We can't just stand here!" Fiona cried out; her eyes wide with terror.

The officer radioed her team, her voice tense. "What's happening in there? Report."

Static crackled over the radio, followed by a garbled voice. "Something's wrong... it's everywhere..."

I felt a chill run down my spine. Was the entity attacking them, just like it attacked us?

The officer turned to us, a stern expression on her face. "Stay here. I'm going in."

Before I could protest, she ran towards the building, turning on her torch as she disappeared into the darkness of the asylum. The commotion persisted, screams and shouts echoing through the air. Fiona and I stood helpless, as we waited for any sign of the officers, our friends, or the entity. The sun continued to rise, casting light over a scene that seemed surreal in its horror. Finally, after what seemed like an eternity, the officers emerged, disheveled, their faces etched with fear. Moving quickly, they ushered us away from the building.

"We're evacuating the area," the tall officer said, his voice shaky. "Something's not right in there. We need backup."

As we were led to the relative safety of the police car, I looked back at the asylum. The building stood silent, menacing, so many secrets hidden within. Our friends were still in there, along with the entity. I knew this was far from over and that we needed to go back inside. We needed to save them. A second police car arrived breaking what had built into a tense silence. Four more officers stepped out, their presence adding to the sense of urgency. They quickly joined the first group of officers, gathering in a tight circle. It was clear they were conducting a briefing. Animated gestures and serious expressions were exchanged among them, showing they were likely discussing strategies for their next course of action. Their body language suggesting a mix of fear and apprehension.

The female officer drove us back to the police station; the ride was a blur of flashing lights, muffled radio chatter and confusion. Fiona sat beside me. Her body trembling, her eyes fixed on the passing scenery but not really seeing it as she was lost in her own haunted thoughts. Upon arrival at the police station, they ushered us into a stark, fluorescent-lit room. The walls were bare, the atmosphere sterile and cold. Another officer brought us coffee, but it remained untouched, the steam swirling into nothingness. A man entered the room, his face one of professional concern. "I'm Detective Harris," he said, taking a seat opposite us. A female officer entered and asked Fiona to follow her.

In the sterile interrogation room, Detective Harris sat across from me, a sceptic whose recent experiences turned that scepticism into a haunting belief. Between us, the start of a case file on Ravenswood Asylum. It lay open, its pages holding our tales of last night's harrowing events.

Detective Harris, with a voice tempered by years of navigating the blurred lines between facts and fiction, spoke, "Steve, take me back to the beginning when you and your friends decided to go ghost hunting at Ravenswood?"

With my hands clasped tightly together, I nodded. "Well Detective. It was supposed to be just another investigation. We had been in there the two nights previously, but... last night was different."

"Different how?" Harris prodded, his pen poised above his notepad.

"The atmosphere," I said, my voice barely above a whisper. "It was as if the air was thick, charged with something... I don't know... something foreboding. We tried to shake it off, thinking it was just part of the experience."

"And the voices?" Harris asked, his scepticism momentarily set aside.

I shivered at the memory. "They had started as whispers, incoherent, indiscernible. We thought we had found something with the EVP recordings, but then the doors... they began slamming shut on their own, trapping us inside. I think that's when we started to realise it wasn't just a normal investigation anymore."

Harris leaned forward; his interest piqued. "You mentioned an evil spirit. Tell me more about that."

I met the detective's gaze, my eyes reflecting the terror of the night. "Detective, I never believed in spirits or ghosts, but what I witnessed in there, it felt... It was real. The sudden cold spots, the way something seemed to follow us, playing with us... It felt personal. It wanted to harm us and it did, it possessed our friend Tom's body. It used his body to come after us, he's still in there."

"The officers we sent in also reported strange things happening. Voices, unexplained banging. However, there was no sign of your friends. Could they have got out via another route and made their way home?"

My desperation was building. "I know how this sounds, Detective. But you have to understand, whatever is in the asylum is holding them back. It's not just a story; it's happening, and it's dangerous."

Detective Harris sat back, his mind a whirlwind of thoughts. The evidence before him challenged the very foundation of his beliefs. "We're going to continue our search, Steve. If your friends are in there, we will find them. You have my word."

My gratitude was clear, but my eyes remained shadowed by doubt, because of the events of the previous night. "Thank you, Detective. I just hope it's not too late."

As the interrogation came to a close, Detective Harris couldn't shake the feeling that this case was blurring the lines between the known and the unknown. It would challenge everything he thought he understood about the living and the dead.

He left the room, a few moments passed when the female officer brought Fiona back into the room.

Harris addressed both of us. "Neither of you are to go anywhere near the asylum. It is now being treated as a crime scene. If either of you go there, make no mistake, you will be arrested. Have I made myself clear?"

"Yes, detective, perfectly clear." I replied, but not with any conviction.

We left the police station and started walking, I guided Fiona towards my flat. She turned to me, her eyes brimming with tears. "Steve, we can't just do nothing, our friends... we have to do something."

I nodded, my mind racing with plans and possibilities. "We'll find a way back in, Fiona. It's obvious the police don't believe a word we're telling them. It'll be down to us to save everyone."

Back at my flat, our thoughts heavy with a mixture of fear and guilt, we sat in silence, the events of the night replaying in our minds like a horror film with no end. Fiona was the first to speak, her voice shaky. "What if... what if they don't make it out? What if that thing...?"

"We cannot think like that," I said, interrupting firmly as I attempted to push away the gnawing fear in my gut. "We've seen what it can do, but we also know it has weaknesses. We're not helpless."

Fiona nodded, wiping away her tears. "We need a plan. Something fool proof."

I paced the room, my thoughts swirling. "First, we need to find someone who can help us. A demonologist or an exorcist. We cannot do this without professional help. surely you someone? Haven't you heard about anyone?"

We spent the next few hours scouring the internet, delving into forums on the supernatural. Looking at ancient texts on demonology, and accounts of hauntings. The more we read, the more the pieces started to fit together. This thing wasn't just an angry spirit; it was something older, something far darker. Fiona held her phone in her hand, her fingers were trembling slightly as she scrolled through her contacts.

"There is someone I could ring. I think she might know who could help us. I'll calling my friend Sarah. She's got contacts, people who know about the paranormal. She could put us in touch with someone who can help."

The phone rang once, twice, and then a cheery voice answered. "Hello Fiona, long time no hear."

Fiona's response was urgent. "Sarah, it's important. We need a demonologist or someone who knows about evil entities... an exorcist maybe. It's an emergency."

There was a pause on the other end, Sarah's tone changed, "What's the matter? What has happened? You sound dreadful."

"It's complicated. I can't explain everything right now. Do you know of anyone who might help?"

"I might know someone. A group of paranormal investigators led by a guy named Denis Clarke. He's a demonologist, quite renowned in paranormal circles."

Relief washed over Fiona's face. "Can you put us in touch with him?"

"Give me a few minutes. I'll send you his details."

After the call, the room was silent, save for the ticking of the clock. Every passing second seemed like a betrayal to our friends trapped in that nightmare. True to her word, Sarah sent a text with Denis's contact information. Fiona wasted no time dialling the number.

Fiona's voice, shaky yet urgent, broke the silence of the room. "Hello, is this Denis Clarke?"

On the other end of the line, a voice replied, calm and measured. "Yes, speaking. Can I help you?"

Inhaling deeply, Fiona dived into her story. "Mr. Clarke, my name is Fiona. My friends and I, we've encountered something horrifying at an old asylum on the outskirts of Stonebridge."

"Go on, I'm listening," Denis Clarke encouraged, a note of intrigue in his voice.

"We are a group of amateur ghost hunters. We went there, exploring, following rumours we'd heard. But when we got inside we found something more, something evil. A dark presence, an entity. It... it took control of my friend, Tom, and we think it has our other friends trapped in there, too."

Denis's voice was steady, professional. "I see. Can you describe this entity to me? Any specific occurrences or signs? Did it give you a name?"

Fiona's voice quivered as she recounted their ordeal. "Its presence was suffocating. It felt like pure evil. We didn't get any name. Tom... our friend. He changed before our eyes, his body contorted, his eyes... they were filled with evil. We tried to fight it, with prayers, but it was too strong. It spoke in a raspy deep evil tone."

Denis's interest was piqued. "Interesting. And you say there are others still trapped in the building?"

Fiona began to cry, "Yes. Two of us managed to escape, but our friends are still inside. I fear for their lives. We need your help, Mr. Clarke. We have to go back there, but we do not have the necessary tools or knowledge to confront that thing by ourselves."

"It sounds like a powerful entity, possibly a malevolent spirit or demon. I must warn you, dealing with such forces can be extremely dangerous. Whatever you do, do not go back in there on your own." Denis replied, his tone serious.

"The police have it cordoned off as a crime scene. We know the risks. But we can't abandon them. This is unlike anything we've ever faced," Fiona insisted.

"I Understand. My team and I have dealt with similar cases. We'll need to prepare carefully. What's your address?"

Fiona's voice was tinged with desperation as she gave him my address.

"Ah, you're quite a distance from us, we'll see you tomorrow. For now, we have to formulate a plan and gather the necessary resources."

"Thank you, Mr. Clarke. We're at our wits' end. We'll help too, we're prepared to do whatever it takes."

"The best thing you can do is rest for now, Fiona. Conserve your strength. Tomorrow, we'll start to better understand the situation and figure out how to confront this entity."

"Thank you. We'll see you here tomorrow."

"Stay safe tonight. Remember, entities like this can sometimes reach beyond their confines. Be vigilant."

"We will, thank you. Goodnight, Mr. Clarke."

As the call ended, Fiona was left with a confusing mixture of relief and a looming sense of dread. She explained the conversation to me and informed me the team will come here sometime tomorrow.

I exhaled deeply, my breath escaping in a relieved sigh. "Well, that certainly eases my mind a little."

After that call, the evening waned into night, casting a solemn shadow over my flat. The weight of the last 24 hours events hung heavily, a sense of unease neither of us could shake.

"Fiona, you can take the bed," I offered. "I'll crash on the couch. We both need some rest before tomorrow."

She nodded, her eyes reflecting a deep weariness. "Thank you. I just hope I will be able to sleep."

Fiona made her way to the bedroom. Shutting the door, she left me alone with my thoughts. As the clock ticked past midnight, Fiona fell into a restless sleep. A nightmare took hold, dragging her back to the dark, menacing corridors of the asylum. The silence was suffocating, broken only by her own ragged breathing. Wandering the halls, calling out for her friends. "Tom? Carl? Where are you?" Only her voice echoed back, a hollow reminder of her solitude. The walls closed in around her; the darkness pulsating with an unseen evil. She felt the entity's presence, its sinister aura enveloping her, an icy dread settling in her heart. In a room, she found a mirror. Looking into it her reflection was twisted, her face contorted in horror. The glass cracked, spider-webbing outwards with an ominous creaking sound. Shadowy hands reached out from the broken mirror grasping at her. Fiona tried to scream; her mouth opened wide, but no sound came out. Frozen in terror, her body refused to obey her desperate urge to flee. The hands wrapped around her, pulling her through the mirror. Now she was in a room with no doors, no windows, just endless mirrors. Her reflections stared back at her, each one more grotesque than the last. A voice whispered in the darkness, its tone mocking, and cruel. "You can never leave. You belong to me now."

Fiona's heart raced, panic clawing at her throat. She looked around, searching for an escape, but the room stretched on infinitely in every direction. She jolted awake, her body drenched in sweat. She shouted for me. I sat bolt upright and took a moment to gather my thoughts. 'Did I just hear a shout?' I thought to myself, not sure what was happening. Then I heard her cry out again, I ran into the bedroom, not knowing what I might find. Fiona lay there, her breath coming in shallow gasps.

"Sorry Steve, it was just a nightmare, or at least I think it was, it felt ominously real," she said, tears running down her cheeks.

We glanced at the clock: 3 am. I sat on the edge of the bed. "You're okay, you're safe. You're in my flat, remember?"

Fiona sat up and flung her arms around me. "It was horrible. I was trapped in a mirror like Janet, only there was no way out."

"It's okay, don't worry it was just a nightmare. Try to get some sleep. We're going to have a long day ahead of us."

Fiona wiped away her tears and laid back down. "I'm just through the door in the living room. Go on, close your eyes and try to get some sleep."

"Please leave the light on."

I smiled reassuringly, "Of course, I'll see you in the morning."

Fiona lay there for a while before falling back into a fitful sleep. As her eyes fluttered closed, the tranquillity of the waking world faded, and she was plunged back once more into the depths of her nightmarish realm. The room of mirrors awaited her return, its endless reflections twisting and contorting her face. Her breath, each inhalation a struggle against the suffocating dread enveloping her. The mirrors closed in, their surfaces alive with mocking, distorted images of herself. The whispering voice spoke again, a sinister hiss slithering through the air. "Running is futile. You're part of this place now."

Terror gripped her as she stumbled through the labyrinth of mirrors. Her reflections sneering and jeering in silent judgment. The chilling sensation of being watched, of being hunted, was relentless. The entity's presence was a terrifying force. In a desperate bid for escape, she pounded on a mirror; her fists leaving bloodied smears on the cold, cracked surface. "Let me out!" she screamed, her voice cracking under the strain. But the mirror merely rippled like water, distorting her image further into a grotesque caricature. Faces emerged from the other side of the glass, their features twisted in agony, eyes hollow with despair. They reached out towards her, their touch felt as cold as death. Fiona recoiled, stumbling backwards, her heart pounding in her chest. The mirrors spun around her, a carousel of horror from which there was no respite. She screamed as if her life depended on it.

I ran into the bedroom. "Fiona! Wake up, you're having another nightmare. Fiona!"

She woke with a jolt, disorientated she looked at me, then looked all around the room. My face was etched with concern as I sat by her side, my voice a mixture of worry and concern. "Fiona, it's okay. You're safe. It was just another nightmare."

Fiona's breathing was erratic, her eyes wide, filled with terror as she struggled to distinguish reality from the horrors of her dream. This room, my bedroom, felt so much safer than the dark, twisted world she had just escaped from. She felt her heart racing uncontrollably while clutching at her chest. "It... it was there, in the mirrors. It was like being trapped in hell," she stammered, her voice trembling. "I'm scared to close my eyes. I know it's there, waiting for me."

"It's the stress, Fiona. Everything we've been through. But it's over, for now. You're here, with me, in my flat."

Fiona nodded, trying to steady her breathing, to ground herself in the reality of my room. "I'm sorry. I didn't mean to wake you."

"Don't apologise," I reassured her, my hand gently squeezing her shoulder. "We're in this together, remember? Whatever it takes to get through this."

Fiona managed a weak smile, her eyes still haunted by the remnants of the dream. "Together," she repeated, her voice a mere whisper.

I stood up, moving to the window. "I'll make us some tea. It might help calm our nerves."

As I left the room, Fiona's gaze lingered on the space where I had been sitting. The nightmare was so vivid, so real. She shivered, pulling the duvet tighter around her. The entity's words echoed in her mind, a chilling reminder of the darkness which still lurked within the walls of the asylum. The room felt colder now, the shadows darker. Fiona knew sleep would be elusive for the rest of the night, but she felt a strange comfort in that. She wrapped the duvet around herself like a protective cocoon and went into the living room. The darkness seemed to press in around her, each shadow a reminder of the horrors she had faced. Settling on the couch, her mind was full of fear.

I returned, two steaming mugs of tea in hand. "Here," I whispered, handing her a mug. "It's not much, but it will help."

Fiona accepted the tea, the warmth of the mug seeping into her chilled fingers. She took a sip. The herbal blend a minor comfort against the night's terrors. I sat down beside her, hoping my presence would be a steadying force. "We'll get through this, Fiona. We have to believe that."

Fiona nodded, her gaze fixed on the dark window. "It's just so hard. Every time I close my eyes, I'm back there. In that place."

I sighed, my own exhaustion evident. "I know. But we're not alone in this. Denis Clarke and his team will be here in the morning. Then we'll have a plan."

We sat in silence for a while, sipping our tea, lost in our own thoughts. The clock on the wall ticked loudly, marking the passing of time in the otherwise still room. Fiona broke the silence, her voice hesitant. "Steve, do you ever wonder... Are we in over our heads?"

I looked at her, my eyes serious. "Yes, every moment since we left that place. But now we'll have a more experienced team helping us. We can't abandon our friends. We can't let that thing win."

Fiona shuddered, the memory of the entity's presence still fresh in her mind. "I just hope we're not too late."

The night wore on, the darkness outside slowly giving way to the first hints of dawn. We talked in hushed tones, discussing strategies, sharing fears and doubts. It had been a long night, filled with the spectre of the asylum and the unknown horrors which awaited us. As the first light of dawn crept into the sky, Fiona experienced a sense of resolve settling over her. They would face the entity again, but this time armed with knowledge and support. They would fight for their friends, for themselves.

I stood up, stretching out tired muscles. "We should try to get some rest. It's going to be a long day."

Fiona agreed I was right. We tidied up the living room, extinguishing the lights and ensuring the doors were locked. A sense of unease lingered in us, a fear the entity might reach beyond the confines of the asylum. Back in my room, Fiona lay down on the bed, pulling the duvet up to her chin. I settled on the couch, my eyes closing immediately. Fiona lay awake for a long time, listening to the sounds of the town waking up. She felt restless, images of the asylum flickering across her mind. She knew if she slept it would be intermittent, filled with shadows and whispers.

Eventually, exhaustion overtook her, and she drifted into an uneasy slumber. Her dreams were again filled with echoing hallways and distorted mirrors. The entity's mocking laughter a constant accompaniment. With the morning sun rising in the sky, Fiona awoke, a sense of purpose fuelling her tired body. Today, they would return to the asylum. Today, they would confront their fears and whatever was holding their friend's captive.

Now midmorning, a grey overcast sky, created a sombre mood over the town. Our anxious wait was over as a van marked with the logo of 'Clarke Paranormal Investigations' pulled up outside the flat. The moment was upon us, a mix of fear and purpose settling in their stomachs.

"Mr. Clarke, thank you for coming," I greeted them, extending my hand.

He nodded, his handshake firm. "Let's not waste time. I need to know everything, every detail."

Denis Clarke was a seasoned demonologist; he carried an air of quiet authority which was immediately noticeable. In his late fifties, his tall, lean stature spoke of a life spent in both study and fieldwork. His hair was a distinguished silver, neatly combed back and just touching his collar. Lines of experience adorned his face, and his deep-set, piercing blue eyes seemed to miss nothing, eyes that had probably seen more than their fair share of the unexplainable and the terrifying. His skin was weathered, perhaps not just by age but by the many days and nights spent in various locations, researching and confronting entities beyond the ordinary. A short, well-kept beard, was peppered with grey, framed his strong jawline, giving him a scholarly yet practical appearance.

The clothes he wore were unassuming, a dark shirt, sturdy trousers, and rugged boots which looked both comfortable and suitable for unpredictable environments. Around his neck, practically hidden beneath his shirt, was a small, unobtrusive pendant, its significance known only to him. He moved with purpose, each step and gesture deliberate. His hands were those of a worker, with calluses and faint scars, perhaps from years of handling various tools and artefacts in his line of work.

Overall, Denis Clarke exuded a sense of calm confidence. A man who dedicated his life to understanding and battling the forces which lay beyond any normal understanding. His appearance was a testament to his unique and challenging vocation. A woman, introduced as Mia, began setting up a laptop, her fingers flying over the keyboard.

She was a seasoned paranormal investigator, possessing a unique blend of intensity and sharp intellect. In her mid-thirties, she was of medium build which suggested both agility and strength. Striking auburn-coloured hair, cut in a stylish, asymmetrical bob, framed her keen, observant face. Her eyes were a deep emerald green and stood out against her natural fair complexion, which was marked with the faint tan lines of someone who had spent a lot of time outdoors. Mia's facial features were defined and angular, with high cheekbones. She was dressed in functional attire suitable for investigative work. Dark cargo pants paired with a fitted, long-sleeve top, allowing her ease of movement and the ability to carry various tools and gadgets. Finished off with sturdy, waterproof boots, well broken in from countless expeditions.

Mia's overall appearance was of a professional who was serious about her work. Her posture was confident. Another seasoned investigator who'd seen the unexplainable and faced it head-on. "We'll monitor some readings here," she explained. "See if there's any unusual activity. Make sure nothing has followed you home or has made an attachment to one of you."

The third member of the team, Dave, opened his case, revealing an array of vials, herbs, and religious icons. "We're prepared for various types of entities," he stated gruffly. "But, each case is unique."

He was the youngest member of the paranormal investigation team and presented a contrast to his more seasoned colleagues. He was in his early twenties, with a youthful, somewhat boyish appearance. His hair was a messy mop of dark curls, falling into his eyes, which were a bright, curious hazel, wide with interest and excitement. A slim, lanky build gave him an air of being slightly uncoordinated, though his movements suggested an underlying agility. His skin was smooth, the kind that hadn't yet been weathered by years of fieldwork, and sporting a faint, unintentional stubble, a sign of his youth and inexperience.

Alex, the fourth and final member, looked around nervously. "And I'm here to document everything. For the records, you know."

He was the cameraman of the paranormal team and carried an air of practical creativity. I would guess he was in his late twenties and had a lean and agile physique which spoke of his readiness to capture action from any angle. His wind-swept sandy blond hair was pushed back and tucked under a baseball cap which was worn backwards. His eyes were a focused blue, constantly scanning his surroundings, seeming to look for the best shot or angle. With skin boasting a hint of sun-kissed tan from spending long hours outdoors on various shoots. Alex had an approachable, boy-next-door kind of charm, with a ready smile crinkling the corners of his eyes.

Fiona recounted their experiences at the asylum, her voice steady but filled with emotion. Denis listened intently, occasionally asking pointed questions. When Fiona finished, He leaned back, deep in thought. "This entity is powerful. We're not just dealing with a restless spirit. You are right, this is something much darker."

I felt a chill run down my spine. "So, what's the plan?"

Chapter 8

Denis stood up; his expression resolute. "First, as Mia stated, we need to assess the situation here. We need to make sure you two are safe."

His declaration sparked an immediate flurry of activity. Mia continued unpacking an array of devices, each beep, and whir of machinery adding to the already tense atmosphere of the flat. Dave carried out a methodical inspection of each room, his every movement precise, his eyes keenly observing the environment. Alex, had a camera slung around his neck, documenting every step. Mia began setting up more equipment, focusing on capturing any fluctuation in the ambient energy. Denis tried to communicate, using his psychic abilities, with anything which may have connected itself to one of us or followed us home.

Fiona watched with a mixture of fascination and anxiety. "I really hope nothing has actually followed me here." She whispered.

Mia, who was scanning the room with an EMF meter, spoke without looking up. "Entities of this kind can sometimes form attachments. We need to ensure your safety before we tackle the asylum."

Denis glanced over; his face illuminated by the glow of a monitor. "These devices can detect things our eyes can't. They can detect things like hidden electromagnetic fields, temperature changes, and invisible movements. Spirits, especially strong spirits with a malevolent nature can disrupt the physical environment."

"Yes, we use a lot of this equipment in our ghost hunts," Fiona replied.

Denis gave a slightly disapproving look. He wasn't against amateur ghost hunters. He merely wished they had a greater understanding of what they were dealing with.

I stood beside Fiona, my eyes following the team's movements. My flat, usually a haven of normality, now felt like a stage for a supernatural drama.

Dave approached with a handheld thermal camera. "We're looking for any cold spots," she explained. "They can show a paranormal presence." The screen displayed the warmth of the room in a kaleidoscope of colours, but no irregular cold areas appeared.

Denis, meanwhile, took out a small bottle filled with a clear liquid. "Holy Water," he said, sprinkling it in the corners of each room. "Just a precaution. Thankfully there has been no reaction."

After a thorough sweep of the flat, Denis gathered the team in the living room. "The readings are normal. No traces of any paranormal activity. It seems whatever you came across at the asylum has not followed you here."

Fiona let out a breath she hadn't realised she'd been holding. "That's a relief," she murmured.

"We've reviewed the data from our equipment," Denis continued with a serious tone to his voice. "There are no significant EMF fluctuations. No unexplained temperature changes, and the infrared cameras haven't picked up any anomalies, nor did the SLS camera. Based on what we've observed Steve, it seems your flat is clear."

I let out a sigh of relief, the tension in my shoulders eased. "Out of curiosity, what's an SLS camera?"

Denis looked at Fiona. "Fiona, would you like to tell him how it works?"

"Sure. The SLS, or Structured Light Sensor camera, works like a high-tech version of connect-the-dots. It projects a wide blanket of invisible infrared laser lights, creating a grid with over a million tiny points of light. Imagine it was like a net of light covering the room. This grid helps the camera create a detailed map of the room and everything in it. So, if anything moves within this grid, say, a person or something we can't see, it alters the pattern of the light dots. The camera detects these changes letting us know if something is there, even if we can't see it with our own eyes. Spirits appear as stickmen on a screen."

Denis allowed himself a slight smile. "That was an excellent 'non-tech' description. Well done, I'm impressed."

"And what about us? Could this thing be attached to one of us?" I asked.

Denis nodded at Mia, who stepped forward with a small device. "We also conducted a thorough scan for spirit attachments. It's a bit like a thermal camera, but it detects energy patterns consistent with spirit attachments. Both of you are clear."

Fiona's face softened, a hint of relief in her eyes. "So, we're safe? Nothing followed us and nothing attached to us?"

Denis hesitated, choosing his words carefully. "For now, it seems that way. But it's important to remain vigilant. Entities like the one we seem to be dealing with can be unpredictable."

I ran a hand through my hair, my mind was racing. "What do we do now? I mean, if it's not here, then I assume it's back at the asylum. correct?"

Denis gathered his equipment, preparing to leave. "Correct, and our next step is to return there, we need to confront this entity at its source. That's the only way to ensure it doesn't harm anyone else."

Fiona stepped forward, a determined look on her face. "We want to help. Whatever it is, whatever it takes to stop this thing."

Denis looked at us both, a sense of camaraderie building between us all. "Your bravery is admirable. But this next part can be incredibly dangerous. We'll need to prepare thoroughly."

As the team packed up their gear, I felt the atmosphere in the flat shift, the fear not entirely dissipating but there was a new sense of purpose, a resolve to face the darkness head-on and put an end to the terror lurking within the walls of the asylum. Once everything was packed away, Denis started the conversation. "We need to understand the entity's strengths and weaknesses. Then we can make a plan to rescue your friends."

Mia joined in. "We should also consider the possibility of a portal or a focal point of energy. Something must be giving this entity its power."

Dave nodded, adding, "And we'll need to be prepared for a confrontation. From what Fiona and Steve have told us, this thing is going to be dangerous and unpredictable."

I felt a surge of hope amidst the fear. "When do we leave?"

Denis glanced out the window at the darkening sky. "Soon. We must move swiftly but also cautiously."

The team went into a huddle, discussing logistics and strategies. I exchanged a look with Fiona, a silent agreement. We were ready to face whatever lay ahead.

As the afternoon wore on, final preparations were made. Mia would set up a mobile command centre in their van on arrival at the asylum, while Dave would arrange his arsenal of spiritual and paranormal deterrents. Alex was tasked with setting up his cameras, and ensuring every angle was covered.

The atmosphere was tense but focused as they loaded up their van. Denis pulled me aside. "I need you to be prepared for anything. Once we're in there I think things might become dangerous."

"What about the police? They've cordoned off the building."

Denis scratched his chin. "Hmm, we'd better speak to them. Explain to them what's going on. We must get into the building tonight."

Denis pulled up outside the police station, a modern nondescript building blending into the grey, cloud-covered sky. The team sat in silence, each lost in their own thoughts about the task ahead. Denis ventured inside.

At the front desk, a young female officer looked up, her expression one of apathy. "Can I help you?" she asked.

Denis cleared his throat. "I'm Denis Clarke, with Clarke Paranormal Investigations. I need to speak to someone in charge regarding the situation at the old asylum."

The officer's eyebrows raised slightly. She picked up the phone. "I'll see who's available."

Denis waited in the cramped lobby, the walls, adorned with notices and posters, a clock ticking away on the wall in a monotonous rhythm.

A door opened, and a tall, broad-shouldered man stepped out. "I'm Detective Harris. Follow me," he said, his voice carrying a note of authority.

In a small, bland meeting room, Denis explained the situation. "We believe there's a malevolent entity in the asylum. We need access to conduct a thorough investigation."

Detective Harris listened; his expression unreadable. "You're aware the building is off-limits to the public. It's a safety hazard, and we have it on good authority people have disappeared in there. It is now a crime scene."

Denis nodded. "We understand, but time is critical. We have the expertise to handle this."

"I can't let you into an active crime scene."

"I appreciate what you are saying, but if we don't get in there, it could be all over for those people trapped in there. Then you're looking at a murder scene rather than a crime scene, murders you will never crack. I ... we, have worked with the police, solving many cases."

"I have read the reports from the officers who investigated the building this morning. Three of the officers have vowed never to step foot in the building again. Their report, I must admit... certainly made strange reading."

Denis leaned in closer, the intensity in his eyes unwavering. "Detective Harris, what those officers encountered was not just a fleeting shadow or an unexplained noise. They faced something which defies all logic, something which has been lurking in the depths of that place, growing stronger. It also apparently has taken hostages or may have killed them. We need to make certain one way or the other at the very least, if they are still alive, try to rescue them. Unfortunately, this is something the police cannot do by themselves."

Harris, unmoved, responded with a firm tone. "Mr Clarke, you're asking me to sanction an expedition into a crumbling building based on hearsay and ghost stories. My hands are tied by protocol and the law. I can't just ignore that."

Denis's voice grew more direct, more urgent. "But isn't it your duty to protect the public? To investigate threats, regardless of how unconventional they may seem? We are not just talking about a physical hazard here, Detective. We are talking about something that might harm more than just those trapped inside."

Harris's face remained stoic, his voice steady. "The law doesn't account for supernatural threats, it deals with the tangible, with explainable events. I can't authorise a mission based on speculation and fear."

Denis leaned back, his frustration was clear. "Fear, Detective? Yes, there is fear. But it's not baseless. The evidence is there, in the testimonies of your own officers. They were trained to handle danger, yet what they saw in there, in those few minutes, terrified them beyond words. Isn't that worth investigating?"

Harris sighed, a hint of weariness creeping into his voice. "Look, I've read the reports. Yes, they're unnerving, but they're also vague and subjective. I need more to go on than just their word."

Denis's tone hardened. "What more do you need? A body? Are you going to wait until you have proof that whatever is in there has taken a life before you act? We have a chance here, Detective, a chance to confront this threat head-on, with people who are experienced and prepared for exactly this kind of situation."

Harris shook his head, unconvinced. "Prepared? How can anyone be prepared for something which may not even exist? You're asking me to gamble with lives on ghost story."

The room's tension seemed to thicken, pressing in from all sides. Denis spoke again, his voice laced with determination. "It's more than a ghost story, Detective. We've seen the effects of these entities before. We've helped people, saved them from things science can't explain. I'm asking you to trust me, to trust that I know what I'm doing."

Harris leaned forward, his eyes searching Denis's. "And if I do this, if I let you in there, what then? How do I justify it if something goes wrong? You're asking me to put my career on the line."

Denis met his gaze, resolute. "I'm asking you to do what's right, Detective. To protect people. Sometimes it means taking risks, stepping into the unknown. I promise you; we will be taking every precaution. We'll do everything in our power to ensure everyone's safety."

Harris remained silent his eyes reflecting the weight of the decision. Finally, he spoke, his voice serious with responsibility. "Alright, Denis. I'll grant you access. But understand this; I'm putting my trust in you. If anything happens, if anyone gets hurt, it's on you."

Denis nodded, a solemn expression on his face. "I understand, detective. You won't regret this. We'll handle it with the utmost care."

Harris stood up, extending his hand. "One more condition. One of my officers will accompany you. Not just for oversight, but for communication. If anything goes south, I need to know immediately."

Denis stood and shook his hand, a mixture of gratitude and apprehension in his eyes. "Agreed, detective. I'm happy to work together on this. Thank you for trusting us."

As Harris left the room, Denis let out a breath, that first small battle had been won, but the war... the war against an unseen and unknown enemy, was just beginning.

As we left the station, the sky turned a darker shade of grey, heavy with the promise of rain. We drove in silence; tension mounting as we neared the asylum.

The building loomed ominously against the darkening sky, its windows like vacant eyes staring back at them. Officer Johnson, a tall man with a serious expression, was waiting by the building.

"Hello, you must be Mr Clarke, I'm Officer Johnson,"

Denis greeted him. "Thank you for joining us, and please, call me Denis."

Johnson nodded; his gaze fixed on the building. "Just doing my job. Lead the way."

"Not so fast. Don't be too eager to go inside. We need to set things up, safety first."

"Absolutely. Can I do anything to help?"

"Not really, but we will all need to discuss tactics before we enter the building. First, my team needs to go in and set up the equipment. It shouldn't take them long. They are well versed in these situations."

Unpacking their equipment, the team worked efficiently. On reaching the asylum's entrance, the door creaked open, revealing its dark, silent halls. Stepping inside, the beams of their torches cut through the darkness. The atmosphere was fraught with a sense of foreboding.

The team, a tight-knit group of seasoned paranormal experts, stepped into the decrepit building, each footfall echoing through the empty halls. The atmosphere was laden with the stench of mould and the residue of long-forgotten despair. Their equipment, an arsenal of modern ghost-hunting technology, seemed out of place amidst the peeling paint and rotting debris.

As they unpacked their gear, a sudden thud resonated from somewhere in the building, freezing them in their tracks. The sound was hollow as if something substantial had been dropped on the rotting floorboards above them. The thud was followed by a scraping sound, a slow dragging noise making its way across the floor, sending shivers down their spines.

Alex clutched his video camera tighter, its red recording light a solitary point of colour in the murky darkness. He panned the camera around, capturing the anxious faces of his companions, their eyes darting towards the ceiling, then to each other.

"I take it everybody heard that?" whispered Mia, her voice barely rising above a breath, her eyes wide with a mixture of fear and excitement.

Dave nodded, his hand instinctively reaching for the EMF detector. "Stay sharp. We knew this wouldn't be easy."

They continued their setup, each movement deliberate. Every creak and groan of the ancient structure clawed at their senses. The atmosphere was charged, a tangible anticipation mingling with the musty air.

A faint cry pierced the silence, distant but unmistakably human. It was a sob, filled with such despair it seemed to resonate in their very bones. Spectres at the periphery of their vision, seemed to move ominously, slithering and shifting, as if the darkness itself was alive.

"Keep it together," Mia said, her voice steady but her eyes betraying her concern. "This is what we're here for. We need to find the source."

The team split up, each taking a different direction, their torches cutting swathes through the inky blackness. Alex continued to record, his camera an unblinking eye in the face of the unknown.

As Denis and Mia ventured deeper into the building, the temperature plummeted, their breaths materialising in the frigid air, the EMF detector in Denis's hand buzzed, its lights flickered erratically.

"There's something here," Muttered Denis, his eyes scanning the darkness.

They walked down a corridor where doors hung off their hinges, leading to empty rooms filled with haunting memories. A sudden movement caught Mia's eye, a fleeting shape darted across the end of the hallway.

"There!" she gasped, pointing.

Denis moved towards it, his footsteps deliberate. As they approached, the air grew even colder, the very atmosphere constricting around them like an unseen hand gripping their throats. A door slammed shut with a thunderous bang, reverberating through the hall. Mia screamed, a short, sharp sound of fear, "Sorry, it took me by surprise." she said sheepishly.

"It's okay," Denis said, though his voice betrayed his own fear. "Like Fiona said, it's trying to scare us; it wants to feed off our fear. We can't let it. I can sense it, it's pure evil. We need to get set up, then get out and regroup."

In another part of the building, Alex, and Dave had set up equipment and static cameras on the upper floors.

"Did you see that?" Alex whispered, his voice trembling as he reviewed the footage. On the screen, a figure appeared for a mere second in the background, a shadowy form seemed to gaze directly into the camera before vanishing.

Dave swallowed hard, his face pale. "We need to show this to Denis."

As they turned to leave, the floorboards groaned underfoot. Then, with a deafening crack, the floor gave way beneath Dave's feet. He plummeted downwards with a horrified yell, disappearing into the darkness below.

"Dave!" Alex screamed, pointing his camera and rushing to the gaping hole in the floor. Peering down, he saw only darkness. A soulless abyss staring back at him.

Denis and Mia, hearing the commotion, rushed to the scene. "What happened?" Denis asked, his face full of fear and concern.

"Dave fell through the floor," Alex stammered, his eyes wide with shock.

Without hesitation, Denis stepped forward and shone his torch into the dark depths, the beam, cutting through the darkness. "Dave, are you alright? ... Dave, can you hear me?"

"Yes, I'm alright. Be careful or you'll be joining me."

The team rushed to the floor below to check if Dave was injured. "Dave, call out... which room are you in?" shouted Mia.

"Here... I'm in here!" came the reply.

Denis entered to the room first. "Are you okay?"

"Believe it or not, I think I am, that wardrobe broke my fall."

Denis's torch beam danced around the room, illuminating a scene straight out of a nightmare. Dust swirled in the room, creating ghostly shapes in the dim light. The wardrobe, a huge piece of Victorian furniture, lay shattered under Dave, its once-sturdy frame now a heap of splintered wood.

Dave lay awkwardly, sprawled across the remnants, his face pale and drawn. "I think I've twisted my ankle," he grimaced, trying to shift himself into a less painful position.

Mia rushed to his side. "Don't move, Dave. We need to check you for injuries."

As Denis and Alex looked on, they could feel the overbearing atmosphere of the building pressing down on them. The darkness around them felt alive, an unseen presence watching, waiting. A low, rasping growl echoed through the room, sending chills down their spines. Denis spun around, his torch sweeping across the walls, searching for the source. The growl grew louder, a sound so primal and full of hatred it seemed to vibrate in their very souls.

"Denis... what is that?" Mia whispered, her voice quivering.

Denis didn't answer, his eyes were scanning the darkness. The growl morphed into a series of chilling whispers; words indiscernible but dripping with malice.

Without warning, the temperature in the room plummeted, their breath turning to mist in the frigid air. The torch flickered, casting eerie, dancing silhouettes reaching out towards them.

Alex's camera, forgotten in the chaos, suddenly started recording again, its screen flickering with static. Through the crackle, a voice could be heard, a voice not quite human, its tone laced with hatred.

"You are not welcome here," it hissed, the words distorted but unmistakably threatening.

Denis stepped forward, his protective instincts driving him. "We mean no harm. We're just here to help our friends."

The room fell silent, the oppressive atmosphere intensifying. In a sudden explosion of movement, a swarm of flies burst forth from the shadows. The room was instantly thick with them, buzzing furiously, a black cloud of winged terror. They swarmed around the team, a living, writhing mass consuming the light and air from the room.

Denis swatted at the swarm of flies, but there were so many that his actions had no effect, and they soon covered him. They crawled over his skin, across his face, in his eyes, their tiny bodies so numerous, they made it difficult for him to breath. Mia was screaming, her arms flailing wildly as she tried to fend off the swarm, her voice barely audible over the deafening buzz.

The flies were everywhere, covering the walls and ceiling as well as the team, turning the room into a writhing black mass. Denis's torch beam could not penetrate the swarm but it cast eerie outlines on the flies which looked like dancing demons in the chaos.

Dave, still lying injured on the floor, tried to shield his face, but there were too many, they covered him like a living shroud. His cries were muffled under the mass of insects, his body barely visible under the swarm.

Alex, in a panic, tried to film the scene, but the swarm was so thick they covered the camera's lens, blocking it with their wriggling bodies. He stumbled backwards, crashing into a wall, his mind reeling in terror.

"Out, now!" Denis yelled, his voice commanding. He grabbed Mia by the arm, pushing her towards the door, fighting through the dense mass of flies he lifted Dave to his feet and helped him out of the room. They stumbled into the hallway; slamming the door shut behind them with a resounding thud.

For a moment, they stood there, gasping for breath, their hearts pounding in their chests. The sound of the flies was muffled behind the door, but the memory of their touch, their buzzing, lingered like a nightmare. Mia brushed at her hair with her fingers. She could still feel them crawling all over her. Denis spoke, his voice barely above a whisper, "You know what this means?"

"A demon!" Mia replied.

Denis's eyes met Mia's. "Yes, a demon. It's something so dark, so ancient, it's beyond our understanding. This is no mere haunting. We're dealing with something that's pure evil."

The corridor in which they stood seemed to close in around them, the shadows deepening, stretching their long fingers towards them. The air charged with an unseen energy made their skin crawl. Mia caught her breath, her mind reeling from the horror they just witnessed.

"This is going to be a hard fight. Are you all prepared for what is coming?" Denis asked. His words were more of a warning than a question.

Mia shivered at his words, the truth of them echoing in the hollow emptiness of the building. The sound of their own breathing suddenly seemed unnaturally loud.

They moved cautiously back towards the main hall, their torches cutting through the darkness. Every shadow seemed to move; every sound seemed a potential threat. The building itself felt alive, aware of their presence, danger hanging around them like a shroud.

As they entered the main hall, a gust of wind swept through the room, their torches turned off in a chorus of clicks. Darkness enveloped them, a darkness so complete it felt like a physical force.

Mia cried out; her voice swallowed by the oppressive blackness. "Denis!"

"I'm here," his reply came, a low whisper in the dark. "Stay close."

They fumbled in the darkness, hands searching for each other. When they finally touched, there was a moment of comfort, a human connection amid overwhelming fear.

A low, mocking laughter suddenly echoed through the hall, bouncing off the walls and filling the space with dread. The sound was neither male nor female, a chorus of voices speaking of suffering and pain.

"You cannot escape," the voices hissed, the words slithering into their ears like tiny serpents. "This is our domain."

Mia felt tears stinging her eyes, her heart racing with terror. "What do we do, Denis?"

Denis's voice was steady, but she could hear the underlying fear. "Sticking to the plan is a priority. We get out, now, and regroup. We can't let it break us."

The darkness seemed to press further in on them, a suffocating blanket. They moved slowly, hands clasped tightly, knowing this darkness of unseen horrors was far more terrifying than anything they had experienced before, or even imagined.

Their footsteps echoed in the silence, a slow, rhythmic sound bouncing back towards them, appearing to taunt them. The mocking laughter continued, a haunting soundtrack to their nightmare, each chuckle a reminder of the danger lurking somewhere in the dark.

They navigated the darkness, every sense heightened, every movement, every noise, a potential threat. The building seemed to whisper, the voices of the damned calling out in a chorus of misery and despair.

In the heart of the darkness, in the very depths of fear, they knew they were not alone. Something was watching, something was waiting, a dark spectre following their every step.

"Stop." Said Dave, "I have an idea," he reached into his pocket and took out a vial of Holy Water and sprinkled it in front of them. Howls and groans emanated from the darkness as it retreated.

"Head for the exit, now!" Yelled Denis.

Dave led the way, sprinkling the Holy Water, cutting a swathe through the thick, overbearing air that clogged the corridors. Each droplet sizzled as it hit the ground, sending up tiny wisps of steam, as if the very floor of the asylum rebelled against its sanctity. Before them, the hallway extended, a path filled with gloom and whispers. The walls themselves pulsating with a life force of their own. The peeling paint and cracked plaster resembling the decaying skin of some monstrous being. Faint echoes of anguished cries reverberated through the air, cries of despair seeming to emanate from the very bones of the building.

Denis followed closely. Mia clinging to his arm, her eyes wide with terror, every shadow a lurking menace, every creak a harbinger of doom. Alex was close behind, clutching his camera, but too afraid to film the moment. As they advanced, the corridor grew colder, a chill seeping into their bones, a coldness not of this world. The laughter continued, a taunting, echoing chorus coming from everywhere and nowhere.

"Keep moving," Denis urged, his voice barely above a whisper. "We can't let it intimidate us."

But their fear was real, a living thing clinging to them. Dave's hand trembled as he continued to sprinkle the Holy Water, his usual calm demeanour gone, shattered by the unspeakable horrors they faced. Suddenly, the laughter ceased, replaced by a deafening silence. The darkness seemed to thicken again, a barrier clouding their vision and dulling their senses.

Without warning, their torches flickered back into life illuminating a woman, or what was once a woman standing in front of them. Her face was gaunt, with eyes like hollow pits of despair, her mouth twisted as if in a silent scream. She wore a tattered gown of a Victorian Nurse; the fabric stained, her skin ashen and stretched tight over her skeletal frame.

Mia gasped, her hand flying to her mouth in horror. "Who is she?"

The apparition raised a bony hand, a slender finger pointing down the corridor, her mouth moving in a silent scream. Denis took a step forward, his heart pounding in his chest. "Do we go that way?"

Dave hesitated; his faith shaken by the nightmarish reality they faced. "I... I don't know. It could be a trap."

The apparition's gaze bore into them, a force that seemed to pierce their very souls. Her eyes, devoid of life, yet filled with an unspeakable sadness, held them in a paralysing trance.

The apparition pointed down the corridor again as she vanished, dissipating into the darkness like smoke.

Denis took a deep breath, steadying his nerves. "We have no choice. Let's go that way, now!"

It was the right way, they reached the front door and rushed out of the building running towards their van. As they reached it, they were met by officer Johnson, Denis's gaze lingered on him, his eyes piercing through the dim light like shards of ice.

"What the hell went on in there? I could hear screaming, shouting." Said Johnson

"And you didn't think to investigate?"

"I did, I nearly came in, but…"

"I need to know I can trust you, Officer Johnson. In there," he said pointing back towards the ominous structure looming behind them, "it's a different world. It's a world where the rules of reality are twisted, contorted by something ancient and malevolent."

Officer Johnson was a tall man with a sturdy build and a face not yet hardened by the cruelties of life. He swallowed hard. His voice wavered slightly as he replied, "I understand. I've seen my share of horrors on the job, but this… this is something else."

Denis's expression softened momentarily, recognising the trepidation in the officer's eyes. "It's more than something else, officer. It's a place where the veil between our world and the next is so thin, you can hear the whispers of the damned. You'll see things, hear things. Don't let them get into your head. Stay focused, stay close."

Johnson nodded, his resolve strengthening. "I won't let you down."

Denis turned towards the imposing structure, "This place, it feeds on fear, no doubt about it. It twists your mind, shows you things, things which can break even the strongest person's will." Denis's face was one of grim determination. "An entity, ancient and dark, a collector of souls, a weaver of nightmares.

It's been here, growing in power, feeding on the pain and madness which these walls have absorbed over decades."

Johnson felt a chill crawl down his spine, the night air suddenly intense, suffocating. "How do we fight something like this?"

Denis's eyes turned to the decaying facade of the building. "With knowledge, with courage, and with an unwavering faith. We confront it, challenge it, and if we're lucky, we'll banish it to Hell, back where it came from."

Johnson took a deep breath, trying to steady his racing heart. "And if we're not lucky?"

Denis's gaze was, unflinching. "Then we become another scream within those walls, another lost soul for it to torment and feed off for ever more."

Johnson could feel the weight of their task starting to bear down on him, a burden far heavier than any he had experienced in his life. Yet, alongside his fear, was a burning determination, a desire to face the darkness and emerge victorious.

Chapter 9

It was agreed that myself and Alex would man the command centre. Within this mobile sanctuary, a myriad of screens blinked into existence. Outside a creeping mist now enshrouded the asylum and everything around it, slithering across the ground with a life of its own. It had brought with it a chilling silence, thick and unyielding, transforming the world outside into a realm of ghosts and shadows. It created a landscape where the unknown lurked behind every twist of vapour. Dave stared at the mist for a few moments, "Do you think this has anything to do with what's going on in the building?"

Denis smiled and shook his head, "No, I think you have been reading too many James Herbert books. It's just fog."

"Hmm." muttered Dave, disbelievingly.

Within the cloak of the mist, Denis, Mia, Dave, Fiona, and Officer Johnson, their designated guardian from the local constabulary, prepared to breach the threshold of the forsaken edifice. Their arsenal was not of flesh-piercing bullets or blades, but of a more ethereal nature, Bible's, Holy Water in vials that shimmered under the scant light, and crucifixes, each a personal sentinel against the darkness. Denis, who had taken on the role of the group's leader, clutched his own crucifix, an imposing emblem that had been sanctified by the highest ecclesiastical order, promising a might beyond the ordinary.

"Remember, faith is our fortress," Denis murmured, a steadying voice in the uncertain gloom. "Let these symbols be our armour against the evil that dwells within."

Mia, her features set in a mask of pure determination, nodded. "And let our strength be unwavering," she added, her hand gripping her own crucifix as if to draw strength from it.

The building loomed before them, a monolith of shadows and threats, some whispered, some not so quiet. It's windows like huge blind eyes that refused to reveal the horrors housed within stared down at them. Johnson, his usual confidence subdued by the aura of dread he felt, checked the readiness of his companions. "Are we going to be long in there?" His voice tinged with fear.

Denis turned to face him, "We step not just into darkness, but into a potential battle of souls," his voice barely above a whisper, carrying the weight of their collective apprehension.

Dave and Fiona exchanged a glance, a silent pact of mutual protection, their crucifixes held before them not as weapons, but as shields against the unseen forces that awaited. With a collective breath, they crossed the boundary, the door creaking open like a spectral lamentation, inviting them into the bowels of the building. The darkness seemed to swallow them whole, a living, moving, entity that watched them with malignant intent. They moved forward as one, bound by a shared resolve to confront whatever lay in the heart of this structure, their faith and symbols of sanctity, were their only protection in the engulfing shadows. A pungent stench of rotting flesh permeated the atmosphere, rendering it heavy and suffocating.

"What is that smell?" exclaimed officer Johnson, retching while trying not to physically vomit.

"Evil." Whispered Denis, "Pure evil." Holding his crucifix in front of him, his voice rose in the silence, saying a prayer with a resolute tone. "Saint Michael the Archangel, noble leader of the Heavenly Hosts, we seek your protection as we enter this realm of darkness. Defend us in our struggle against the forces of Evil, against the rulers and powers of this world shrouded in darkness, against the spirits that dwell in places unseen. Be our shield against their wickedness."

Together, in a unified chorus, they solemnly echoed, "Amen."

"Stay close," Denis whispered, his voice barely audible, "And whatever happens, do not let it separate us. That's how it weakens its prey, it isolates them, and then breaks them."

Officer Johnson nodded, every sense heightened, aware of the slightest sound, the faintest movement in the periphery of his vision.

The darkness in the building was absolute, a void seeming to swallow all light, all hope. They moved forward, each step in defiance against the terror seeking to engulf them.

Their footsteps echoed through the silence, slow, rhythmic echoes, multiplying with each step. Officer Johnson' breathing became rapid and shallow, his eyes darted back and forth, trying as hard as he could but with little success to penetrate the impenetrable blackness. Every shadow seemed to move, every whisper of wind a potential threat. The oppressive atmosphere of the building seemed to weigh down on them, an unseen force threatening to crush their spirits.

"Listen," Denis whispered, as he stopped in his tracks.

The group halted holding their breath. From the depths of the building came a sound, a murmur, faint at first, but growing steadily louder, a chant, a chorus of voices reverberating through the halls, the tone neither human nor pleasant. The words were indecipherable, yet they carried with them a sense of ancient malice transcending time, a hatred of everything human.

"What is that?" Mia whispered, her voice trembling.

Denis didn't answer. His face appeared strained as he listened intently, his eyes reflected the terror gripping his heart. He knew they were not alone. They were being stalked, hunted, something lurking in the dark wanted them. The chanting grew louder; the voices merging into a cacophony of evil which resounded off the walls. The temperature dropped rapidly, a sharp chill that continued dropping with each passing second until their breaths materialised in the frigid air.

Denis held his large crucifix in front of him, and took a deep breath, "Everyone stay together behind me." Then, in a louder, more confident voice, "In the revered name of Jesus Christ, our formidable guardian and divine leader, fortified by the wisdom of the Immaculate Virgin Mary, Mother of God, strengthened by the valiant Michael the Archangel, and the blessed Apostles Peter and Paul, along with all the Saints. With the resolve imparted by our steadfast belief, we courageously confront and dispel the spectres and illusions cast by this malevolence. God asserts His power; His foes are dispersed. Those who oppose Him retreat from His overwhelming aura. Just as smoke is swept away by the breeze, so too are you scattered. As wax dissolves under the intensity of the flame, so the wicked wither away in the presence of God. Witness the emblem of the Lord's conquest, flee you, assembly of foes. The lion from the tribe of Judah descended from David, heralds triumph. Let your benevolence, Lord, envelop us, as boundless as our trust in you. We banish you, all impure spirits, every demonic power, each incursion from the abyss, all maleficent congregations, gatherings, and factions. In the name and under the supreme command of our Lord Jesus Christ, we unite in strength, ordering you to depart, to dissipate, to cease your existence amidst us. This sanctuary is now restored in the radiance of God's grace and compassion. Amen."

The chanting from around the building stopped, replaced by total silence. But, as suddenly as it had ceased, it resumed, this time louder and more insistent than before. The voices were joined by a series of thuds and scrapes, as if something was being dragged across the floor above them.

Officer Johnson instinctively reached for the hand of Mia, a meagre comfort against the unseen terrors surrounding them. "Should we turn back?" he whispered, failing to hide the fear in his voice.

Mia shook her head, her determination a beacon of light in the overwhelming darkness. "We can't. We must find the source of this evil and confront it. It's the only way to save everyone."

Denis repeated the prayer with increased fervour and conviction, louder this time, flicking Holy Water in front of them as they advanced. "In the revered name of Jesus Christ, our formidable guardian and divine leader, fortified by the wisdom of the Immaculate Virgin Mary, Mother of God, strengthened by the valiant Michael the Archangel, and the blessed Apostles Peter and Paul, along with all the Saints. With the resolve imparted by our steadfast belief, we courageously confront and dispel the spectres and illusions cast by malevolence. God asserts his power; His foes are dispersed. Those who oppose Him retreat from His overwhelming aura. Just as smoke is swept away by the breeze, so too are you scattered. As wax dissolves under the intensity of the flame, so the wicked wither away in the presence of God. Witness the emblem of the Lord's conquest, flee you, assembly of foes. The lion from the tribe of Judah descended from David, heralds triumph. Let your benevolence, Lord, envelop us, as boundless as our trust in you. We banish you, all impure spirits, every demonic power, each incursion from the abyss, all maleficent congregations, gatherings, and factions. In the name and under the supreme command of our Lord Jesus Christ, we unite in strength, ordering you to depart, to dissipate, to cease your existence amidst us. This sanctuary is now restored in the radiance of God's grace and compassion. Amen."

The chanting stopped again as if affected by the prayer. The group continued to move forward. Their torches' beams flickering, casting eerie, dancing silhouettes that seemed to reach back towards them. A figure materialised within the torch light. It was the figure of a child, or what once was a child. Its eyes hollow, its face contorted in an expression of eternal suffering. Tattered clothes hung loosely on its skeletal frame, its skin ashen and barely covering its bones. The figure pointed down the corridor, its mouth moving in silent speech. Then, just as simply as it appeared, it withdrew back into the darkness.

Denis took a deep breath, steadying his nerves. "I think we should go that way. It looked like it was trying to show us something."

Together they moved cautiously down the corridor, as they rounded a corner, they came to a door, its surface scarred with long, deep scratches. Denis hesitated, his hand hovering over the handle. "This is it," he said in a whisper. "It's here... What lies beyond this door... is not of this world."

With a deep breath, he pushed the door open, revealing a room engulfed in darkness. The beams of their torches struggled to pierce the gloom, what they showed was a scene of utter desolation. Broken furniture lay scattered across the floor, and on the walls were strange symbols painted in a substance that looked ominously like blood. A sudden loud bang echoed through the room, making everyone jump. A shadow, even darker than the surrounding darkness, moved across the room, its form shifting and changing, never quite revealing itself.

Johnson' voice trembled, "What... what in the name of heaven... or hell... is that?"

Denis moved forward, his eyes scanning the room. "It's not of this world officer. This is the heart of the haunting. If there truly is a presence here, I think this is where it will manifest."

As if it had been listening, the temperature in the room plummeted, their breath once again turning to mist as it left their lips. The darkness pressed in on them, suffocating them in a blanket of fear. As they looked at the symbols on the wall, they began to glow. A blood red light cast the room with a hellish hue. The shadow moved faster, circling them, like a predator stalking its prey. The five of them turned repeatedly, spinning, trying desperately to keep an eye on the swirling black mass whirling around them.

Denis's voice was firm in the ensuing chaos. "Stay together. Everyone, join hands if you need to, but don't let it divide us."

The shadow lunged forward, a formless mass of darkness and malice. The group jumped as one and huddled even closer together, their fear feeding the entity. As the shadow circled around them once more, Denis's voice rose above the terror, a prayer of protection against the darkness threatening to consume them.

"O Almighty and Everlasting God, shield and protector of all who seek your refuge, I call upon your boundless mercy. In this hour of darkness, we stand at the threshold of the unknown, facing forces unseen and powers untold. Surround us with your divine light, be our fortress against the darkness that encroaches. Guide us with your wisdom, arm us with Your strength, so we may tread safely through realms uncharted, and challenges unspoken. Bless us with your Holy presence, shield us with your celestial guardians, let the mighty Archangel Michael be our defender in battle, his sword a beacon of your eternal light. May the pure and unwavering courage of Saints Peter and Paul inspire our hearts and steady our resolve. Cast a circle of protection around us, a barrier impenetrable by evil. Let no malevolent spirit or corrupting influence breach this Holy perimeter. In the face of adversity, in the presence of danger, let us feel your comforting embrace, O Lord. As we venture forth into the night, into the heart of this maelstrom of darkness, we place our trust in you, O God. Watch over us, guide our steps, and bring us back into the warmth of your light.

In the name of Jesus Christ, our Saviour and Redeemer, we pray. Amen."

They looked around the room, then at each other. Did the room's atmosphere lift slightly? Whatever had been swirling around them had gone.

Daniel's voice croaked with fear. "How do you deal with all this? Doesn't it scare the life out of you?"

"It most certainly does, but we cannot give in to that fear. Use that fear, make your fear work for you. The biggest battle with your fear is the one in your own mind." Denis replied.

"That's easy for you to say. I've never come across anything like this, and truthfully... I never want to again. I would like to get out of here as soon as possible, please."

Denis nodded, "Mia, Dave, what do you make of all this?"

"It seems to me someone has held a ritual of some sort here and has somehow conjured up these spirits," Mia replied.

Denis's eyes scanned the decrepit room, the darkness clung to the corners like dark spectres. "A ritual, yes," he murmured, his voice a low rumble. "This place has become a nexus for the unnatural, a beacon for the damned."

The atmosphere was filled with echoes of screams and cries from the past as if their torment remained here in the present. The faint sound of scratching against the walls sent shivers down their spines, a sinister reminder they were not finished.

Dave nodded in agreement with Mia. "The energy in here, it's unlike anything I've ever felt before. It's as if evil itself has come to life, invading everything with its sinister presence."

Johnson, visibly shaken, glanced around the room his eyes wide and fearful. "But what can we do? We're mere mortals against... against whatever that was."

Denis placed a reassuring hand on the officer's shoulder. "We have knowledge, and with knowledge comes power. Entities like that feed on fear, on uncertainty. We must stand firm, united in our resolve, that will give it nothing to feed on."

The room seemed to respond to Denis's words; the air growing even colder, the gloom growing even deeper. Low, mournful wailing echoed through the halls, a sound filled with so much sorrow and pain it clawed at their hearts.

The wail grew into a cacophony of voices, a chorus of the damned which filled the room with a sense of despair. The walls themselves vibrated with the intensity of the sound, the foundations of the building shuddering under its weight.

Fiona spoke out, "Do you want to cross over?" She yelled in an attempt to be heard. "Do you want to find everlasting peace?"

Mia clutched her crucifix, her lips moving in silent prayer. "These spirits, they're trapped, tormented. We need to release them, we need to break the bonds which are holding them here."

Denis nodded; his eyes widened with determination.

"We need to find out who did this. Who could be so stupid as to conjure up this evil? More importantly, we need to find out the demon's name." Denis's voice was filled with anger.

"Why do you need to know its name?" Asked officer Johnson.

"Knowing its name gives us power, knowing its name, we can banish it back to Hell," Denis replied.

Fiona looked at Denis. "I have an idea who might have done this. It's only an idea. I have no proof yet. Someone who might benefit from a haunted building, perhaps?"

Denis smiled. "Okay, let's get out of here, let's vacate this building and review our footage back at the van."

Officer Johnson looked at the group with eager anticipation. "You mean we're getting out of here?...Now!"

Fiona smiled. "Yes, it's time to go. Time to review our evidence and do some research, and you might just be the person to help us."

Relief washed over his face, his eyes reflecting a mix of fear and gratitude. "I've never been happier to hear those words. Let's go."

The group began their cautious retreat, each step echoing through the dimly lit corridors. Silhouettes flickered at the edges of their vision, shadowy forms were there one moment and gone the next before you could really see them, it was as if the darkness itself was watching them. Denis led the way. Faint sounds followed them, words spoken in a language not of this world, sinister whispering coming from the walls. The moment they neared the entrance, a cold wind swept through the building, the temperature plummeting in an instant. Their breaths were a ghostly fog in the beams of their torches.

Mia shivered, pulling her coat tighter around her. "It doesn't want us to leave," she whispered.

Officer Johnson glanced nervously over his shoulder. "Can it stop us?"

Denis shook his head. "No, but it can try to intimidate us. Keep moving. Don't let it sense your fear."

They quickened their pace as they hurried towards the exit. The whispering grew louder, a host of voices filling the air with dread. The building groaned around them, its structure protesting their departure. Finally, they emerged into the night, the fresh air, a striking difference to the suffocating atmosphere in the asylum. They hurried across the grounds to the safety of the command centre, their converted van parked at the edge of the property. Inside the van they found a semblance of normality with the hum of computers and the soft glow of monitors.

Dave looked at Alex and me, his expression a mix of urgency and hope. "Tell me you got it on camera? You definitely have footage, don't you?"

Alex, fumbling with the screens, nodded vigorously, his hands trembling slightly. "Yes, yes, we got it. Everything. The darkness, the voices, we even caught the temperature drop on the sensors. It's all here." His voice held a tremor of excitement tinged with fear.

I leaned in. "The footage is unbelievable, Dave. There's stuff here... stuff you just can't explain. You can see things moving, you can hear voices when no one is around, voices that we could not hear whilst we were in there."

The group huddled around one of the screens, their faces illuminated by the flickering light. As the footage played back, the eerie silence of the van was filled with the sounds they captured while they were in the asylum. The unholy wailing and the chilling whispers emanated from the speakers.

Mia's face lit up as she watched. "This... this is way more than I expected. The activity is off the charts. I've never seen anything like it before." Her excitement was uncontainable.

Denis, his eyes fixed on the screen, nodded solemnly. "This is definitive proof. We're not just dealing with mere ghosts or spirits. This is real evidence of something evil, something more powerful existing in there."

Officer Johnson, who had been watching over their shoulders, swallowed hard. "I've seen a lot in my time on the force, but this... this is something else."

As the footage continued, a chilling scene unfolded on the screen. The camera panned across the room, briefly revealing a dark figure. It moved around then lingered for a moment staring at them before vanishing.

Everyone in the van fell silent, the implication of what they were seeing weighing heavily upon them. The figure, so fleeting yet so clearly present, was proof of the unknown they were dealing with.

Denis broke the silence, his voice determined. "We need to analyse this footage, every frame. Look for patterns, symbols, anything which can give us a clue what we're dealing with. Can you freeze-frame the spectre? I would like a closer look at it."

Alex rewound the recording, and they all gazed at the screen. Looking back at them was a black murky figure, blood-red eyes staring back at them. Denis's gaze turned to Fiona, a sense of urgency flickering across his face. "Fiona, you mentioned something about knowing who might have held a ritual in the building?"

"Yes," Fiona replied, her voice tinged with curiosity. "The new owner, Ron. There's something about him. He was quite insistent we did a ghost hunt and record what we found. His plan is to convert the building into a haunted museum and attract ghost hunting teams from around the world, including those on television. He said it would be perfect publicity."

"Hmm... that's very interesting," Denis mused, the cogs in his mind turning. "We, and by we, I mean you, Officer Johnson, will need to bring him in for questioning. If it was him who performed a ritual, we need to know what he conjured up, and, importantly, as I said before, the name of this demon."

The silence that followed was unnerving. The figure they had glimpsed, so elusive yet undeniably there, a chilling indication of the unknown horrors they were grappling with, appearing as a spectre visible on the screen. Was this the demon or merely one of its minions? Mia nodded to herself, her fingers flying over her laptop keyboard. "I'll start enhancing some of these images, see if I can get a clearer view of the figure."

With my gaze fixed on the screen, I added, "There's something about that figure. It feels familiar, like a piece of a puzzle we've seen before but can't quite place."

As the team delved into their work, the van became a hive of activity. Each person researching a different aspect of their findings. Outside, the shadows seemed to shift and whisper themselves, as if the building itself was conscious of their research, patiently biding its time, the spectre lying in wait. The atmosphere inside the van was one of tense concentration, each member of the team lost in their own thoughts, and their own fears. The van was heavy with the electric buzz of technology mingling with the sense of a looming, unseen threat. Denis leaned closer to the screen, his eyes straining to scan every inch of the footage for any clue, any sign which might help them understand what they were up against. His heart raced with anticipation. He knew they were on the brink of something monumental, yet dark and terrifying, something which defied all logic and understanding. The night crept on; hours ticking by with agonising slowness, outside, the wind blew, its mournful howl a fitting acoustic backdrop to their grim task. The trees around the asylum swayed, making eerie sounds. Their twisted branches creating shadows that danced in the moonlight.

Mia gasped, her fingers freezing on the keyboard. "There! Look!" she exclaimed, pointing at the screen. From the dark hallway, a shape took form in the footage. It was humanoid, yet grotesquely distorted, its limbs elongated and bent at impossible angles. An icy chill ran through Denis's body as he stared at the figure. It was like nothing he had ever seen before, a nightmarish entity, its eyes hollow and soulless, its mouth a gaping orifice of darkness.

As I leaned in, my face paled, my voice was barely a whisper. "What is that thing?"

Denis shook his head, unable to tear his eyes away from the screen. "I don't know... but I have a feeling it knows we're here to send it back to wherever it came from."

We fell silent once more, the only sound in the van was the relentless tapping of Mia's fingers as she worked to enhance the image further. The figure on the screen became clearer, more menacing with each passing second.

As they watched, a sudden movement caught their attention. The figure that had once been static, now moved. Its jerky, unnatural motions sent a wave of terror through the van. It was as if the very fabric of reality was warping around the thing, the room behind it shimmering and distorting in its wake. Denis's heart pounded in his chest, his mind racing with thoughts of ancient rituals and devil worship. They were dealing with something here that was far beyond their understanding, something that defied all laws of nature and reason. And as the figure on the screen reached out towards them, its hand appeared to breach the glass barrier of the screen that stood between their world and its own.

The group felt a thick wave of fear and unease as Denis hurriedly turned off the screen. He stood there, a weary figure against the backdrop of the van's cramped interior. Stretching to dispel the tension knotting his muscles, he made a decision. "I think we should stop now and get some rest."

"Officer Johnson, could you find this Ron and bring him in for questioning? He could be responsible for everything that's happened here, including the disappearance of their friends." He said motioning to myself and Fiona.

"I'll radio the station and have him brought in. We can interview him later this afternoon, after some sleep. Assuming any of us can get any sleep," Johnson's voice trailed off, a grim acknowledgement of the horror which shadowed their every thought.

The van's interior, once a hub of frenetic activity, now seemed like a mausoleum to their frayed nerves. The screens, which had recently flickered with the images of unspeakable terror, were now dark. Emitting a low glow, the van's interior light was the only source of light. Outside, the moon, a pale, uncaring witness to the horrors lurking within the asylum's crumbling walls, was waning fast. Denis sat down heavily, his mind a whirlpool of confusion. The figure they had seen on the screen was etched into his memory, a spectral apparition defying explanation. Its movements were bizarre and puppet-like, as if controlled by an unseen evil power.

Johnson's voice, when he spoke, was a thin thread of sound in the overwhelming silence. "I've got a bad feeling about this, Denis. What if bringing Ron in makes things worse? What if we're poking a hornet's nest?"

Denis turned, meeting Johnson's gaze. The fear he saw there was a mirror of his own. "We have no choice," he said, his voice barely above a whisper. "We need answers, and Ron just might be the key to all of this."

Outside, the wind was picking up, its mournful howl a dirge for the invisible terrors prowling the grounds. The trees surrounding the van swayed and danced in the gale, their branches old and gnarled, writhing and groaning. Every gust seemed to press against the van, as if trying to force its way inside to touch them with its cold, spectral fingers. The team wearily made their way back to town, each one of them exhausted. The ride was silent, the usual chatter and camaraderie replaced by an uncomfortable silence. They were all acutely aware of the long day ahead of them, fraught with unknown dangers and dark discoveries. The first light of dawn painted the sleepy town with soft pink hues. The town, usually a picture of quaint charm, now seemed eerily deserted, its streets empty, its houses dark.

They each headed to their respective accommodation, the need for rest overriding everything else. The comfort of familiar surroundings did little to ease the tension which settled in their bones. Sleep, when it came, was fitful and haunted by nightmares. The horrific sights they witnessed were constantly replaying in their minds. Denis, lying in his bed, found no solace in the soft sheets and fluffy pillows. His mind was a whirlwind of thoughts, visualising the events at the asylum over and over. He knew they were on the brink of uncovering something terrible, something only he, as an ordained exorcist, had a chance of defeating. Mid-morning came all too quickly, its arrival marked by a weak sun doing very little to warm the chill in the air. The team gathered once more at the hotel, their faces drawn, their eyes tired and haunted. There was little in the way of conversation, each was lost in their individual thoughts as they sat and ate their late breakfast, each preparing in their own way to face the day ahead. The hunt for the truth had begun, but at what cost?

Chapter 10

Ron sat in the interrogation room. It felt like a tomb, its grey walls closing in on him, the air thick with invisible pressure. Ron, looking every inch a guilty man, sat hunched over, his pale face etched with lines of fear and regret. Officer Johnson and Denis Clarke sat on the opposite side of the table. Denis, with his steady gaze and unwavering voice, seemed to be the embodiment of the grim reaper of truth.

Without hesitation Denis started his questioning, "Why did you perform the ritual, Ron?" His tone measured yet filled with an undercurrent of urgency. Ron's eyes, wide with terror, flickered around the room, desperately seeking an escape that didn't exist. "I... I didn't," he stammered, his voice quivering with denial. Denis leaned forward, his gaze sharpening. "I don't believe you. It seems like a very convenient money-making scheme, doesn't it? Transforming an ordinary Victorian building into a captivating haven for ghost hunters, infused with a touch of supernatural charm. But you delved too deep, didn't you Ron. You've stirred something ancient, something evil, and something of which you know nothing about."

"I didn't, I wouldn't know how," Ron protested, his voice a mere whisper in the crushing silence of the room.

Officer Johnson, who had been a silent observer until now, interjected, his voice slicing through the tension like a blade. "Ron, the evidence speaks for itself. We've found this book in your office. The symbols drawn in circles on the asylum's walls and floor match perfectly what is inside this book. You can't keep denying your involvement, it's pointless"

Ron's face drained of colour, his lips trembling as he struggled to form words. "Yes, the book... but I never... I mean, I just read it..."

Denis's expression was one of serious concentration. "Reading such texts is not a passive act, Ron. You invited something into our world. Tell us, what ritual did you perform? What did the spirits say? Especially the demon"

Ron's eyes darted to the table, his fingers tracing invisible patterns on the surface. "It... it spoke of a ritual to awaken the 'Soul Collector'. I thought it was all myth, folklore and stories."

Denis's eyes narrowed. "The Soul Collector? Do you have any idea what you've done? That's more than a ghost or spirit Ron. You've invoked an ancient evil, one that predates our oldest myths."

Johnson leaned back, a look of disbelief crossing his rugged features. "This is beyond my jurisdiction. If what you're saying is true, then we're dealing with pure evil. And what about the missing people? Will they have lost their souls? Will they even be still alive?"

Ron's voice was now a hushed, haunted whisper. "I just wanted to make the asylum popular. I didn't believe any of it was real. But then things started happening, noises, strange noises, shadows moving in the darkness, visitors speaking of feeling watched, and sometimes touched."

Denis rose from his chair, his movements deliberate, like a predator closing in on its prey. "You've opened a door that you cannot close, Ron. This entity, this Soul Collector, has been awakened, and it seeks a conduit, a way to manifest fully in our world... it starts by collecting souls."

Johnson, a man accustomed to the black-and-white of law and order, struggled to digest the gravity of the situation. "What are you suggesting we do, Denis?"

Denis's gaze returned to Ron, a mixture of pity and resolve etched into his features. "We must go back to the asylum. We must confront what this man has unleashed. And we must try to banish it before it grows too powerful."

Ron shuddered, his mind racing with images of the asylum's dark, echoing corridors and the sense of an unseen presence that now seemed so real and menacing. "What if we can't? What if it's too late?"

Denis's voice was firm, a symbol of hope in the swirling maelstrom of our fear and uncertainty. "Then we must be prepared to face the consequences of your actions, Ron. We cannot allow this entity to roam free. The book you found in his office. I'll need to study it." He said, pointing to the book on the table.

Ron shivered, as if the very mention of the book sent an icy shiver down his spine. "I only meant ghosts for come through. Nothing evil, nothing like this. I just... I..."

"You opened a doorway for something unspeakable," Denis pressed, his voice a low rumble in the otherwise silent room. "An evil that has probably claimed lives. Do you comprehend the severity of what you've done?"

Tears began to flow down Ron's cheeks, his whole-body trembling with sobs. "I didn't mean for any of this. I thought it was harmless, a bit of a thrill for the ghost hunters. I never imagined..."

Denis leaned in closer, his eyes never leaving Ron's face. "What did you summon, Ron? What is the name of this creature?"

Ron shook his head, his voice a mere shadow. "The book didn't specify. Just symbols and incantations in a language I didn't understand. I thought it was all just a bunch of nonsense. I just thought I'd give it a go to see if anything would happen."

Denis's mind was a whirlwind of thoughts, piecing together the fragments of a puzzle that was as ancient as it was terrifying. They were dealing with an entity that defied human understanding. A dangerous force unleashed through Ron's ignorance was now free in their world.

The air in the interrogation room was oppressive as the weight of the dark tale unfolded within its four walls. Ron's story, a blend of naivety and unwitting wrongdoing, was like a key turning in a lock, opening doors that should have remained closed forever.

Denis's interrogation continued, his questions probing deeper into the heart of the darkness that Ron had unleashed. "Describe the ritual, Ron. What exactly did you do?"

Ron's voice was now a cracked hoarse whisper and his eyes were wide, as if he feared that speaking the words might bring forth the horrors again. "I... I just followed the instructions. There was a circle... symbols... I lit candles. I read the words out loud. It felt like a game, I swear. I never thought it would work."

"But it did work, didn't it, Ron?" Denis's voice was like ice. "You invited something into our world, something that doesn't belong here."

Ron nodded, his face full of despair. "Yes, it worked. That night, I heard noises, footsteps, whispers. I thought it was my imagination, but then... then things started happening. Objects shifting, shadows moving in corners, the temperature dropping, door slamming, that's when I ran for it..."

Denis felt a chill run down his spine, "You unleashed a demon, Ron. A demon that we now have to deal with and hopefully banish."

The questioning stretched on, time seeming to warp and bend within the confines of the room. With every word Ron spoke, the reality of their situation became more terrifying, more urgent.

When Denis finally stood to leave, the burden of their next steps weighed heavily upon him. They faced an unknown, ancient evil, a shadow from beyond the veil that Ron had carelessly invited into this world. They were up against a foe shrouded in mystery; a demon born from the whispers of the night.

Denis's hands trembled slightly as he picked up the ancient book from the desk. It was an ominous-looking book; its leather cover was cracked and faded, the pages within yellowed by time and shrouded in an air of malicious intent. Denis knew that within its tattered pages lay the key to understanding the demon they were up against. Officer Johnson watched him intently; Denis's expression was one of apprehension. "This might be our only chance to figure out what we're dealing with," he said in a voice that betrayed his apprehension. "We'll study this thoroughly," he assured. "Whatever this... this thing is, it's somehow linked to the asylum's past and this book. We need to uncover its nature and hopefully its name before we can even think of confronting it."

The walk back to the rest of the team was silent. Denis's mind was overwhelmed with his thoughts, remembering the book's enigmatic symbols, ritual diagrams, and unnatural creatures. Arriving at my flat, which had somehow become the team's makeshift headquarters, Denis laid the book on a table.

The team gathering round, their faces were etched with concern and curiosity as they peered at the ancient text.

"We're dealing with something that goes beyond our usual level and understanding of ghosts or hauntings." Denis began, his voice steady but his hands betraying a slight tremor. "This demon, I think it's something ancient, something very dangerous."

The team listened as Denis recounted what he had learned from Ron, and what he suspected from his initial glance through the book. The atmosphere was tense; each member knew they could be on the brink of uncovering truths that might be better left hidden. As they delved into the book, deciphering the arcane language and piecing together the fragments of information, the room seemed to grow colder. It was as if the very act of reading the book had caught the demon's attention. The team exchanged worried glances, the idea that they were dealing with a demon and not just a restless spirit, was something far more ancient and powerful, and terrifying.

"We need to figure out how to banish it back to where it came from," Denis continued, his voice laced with urgency. "If this thing is as powerful as I think it is, or at least it could yet become, it would pose a threat not just to the asylum, but to the entire town."

The team worked tirelessly, poring over the book, cross-referencing its contents with historical records. Hours passed, as they immersed themselves in a world of forgotten legends and dark rituals. As the day waned, Denis's eyes were drawn repeatedly to a particular passage in the book, a ritual that seemed to resonate with the events they were witnessing. "This could be it," he murmured, his finger tracing the ancient script.

In the dimly lit flat, their sense of urgency was rising. Denis's face was illuminated by a small lamp on a table to his right. His brow furrowed, he poured over the book, his eyes tracing the lines of cryptic script. The book had to hold the key to their salvation. Mia, her face etched with concern, leaned over Denis's shoulder, studying the passage. "It's calling for a series of ritualistic steps, some of which are... well... unsettling to say the least," she said, her voice a whisper in the heavy silence.

Dave, sitting across the room, his arms folded, looked up. "Unsettling how?" he asked, his curiosity piqued. Denis closed the book gently, a sense of resolve hardening in his eyes. "We need to create a binding circle, one that will contain the entity and force it back into its own realm. But the ritual... it requires more than just incantations and diagrams."

Fiona, her hands clasped tightly together, spoke up. "What do you mean more? What else does it need?"

Denis hesitated, his gaze meeting each of theirs in turn. "A part of ourselves. Something meaningful, a sacrifice of sorts. It's the only way to give the ritual the power it needs."

The room fell into a sombre silence, the magnitude of Denis's words weighing heavily upon them. We all knew that what we were about to undertake was fraught with danger, a dance on the razor's edge between light and darkness. Mia broke the silence, her voice tinged with a mix of fear and determination. "What kind of sacrifice are we talking about? It's not... It's not literal, is it?"

Denis shook his head and exhaled, puffing out his cheeks, a grim expression on his face. "No, not literal. But it must be of deep personal value. An object that ties us to this world, something that holds a strong significance to us."

Dave leaned forward. "You're saying these ritual needs something that's a part of us? That's a heavy price."

Fiona, her fingers nervously twisting a lock of her hair, added, "And if we do this if we make this sacrifice, are we sure it will work? That it will banish the entity?"

Denis's gaze drifted to the book, its ancient pages holding secrets of a time long forgotten. "Nothing is certain," he admitted. "But it's our best chance. We need to understand more about this thing, its origin, and hopefully its weaknesses."

The team quietly nodded in agreement, the danger of the task ahead making their decisions even more crucial.

"We need to research," I said, breaking the silence. "We can't go into this blind. We've got to determine precisely what we are dealing with."

Mia stood up, her resolve returning. "I'll start digging into the asylum's records. There must be something in the public archives, old newspaper articles, anything that can give us more insight. Fiona, would you like to help me, please?"

"Yes, of course. But, while we are researching all of this, what about our trapped friends?"

Denis turned to face Fiona, "Hopefully, they are strong and merely trapped in there, between worlds. We can't rush into this and risk all our lives too."

"Can we get them back?"

Denis shook his head slightly. "I don't know, I hope so." His face betrayed his doubts.

The thought unnerved me, but I nodded. "I'll help. There must be something I could do?"

Fiona with a questioning look in her eyes. "And what about the book? Is there more to it can tell us?"

He opened the book again, his eyes scanning the symbols and cryptic text. "There's a lot here, layer upon layer of information and hidden meanings. I need to translate more of it, understand the context. We're dealing with something ancient, something strong, something I have never come across before."

The team set to work. Papers were strewn across every available surface; laptops open with screens glowing as they delved into the dark history of the asylum and the mysterious entity they were facing. Time passed fleetingly as they immersed themselves in their grim task. Dave and I spent hours researching old newspapers in online archives. We discovered terrifying accounts of mysterious events at the asylum. The stories included tales of patients being experimented on by Dr Ravenswood, and much more.

Mia and Fiona returned from their fact-finding mission armed with a notepad filled information. Their eyes bleary from the strain. They had sifted through historical texts and occult references and had pieced together the puzzle of the entity's origins. References to ancient rituals and to beings summoned in Victorian times had also been recorded by them in their notepads.

Denis diligently translated the book, revealing unsettling passages. They described sacrifices offered to appease sinister beings, the fragile boundary separating realms, and the immense power needed to control such a formidable foe. As the afternoon wore on, a picture emerged, a tapestry of horror and madness woven throughout the history of the asylum.

This entity was not merely a spirit. It was older and posed a greater threat. It had been summoned from the depths of darkness and was now bound to the asylum by recent rituals performed by Ron.

"We're dealing with something that's been around for many, many centuries," Denis stated, his voice now heavy with fatigue. "It's now not just part of the asylum; it has become the asylum. And it's reaching out, feeding on fear, growing stronger."

The team looked at each other, the enormity of their task settling upon them like a shroud. They were battling a force that had been strengthened by the very fabric of the asylum's tragic history.

Secrets had been discovered that should have been left buried, but there was no turning back now, the entity, a demon whispered into the present from deep in the past, was a threat that could not be left to grow any stronger.

"Now, we can start to plan," Denis said, his voice resolute despite the exhaustion etched on his face. "Now we know what we're up against. We need to use that knowledge to our advantage."

Mia, her eyes tired from hours of research, nodded in agreement. "We need to be strategic. That thing, it's been dormant for so long, and now this idiot comes along and reawakens it. We need to find its weaknesses, then exploit them."

Fiona chimed in, "The rituals from the past, are something the Victorians were deeply into. They obviously did not know what they were doing, or how dangerous it could be."

Denis, his eyes still on the book, added, "We need to be careful with the sacrifices we choose for the ritual. They need to be meaningful, but we can't let this thing take more from us than is necessary."

The rest of the afternoon was spent formulating a plan, piecing together the information they had gathered into a coherent strategy. As they prepared for the ritual, they continued to research the asylum's history and the demon's origins. They were no longer floundering in the dark; they had a direction, a purpose. But each knew that the road ahead was fraught with danger. This demon, a shadow from the beginning of time, would not be easily banished. It would fight to maintain its foothold in this world.

They worked hard, their resolve hardening, their hope rising with each new piece of information they uncovered. A team united by one common goal, bound by the knowledge that they were the only ones who could face this darkness and send it back to Hell.

"We are going to need a lot of Holy Water. We need to use it to force it into the mirror room and send it back through the portal, then close that portal forever."

Fiona sat up. "We have a large church here. I think the priest there would bless as much as we need."

Her suggestion was met with nods of agreement from the rest of the team. The use of Holy Water seemed a fitting counter to the unholy presence they were dealing with. Alex spoke up, "It's not just about getting the Holy Water. We need to figure out the logistics of trapping this thing in the mirror room. That place... it's like a nexus of paranormal activity."

Mia, her hands wrapped around a steaming cup of coffee, added, "Not to mention the maze of corridors and rooms."

Dave, who had been quietly listening, chimed in, "But how do we ensure it goes back through the portal and not just dissipates into the asylum? We need something to guide it, to control its path."

Denis, still poring over the ancient book, looked up. "There's mention here of a binding ritual, one that can be used to direct an evil spirit. It's complex and dangerous, but with the Holy Water weakening it, we might just be able to pull it off."

The team pondered the idea. Despite the risks, it remained their best choice. "We'll need to be precise," Denis continued. "Any error could mean disaster. We need to rehearse this, make sure everyone knows their part. But, I think we need to leave that until tomorrow. Everyone's tired and we all need a good night's sleep. We have to be fresh in the morning, at our very best."

Reluctantly, everyone agreed to postpone the rehearsal until the following day. We all knew the task was immense and that clear minds were essential. They began to gather their notes and research, preparing to leave my flat. As they stood, ready to depart, Mia voiced the concern that lingered unspoken in each of our minds. "Are we sure we're ready for this? This isn't like anything we've ever faced before."

Denis, closing the ancient book, looked at each of them in turn. "We have no choice but to be ready. This thing, it's not just a threat to us or to the asylum. If we don't stop it, the consequences could be catastrophic."

The drive back to the hotel was a quiet one, each member of the team lost in their own thoughts, each going over the details of the plan, the ritual, and the potential dangers they would face. Dave tried to offer some words of reassurance. "We've got a solid plan. We just need to stick to it, trust in each other."

Mia smiled, though the worry in her eyes was evident. "Thanks, Dave. I'll see you in the morning. We've got a big day ahead of us tomorrow."

Denis had a restless night. The ancient book lay on his bedside table, its secrets haunting his dreams. Visions of the asylum, the entity, and the mirror room played out in his mind, a relentless reminder of the task that awaited them.

Fiona, too, found sleep elusive. She lay in her bed, staring at the ceiling. Morning came too quickly. As the team reconvened at my flat, each wearing the signs of a sleepless night, I made them strong cups of coffee and they began their rehearsal. Denis led them through the binding ritual, making sure each member understood their individual role. The timing of each incantation, the placement of every symbol, each detail vital to their safety and success. They practised the steps over and over, including the movements around the mirror room, and the handling of the Holy Water.

Dave and Fiona worked on the logistics of trapping the demon by using the layout of the asylum to their advantage. Mia and I focused on contingency plans, what to do if something went wrong, how to protect ourselves and each other. As the day progressed, a sense of confidence began to build among us. we were a team, united in our purpose, each of us bringing our own strengths to the table.

But, underlying our confidence, was the knowledge of the danger we faced. We were about to confront a force of pure malevolence. An entity that had lurked in the shadows of the asylum, preying on the vulnerable for decades, perhaps longer, before Ron had released it. It was a being that defied understanding, a creature of nightmares and madness. As the final rehearsal came to a close, Denis looked around at his team, a sense of pride mixed with fear in his heart. "We're as ready as we'll ever be," he said, his voice firm. "Tonight, we face this thing. Tonight, god willing, we end it."

Denis's van alarm shattered the morning stillness. Its ear-piercing sound was a jarring intrusion into their tense planning session. Denis, with a furrowed brow, rushed to the window to investigate. On the street below, two figures stood near his van. He hurried downstairs, determination etched on his face, ready to confront them.

"Who are you? Are you responsible for the alarm going off?" he demanded, clicking his key fob to silence the alarm's piercing cry.

A woman, her face framed by shadows beneath the hood of her coat, stepped forward with an apologetic yet resolute expression. "I'm sorry for that, yes, I set the alarm off. My name is Julie. I'm a psychic medium, and this is Father Lucian Ambrose, an ordained priest, and exorcist. We were informed you would need our help."

Denis, taken aback by the claim, responded with a mix of scepticism and intrigue. "I'm sorry, who? And we have not asked for any help."

Father Ambrose, a figure both imposing and serene, spoke with a voice that seemed to resonate with a hidden depth. "We understand your hesitation, but we come with knowledge and skills that may be of use to you. The darkness you're about face is not something to be trifled with."

"I know, and for your information, I too am an ordained exorcist."

"Yes, we are aware of that. But nonetheless, you will need our help." The priest replied.

"And just who was it that said we needed your help?"

Julie gave a slight enigmatic smile, "The spirits told us."

Denis, his mind racing with the possibilities and risks, gestured for them to follow him back into the flat. As they entered, the room fell into a hushed silence, the team members confused, eyeing the newcomers with curiosity. Julie was the first to speak. "We are here to help. The spirits informed us that you will need our help to defeat the demon you intend to destroy."

Mia's brow furrowed. "The spirits told you? And how do we know you are who you claim to be?"

Julie answered, her gaze steady. "The spirits speak in ways that are not always clear, but the urgency was unmistakable. This thing you face, it's unlike anything you've encountered before. Please, check our credentials; they are easily found on the internet."

Mia, her eyes fixed on the screen of her laptop, spoke up. "It would appear they are who they say they are. Their names, photographs, and exploits are indeed on several websites, and we are dealing with an entity that's not just haunting the asylum. It's actively hostile and possibly dangerous, I think we need all the help we can get."

Denis, weighing his options, welcomed the help. "Alright, let's hear what you have to say. We're planning an exorcism tonight, and yes, you're right Mia, we do need all the help we can get."

Chapter 11

Father Ambrose spoke first. "We need to do a walk-around first, find out what we are dealing with, and how many spirits we will be fighting. Not all the spirits in the building will be on the side of the demon, nor protecting it."

I looked at Father Ambrose. "But you mean it could have an army of spirits helping it?"

"Sort of, it will be in control of some lesser spirits that it will hide behind."

Julie closed her eyes. "You're Steve. You were a sceptic at the start of all this, correct?"

My brow furrowed as I thought about her statement. "Yes, I never believed in ghosts or demons before, and your point is?"

"Someone has been trying to reach you for years, but your scepticism has prevented them from coming through."

"Someone's been trying to reach me, like… Who?"

Julie, her eyes still closed, raised her head and cocked it slightly to her right. "Emily, your sister, Emily. She died in a house fire…"

The colour drained from my face, my mind a mix of confusion and dawning realisation. "Emily?" I stuttered, "But how? I mean, she died years ago…"

Father Ambrose nodded solemnly, acknowledging Julie's insight. "Some of these spirits, like Emily, might not be malevolent, but unlike Emily they are trapped there, ensnared by the same darkness that holds your friend."

My face was a mix of confusion and dawning realisation, "Emily? But how? I mean, she died years ago… and has never been to this asylum." I stuttered.

"Emily has been trying to reach out to you, to communicate, but your disbelief formed a barrier. Now, in this place, she has followed you to protect you and she's trying to protect your friends."

Father Ambrose interjected, "This is why our walk-around is crucial. We need to understand not just the forces at play, but also the other trapped spirits. They could be key in understanding the full extent of what we're dealing with."

Fiona, absorbing the gravity of the situation, spoke up. "So, this demon, it's using these spirits? Holding them hostage, as it were?"

"Exactly. It feeds off their energy, their unresolved emotions. They are both its shield and its sustenance."

My confusion was increasing under the weight of recent events, "So, what do we do? How do we help these spirits... and Emily... and stop the demon? Can you speak with Emily? Can I speak to her? Tell her to leave that place."

"It will be better if I try when we get to the asylum. If she is protecting your friends, she may not have the strength to come through to me here."

Father Ambrose spoke again, determination lighting up his eyes. "First, we identify the spirits bound to this place. We understand their stories, their pain. This knowledge will give us some power. Then, we will be confronting the demon, armed not just with our faith, but with knowledge that will weaken its hold on this place."

Julie added, "And in doing so, we can provide peace to all those lost souls, allowing them to move on, breaking the demon's hold on them. Which will weaken it even further."

"And what about Emily?"

"I feel she is alright, hiding in the shadows, protecting your friends. I sense they are still alive. But they are lost between our two worlds. Emily is doing her best to help them."

My expression softened, a glimmer of hope piercing through the fog of my mind. "Emily is... protecting them? She's been dead for years. How is that even possible?"

Julie, her voice calm and soothing, replied, "In the spirit world, time doesn't flow as it does here. Spirits, especially those with unresolved ties to the living can linger, their essence tied to places or people. Emily's connection is to you, her desire to reach out, has given her a unique strength."

I rubbed my temples, trying to process this new reality. "But she died in a fire. How can she now be a protector?"

Julie sighed softly. "Death often frees a spirit from the physical constraints and fears of the living world. Her death was tragic, but in the afterlife, she has found a purpose. Her love for you, and her desire to protect you, have given her this role."

My mind was racing, a whirlwind of emotions. "And she's been trying to reach me all this time?"

"Yes," Julie responded in a gentle tone. "Your scepticism, while understandable, created a barrier. It was one that Emily had no way to penetrate, until now. Because of the rituals someone carried out here, this asylum is now a nexus, a point where the veil between worlds is thinner. Your evolving belief has made it easier for her to reach out to you, you just haven't been listening."

"I'm listening now. Can't I just speak to her?"

"Not at this moment in time. It's not like calling someone on the phone. She will contact us when the time's right."

Father Ambrose interjected, "Denis, we need to conduct a walk-around of the building with Julie. When we enter, you and I will guard her. It's essential for Julie to complete this walk-around. She needs to gather information on the entity that we could not otherwise retrieve. Once we have more information, we should split into two teams, working inwards from opposite ends of the asylum, trapping the entity between us. Then hopefully, we can combine our efforts and banish this thing back to hell. I am aware this is your investigation Denis, and that you are an ordained exorcist, but please do not be offended. You will fail without our help."

Denis paused and thought for a moment, "Your presence here is... how shall I put it? Obviously guided. Who am I to contradict the spirits? After all, they are our guardians."

"Thank you for your understanding," said Father Ambrose with a slight smile and a small nod.

Denis glanced at his team. "We should keep the number of people in the building to a minimum. We want to minimise the chances for the demon to find an easy victim. Father Ambrose and Julie will form one team. Myself and Fiona will form the other, as Fiona knows the layout and is familiar to her friends. When we attempted to call them back, they are more likely to trust her."

Alex raised his hand, Denis smiled, "Yes, Alex."

"I think you should all wear body cams. That way we can record what's happening and we can monitor it all from the command centre."

Alex's suggestion resonated through the room, ushering in a sense of practicality amidst the growing unease. Denis acknowledged the wisdom in the idea. "Yes, good idea Alex. Body cams will give us an extra set of eyes. We can document everything, and those at the command centre can keep a vigilant watch over us." He nodded signalling agreement, his voice steady, belying the undercurrent of apprehension. "It will provide us with invaluable insight and evidence."

Father Ambrose, standing at the edge of the group, interjected, his voice tinged with urgency. "We should set off now while we still have daylight, and activity will be at the lowest, this will give Julie the maximum amount of time for her walk-around."

With nods of approval from the team, a silent consensus was reached. There was no time to waste. They swiftly packed their equipment. The van now stocked with an arsenal of both technological and spiritual tools, they set off for the asylum, the mood was one of sombre determination. The priest and Julie followed in their own car, the two vehicles moving towards an uncertain fate. The journey to the asylum was a quiet one, each member of the team lost in their thoughts, mentally preparing for the challenges ahead.

Upon arrival two police officers were sitting in their car, one of them stepped out and raised his hand to stop them from going any further. Denis got out of his vehicle and explained to them why they had returned.

The asylum loomed over them, its dilapidated structure a glaring statement of the darkness waiting within. The team wasted no time in setting up the command centre, something they were well rehearsed in doing. Denis, leading the team, adjusted his body cam, ensuring it had a clear view. The others followed suit, their movements methodical, betraying no hint of the fear gnawing constantly at their resolve.

Father Ambrose, cast his eyes over the foreboding structure. Beside him, Julie clutched her bag of spiritual tools, her expression one of focused concentration. As they approached the entrance, the air grew colder, an icy chill that seemed to signal that something was aware of their arrival. Denis took a deep breath, steadying his nerves. "Remember, everyone, keep your cams on at all times. We need to capture everything we see in there."

Julie and Father Ambrose, each clad in their body cams, gave a nod, their faces set in a grim determination. The small, blinking lights on their cameras were the only signs of life in the growing gloom of the evening. Julie closed her eyes briefly as if in silent prayer, then opened them with a renewed focus. "Remember, this place is not just walls and empty corridors. It's a repository of pain, suffering, and unresolved spirits. Tread carefully, both physically and spiritually."

As they crossed the threshold, the atmosphere shifted. The air inside the asylum was stagnant, thick with the scent of decay and something else, something inexplicably otherworldly.

Julie inhaled deeply. "There's something here that definitely does not want us around. It is lurking in the shadows, watching us, scrutinising our every move."

The three of them walked slowly through the building, their eye's scanning every inch of the shadows, their torches the only form of illumination.

The many corridors of the asylum stretched out before them, a complex network of despair, walls stained with the passage of time, seemed to hold secrets that whispered in the silence. They moved cautiously, every step echoing ominously in the vast emptiness.

Julie, her sensitivity to the unseen heightened in this place, paused periodically, her head tilting slightly as if listening to voices only she could hear. "The spirits here are numerous," she murmured, her voice a hushed whisper. "Some are lost, confused, some in pain and some are angry. Very angry!"

Father Ambrose, his hand gripping his crucifix, replied softly, "Their anger is understandable. This place has seen unimaginable suffering. We must approach them with empathy and caution."

Denis's torch swept across a room, its beam momentarily catching a shape that seemed to flit away into the darkness. He froze, his breath catching in his throat. "Did you see that?" he asked, his voice tense.

Julie looked in the direction Denis was pointing. "Yes, a shadow person. It's not uncommon in places like this. The energies are... How can I put it... they're disturbed. It could be a spirit or simply a manifestation of residual energy."

As they continued deeper into the asylum, the air grew unnaturally cold, even for an abandoned building. Julie stopped in her tracks, her face pale, eyes wide with alarm. "There's something here. It's not just watching us; it's following us."

Father Ambrose whispered a prayer under his breath, his eyes scanning the darkness. "We are in the presence of something that does not wish to be disturbed. We must remain strong in our faith."

The silence of the asylum was suddenly broken by a distant sound, a soft, almost melodic humming that seemed to come from nowhere and everywhere all at once. Denis glanced at Julie, seeking an explanation. Julie shrugged, her expression one of uncertainty. "I don't know. It could be a spirit trying to communicate or something else entirely."

As they turned a corner, their breath visible in the icy air, a clatter echoing from a room somewhere down the hall, caused the three of them to jump. Denis shone his torch towards the sound, nothing was visible, save for an empty, decaying corridor. He spoke quietly, his voice steady despite the eerie atmosphere. "We are being tested. The spirits here they are probing our intentions."

They moved towards the end of the corridor, where the humming grew louder, more insistent. Julie stopped abruptly, her body tense. "There's a child here," she whispered, "a young girl. She's frightened, lost."

Denis experienced a sharp twinge of sorrow. The thought of a child's spirit trapped in such a place was heart-wrenching. "We should help her."

Julie closed her eyes, reaching out with her senses. "I'm trying to connect with her, but there's something interfering. Something dark, something menacing."

"I'm getting pulled towards that room, there," she said pointing, "I feel it's the little girl. She says she wants to show us something."

As the three of them entered the room, Father Ambrose, and Denis scanned the area with their torches. A small bed lay rotting in one corner, a large heavy wardrobe stood against the far wall, the wood suffering from years of neglect. One of the wardrobe doors slowly creaked open.

"She's in there, 'please... look... find me...' I can hear her saying."

Denis cautiously approached the wardrobe and shone his torch through the gap in the door. Not initially seeing anything, he opened the door wider. "There's nothing in here. It's empty."

"She's upset, pleading for us to look properly. She's about nine or ten years old."

Denis looked over every inch of the inside of the wardrobe. "I can't see anything in here." He said as he started to tap the sides and back of the wardrobe with his torch, "Wait... this sounds hollow." He reached out and pushed against one of the wooden panels at the back of the wardrobe. It did not move. He noticed a small change in the colour of the wood at about the halfway point, there was a delve in the surface wood. He pulled hard, trying to slide the panel. It gave slightly. "Wait, I think I may have something." He put the torch down and pulled at the panel with both hands. Slowly, he forced it open. "There's a space behind here." He said, crawling further into the wardrobe to get a better look into the void. He shone his torch into the void... "Woah!" he exclaimed jumping back. He took a deep breath to steady himself and went back for a second look. "Oh my god, there's a skeleton back here, a small one." He crawled back out and joined Father Ambrose and Julie.

"We've have found you. Do you want our help to cross over?... She's saying 'yes,' she's thanking you for finding her. She says she was locked in there for being naughty and then forgotten about."

Father Ambrose stepped forward, his voice gentle yet resonant in the eerie silence. "Little one, we are here to help you. You don't have to stay in this place of sorrow anymore."

Julie, her eyes filled with tears of empathy, knelt as if to be at eye level with the young girl. "Hello sweetie. You are safe with us. We want to help you find peace, to move beyond this world of shadows."

She extended her hands towards the presence of the girl, not to touch her but merely to wrap her in a warm, nurturing energy. "We are going to surround you with light, a light that will cleanse and comfort you."

Father Ambrose joined in, his voice rising in a soft prayer, calling upon any loved ones and guiding angels to come forth and assist in this sacred transition. "May those who have gone before, who hold love for this child, step forward and offer their hands in guidance."

As if in response to his invocation, the air around the wardrobe shimmered with a barely perceptible light, a sense of warmth and love permeating the cold room. Julie spoke softly to the spirit, her words a comforting whisper. "Do you see the light above you? It's a path to a place of peace, where you will be loved and free from all pain. You can go to it, go there and let it guide you home."

The atmosphere in the room shifted, the oppressive feeling of sorrow lifting slightly. The three of them stood in silence, honouring the profound moment of the spirit's crossing. Father Ambrose finally broke the silence, his voice soft yet filled with a deep sense of fulfilment. "She's at peace now. Her time in this realm is complete."

Julie nodded, now tears of joy glistened in her eyes. "She's free, finally free."

Denis, deeply touched by the experience, added, "We did something truly good here today. That should get the demon's attention."

They left the room returning to the corridor. A deep, guttural growl reverberated through the walls. The sound was primal, filled with rage and hatred. Father Ambrose raised his crucifix high, his lips moving in silent prayer. The growl gave way to a series of sharp, rapid knocks that echoed along the corridor, sounding like an eerie Morse code from the beyond. Each knock resonated with an intensity that seemed to vibrate through their very bones. Denis's hand tightened around his torch, his eyes darting around, trying to locate the source of the sounds. "This... this is getting real," he muttered, his voice betraying a hint of fear.

The knocks grew louder, more urgent, as if whatever was creating them was becoming increasingly frustrated at their presence. The air grew thicker with an almost visible sense of menace, the darkness around them pressing in, suffocating.

Father Ambrose's voice, firm and resolute, cut through the tension. "We are not here to harm you. We come in peace and with the light of God."

Abruptly, the growling and knocking stopped. The three stood still, barely daring to breathe. Before anyone could react, a loud banging sound erupted from one of the rooms at the end of the corridor. It was as if something, or someone, was slamming against the walls with ferocious intensity. Father Ambrose stepped forward, his crucifix held high. "In the name of the Lord, I command you to reveal yourself!"

The banging stopped as suddenly as it had begun, leaving behind a silence that was almost deafening. Julie, her eyes closed, whispering softly, words that were a mixture of comfort and invocation. Denis felt a chill run down his spine, a sensation that went beyond the cold air of the asylum. The atmosphere crackled with an unseen energy, evoking a tension that grew by the minute.

As they cautiously moved towards the room from where the banging seemed to have started, the door swung open with a creaking groan, revealing nothing but darkness inside. Denis shone his torch into the room, revealing the usual peeling paint, overturned furniture, and a small, tattered doll lying in one corner. Julie stepped into the room, her body tense, as if bracing for an unseen impact. "This room... there's so much sorrow here. Sorrow and pain," she whispered, her voice trembling.

The air in the room was strangely heavier than it was in the corridor, as if infused with a deeper sense of loss and despair. Denis, following Julie, experienced a wave of sadness wash over him, remnants of the past. Father Ambrose, the last one to enter the room, closed his eyes in prayer, speaking softly, "Lord, protect us and guide us. Help us to bring peace to these lost souls."

Denis glanced back towards the corridor, half-expecting to see something lurking in the shadows. But there was nothing only darkness, a darkness that gave the impression of being watched. A faint giggling echoed through the room, a sound that was both innocent and eerie. The doll, which had been lying still, moved slightly, as if nudged by an unseen hand.

Father Ambrose stepped forward, his crucifix extended towards the doll. "In the name of Christ, I ask you to show yourself. We mean you no harm."

The giggling stopped, replaced by a soft sobbing that seemed to come from the walls themselves. Julie reached out tentatively, her fingers finally touching the doll. "So many children, so much sorrow."

Denis's bodycam captured the scene, the glow of his torch casting long shadows across the room. As they stood there, a breeze swept through the room, causing the papers on the floor to rustle and flutter. A small figure materialised in the corner; a translucent outline barely discernible in the dim light. Julie gingerly approached the apparition, her voice soothing. "You don't need to be afraid anymore. We're here to help you."

The figure flickered, like a candle flame in the wind, its form wavering as if struggling to maintain its presence. Julie continued to edge closer, her movements gentle and reassuring. The spirit was small, the size of a child.

"You've been here for so long," Julie whispered, her voice barely above a whisper. "It's time for you to find peace."

Father Ambrose, holding his crucifix aloft, stepped to Julie's side, his voice a comforting rumble. "Little one, you are not forgotten. There is a place of warmth and love waiting for you, beyond the pain of this world."

Julie extended her hand, offering a symbol of peace. "You don't have to hide in the shadows anymore. There's a light, a beautiful, warm light, where you can find rest. All spirits wishing to cross over, now is the time. Come forward and we will help you cross over."

Father Ambrose began to pray softly, his words a melodic chant that filled the room with a sense of serenity. "May the angels guide you from this place of despair. May they lead you to the paradise you deserve. Walk into the light and find everlasting peace."

The temperature in the room rose slightly, the previously chilly air now had an almost comforting warmth. Julie, sensing the change, spoke with renewed encouragement. "See, there is nothing to fear. Let go of this place and move towards the light. Your family, your friends, they are waiting for you."

Father Ambrose lowered his crucifix, "Go in peace, my child. May your journey be filled with love and light."

Julie, her eyes moist with unshed tears, turned to Denis and Father Ambrose, her voice filled with a mix of awe and reverence. "She is free. After all this time, she is finally free."

Denis, who had been silent throughout the encounter, nodded solemnly, deeply moved by what he had witnessed. "It's incredible. It never seems to amaze me, the awareness of love you get when we help someone cross over."

Father Ambrose placed a reassuring hand on his shoulder. "There's much about this world, and the next, that remains beyond our understanding Denis. Today we've been part of something truly miraculous."

Fiona nodded in agreement, "We certainly have."

The three of them stood in silence for a moment, each processing the profound experience. But then the stark reality of the asylum seemed to press in on them once again, a reminder of the many souls that still lingered within.

Julie closed her eyes. "It's close by, and we have definitely got its attention. I feel it's biding its time... Soon it will show itself and fight. I'm not sensing the others that did not make it out of here. That's not unusual; they could still be in hiding, keeping away from this evil entity."

Denis glanced around the decrepit room, shadows seeming to dance just beyond the reach of their torches. "We need to be extremely careful. This entity... This demon... it's not like any others we've encountered so far."

Father Ambrose nodded, his expression grave. "Indeed. This presence harbours a darkness that is ancient and powerful. We must tread cautiously, with both our minds and spirits guarded."

The silence that followed was heavy, broken only by the distant sound of something scuttling in the shadows, it may only have been a rat, but still a reminder that they were not alone in this forsaken place. Julie slowly opened her eyes, a look of concentration etched across her features. "There's heaviness in the air, a sense of anger and malice. It's watching us, analysing our every move."

Denis shifted uneasily, his hand instinctively reaching for the crucifix hanging around his neck. The sense of being watched, of unseen eyes boring into their very souls, was unsettling. "Do you really think it's planning to confront us?"

Father Ambrose's voice was steady, but there was an underlying tension. "I'd be surprised if it doesn't. Such entities often bide their time, looking for any weaknesses, waiting for the opportunity to strike. We must remain strong."

They continued their walk-around, the beams of their torches cutting through the darkness. The atmosphere within the building was thick with the echoes of past cruelties and pain. Distant cries, shuffling feet, and the rustle of things unseen flitting through the corridors all added to their unease.

Turning a corner, Julie stopped abruptly, her hand raised in a silent signal to stop. "There's something here," she whispered, her voice barely audible. "A gathering of spirits." She paused, lifting her face towards the ceiling, "trapped and tormented spirits."

Denis and Father Ambrose looked at the spot where Julie was focusing. There was nothing visible to their eyes, but the temperature in that area seemed to be significantly lower, their breaths visible in the cold air. The silence was broken by a faint sound, like the soft murmur of voices whispering from the walls. It was an eerie chorus, the words indistinct, filled with sorrow and despair.

Denis's body cam captured the scene, the low light camera seeing in the dark as good as we would see in the daylight. "Can you communicate with them, Julie?" he asked.

Julie closed her eyes again, reaching out with her psychic senses. "I'm trying. They are scared, confused. They don't understand they're no longer living. I feel they are guarding the demon, protecting it."

Father Ambrose began to pray softly, "Lord, we ask for your light to guide these lost souls. Help them find peace and liberation from their earthly bonds."

As he prayed, the whispering grew louder, more insistent. It was as if the spirits were angry at the sound of his voice, wanting him to be silent. Watching the scene unfold, Denis felt a profound sense of humility and responsibility. They were standing at the crossroads between life and death, holding open a bridge for those who had lost their way.

Julie turned to them. "I think it's time to leave here. The negative energy is rising."

Father Ambrose nodded in agreement; his face etched with concern. "Yes, it would be wise to retreat for now. We must regroup and plan our next steps carefully. This entity, it feels more powerful than we first anticipated."

Denis peered into the dark corridor. Shadows seemed to move and shift, as if alive with the energy that Julie had sensed. "Let's make our way back to the van. We need to discuss our findings and prepare for what's ahead."

As they retraced their steps through the desolate halls of the asylum, the atmosphere seemed to grow even more oppressive. With every step the air thickened with an unspoken threat, a sense of imminent danger pressing heavily around them. Julie, her expression one of deep concern, kept glancing over her shoulder as if expecting something to emerge from the shadows. "We've stirred something up here. It's angry that we've sent spirits into the light."

The distant sound of something scraping along the floor echoed through the empty corridors, sending shivers down their spines. They quickened their pace as Father Ambrose continued to murmur prayers under his breath, his faith a shield against the darkness enveloping them. As they reached the main door, a sudden rush of cold air hit them from behind, as if the asylum itself were expelling them from its depths. Stepping into the relative safety of the open grounds, they took a moment to catch their breath, the weight of their experience bearing down on them.

Back at the van, they gathered together, the faces of the rest of the team were a mixture of curiosity and concern. Denis, taking a deep breath, debriefed them on their encounter. "There is something in there, something deeply malevolent. It's definitely not just a simple haunting. This demon is powerful and has a hold on the spirits trapped inside."

Julie added, "It's using those trapped spirits as both a shield and a source of its power. If we can release them, that will weaken it's hold on the asylum."

Father Ambrose, his expression sombre, concluded, "This will be a tough battle, one that will test our strength and faith. But we must persevere. We owe it to the lost souls trapped within those walls."

We all nodded as one, understanding the gravity of our task. The night had only just started, the real challenge was yet to come.

Chapter 12

Denis's voice broke the silence, his tone was decisive. "We need to split up as we planned," he said, his eyes scanning everyone's face. "Father Ambrose and Julie, you take the ground floor. Fiona and I will start on the third floor and work our way down, you can work your way upwards. We need to find the demon and end this nightmare."

Father Ambrose, clutching his crucifix, nodded. "Stay close, Julie. We'll be stronger together."

Julie, her eyes wide with fear but determined, tightened her grip on the torch. "Let's do this," she whispered, more to herself than anyone else.

Fiona turned to Denis, her face pale in the dim light. "Are you sure about this?" she asked, her voice trembling.

"We have no choice," Denis replied, trying to sound more confident than he felt. "We need to find this thing and stop it."

As they entered the building they parted. Father Ambrose and Julie remaining on the ground floor as planned, their footsteps echoing on the wooden floors. Venturing further into the abandoned building the darkness around them deepened.

Disembodied voices whispered from the shadows, a chilling reminder of the asylum's tragic history. Julie shivered, her eyes darting around. "Did you hear that?" she asked, her voice barely a whisper.

"Stay focused," Father Ambrose replied, trying to keep his own fear at bay. "It's just the building." But in his mind added 'or whatever's in it.'

Doors slammed in the distance, the sound reverberating along the corridors. Each noise making them jump; their nerves stretched thin. Moving from room to room, their torches illuminated scenes of past horrors. The air was heavy, not only with the scent of mildew but with something far worse, something rotten and evil.

On the third floor, Denis led Fiona through similar terrors. The disembodied voices mocking them, grew louder with each step. Fiona clung to his side, her torchlight flickering as though the batteries were failing.

"This place is a nightmare," she whispered.

Denis nodded grimly. "We must find this entity and end its reign," he said, his voice filled with determination. They continued their search, each room revealing more of the asylum's gruesome past. Scratched walls, remnants of shackles and dark stains hinting at unspeakable acts.

As they progressed, it was as if the walls were reliving the torments of those who had suffered within. Doors continues to slam behind them, trapping them momentarily in darkness. Each time, they fought to keep their composure, knowing that panic could be their undoing.

They paused in a large room, Fiona's eyes were wide with terror as she whispered, "What if we don't find it?"

"We will," Denis replied, though he could feel his confidence waning. "We have to."

Having covered the ground floor, Father Ambrose and Julie found themselves at the staircase leading to the first floor. "We need to go up," Father Ambrose said. "I have a feeling we're close."

Julie nodded in agreement. They ascended the stairs, each step creaking under their feet. The darkness seemed to grow thicker; the air more cloying as they ascended the stairs.

On reaching the first floor, the whispers became louder, a disharmony of voices, doors were slamming around them. They pressed on, their torches their only solace against the encroaching darkness.

Fiona and Denis, having completed their clearance of the upper two floors were also drawn to the first floor. As they descended the stairs the air was thick with tension, every sound amplified in the silence. They turned a corner and froze.

"There you are," Father Ambrose said, relief evident in his voice. "Any sign of it?"

Denis shook his head. "Nothing yet, but it has to be here. This is the only floor we haven't checked."

A low, menacing laugh echoed through the room, sending chills down their spines, their torches flickered and dimmed, plunging the corridor into near darkness. A figure emerged from the shadows, its eyes glowing with a sinister red light.

"Welcome," it hissed, its voice a distorted mockery of a human's. "I've been waiting for you."

Father Ambrose, his features set in grim determination, confronted the demon possessing Tom, while Denis stood nearby, his expression one of both fear and determination. Julie and Fiona retreated to a safer distance behind Denis who turned to face them, "I think it would be better, safer, if you two went back to the van."

The girls nodded in agreement, and relief, hastily making their way out of the building.

"You have no power here; release this body back to us," Father Ambrose insisted, his voice echoing through the hollow corridors.

The demon, speaking through Tom's body, responded in a deep, guttural voice, a voice dripping with malice: "He's mine." It said, while letting out a chilling chuckle, eerily like that of a small child.

Father Ambrose persisted, his voice firm and commanding. "Tom, this is your body… come forth and reclaim it."

"Tom is not in here anymore," the demon sneered, its voice was a chilling blend of mockery and evil.

"I demand that you leave this body! This body does not belong to you! In the name of the Holy Trinity, I command you to leave!" The words from Father Ambrose were born of faith in the enveloping darkness.

The demon looked directly at Father Ambrose. "No… I like it in here. It's mine now!" Its refusal was as cold as the grave.

"You cannot have him! Tom, I know you are in there… be strong! Demon, I command you to leave! You have no power here," Father Ambrose continued, his voice rising to a crescendo of spiritual authority.

The demon laughed; a sound that was both bone-chilling and despair-inducing. "Your words are weak, priest. You cannot fathom the depths of my power."

Denis stepped forward; his voice shaky but resolute. "Tom, listen to me. You are stronger than this creature. Don't let it control you."

The demon turned its gaze to Denis, its eyes burning with malevolence. "Ah, another soul to collect. Do you think your words can sway him? He's lost in my darkness. It is I who reigns supreme here."

Father Ambrose, undeterred, began to chant in Latin, his words a shield against the darkness. "Exorciso te, omnis spiritus immunde, in nomine Dei Patris omnipotentis, et in nomine Jesu Christi Filii eius, Domini et Judicis nostri."

The demon writhed, Tom's body contorting in unnatural ways. "Your God cannot save you here. All this is mine! It is you who are powerless here."

The air grew colder, the shadows in the room deepening as if feeding off the demon's words. Denis, fighting back his own fear, joined in. His voice intermingling with Father Ambrose's chants. "Tom, hear us. You're not alone in this fight."

The demon roared, a sound that shook the very foundations of the asylum. "You dare challenge me with your feeble faith?" It said laughingly.

Father Ambrose continued, unshaken. "I challenge you with the power of the Almighty. Your reign here ends now!"

As the priest's chants grew louder, the demon hissed, recoiling from the priest as if he were fire.

"You cannot banish me so easily," it spat out, but its voice betrayed a hint of uncertainty, a crack in its otherwise impenetrable facade of evil.

Denis, sensing the shift, pressed on. "Your hold on Tom is weakening, demon. He doesn't belong to you. His spirit is strong."

The demon, now visibly agitated, thrashed within Tom's body. "Lies! He gave in to despair, he gave in to the darkness. He invited me in!"

Father Ambrose, his voice steady and unwavering, countered, "He may have faltered, but the human spirit is resilient. Tom will fight you with our help. His soul is not yours to claim."

The room seemed to tremble as the demon's fury grew, objects rattling and crashing to the floor. "I will not be cast out! I will not return to the abyss!"

Denis, though terrified, found strength in the priest's resolve. "Tom, if you can hear me, fight! Remember who you are, remember the people who love you. Don't let this darkness consume you!"

Father Ambrose raised his cross, a beacon of faith amidst the encroaching darkness. "In the name of the Father, and of the Son, and of the Holy Spirit, I command you, foul spirit, to depart from this servant of God!"

The demon let out an ear-piercing scream, its voice a cacophony of despair and rage. Tom's body began to convulse, the battle for his soul reaching its peak.

"Enough! This is not the end!" the demon howled, its voice echoing through the crumbling halls of the asylum.

But Father Ambrose was unyielding. "It is finished. Your dominion over him is at an end."

Father Ambrose flicked Holy Water at the demon. The demon's screams grew louder, more desperate, as the Holy Water burned into it, searing Tom's flesh.

Denis, his heart pounding in his chest, watched in both awe and terror as the battle unfolded. "Hold on, Tom. You can do this."

The demon's voice was now a mere wail, its presence diminishing. "Curse you, priest! Curse you all!"

Father Ambrose turned to Denis, "Keep it up, we are winning." Then turning back to the demon, "In the name of Jesus Christ our saviour, I command you to return to the bowels of hell whence you spawned."

"No!... I will not go." The demon appeared to be weakening. It started to back away. "Stop! Stop this."

Denis raised his crucifix and walked towards the demon, "Be gone, in the name of our Lord Jesus Christ, be gone."

The demon let out a loud, throaty, evil laugh. Father Ambrose turned to Denis, his face etched with a grim understanding. "It's playing with us," he said, his voice low and steady, yet carrying an undercurrent of urgency. "We're not winning."

Denis, his eyes fixed on Tom's contorted form, nodded grimly. "What do we do now?"

The priest's gaze did not waver from the possessed figure before them. "We must continue. We cannot let it break our resolve. This demon... it's cunning and manipulative. We have to be stronger."

Tom's body, under the control of the dark entity, convulsed, his eyes rolling back to reveal only white. Then, in a voice that was deep, a guttural snarl resonating through the room. "Do you really think you can save him? Pathetic!"

Father Ambrose recited the rite of exorcism, his voice a commanding force in the oppressive atmosphere of the asylum. "Exorciso te, omnis spiritus immunde, in nomine Dei Patris omnipotentis."

The demon laughed, a sound that chilled Denis to the bone. "Words! Mere words! You cannot defeat me with words, priest!"

Denis, despite his fear, stood firm beside Father Ambrose. "Tom is stronger than you. He will reject you!"

The demon, using Tom's body, twisted unnaturally, its face contorting into a grotesque mask of pure evil. "Tom is weak! He invited me in, and now I will consume his soul!"

Father Ambrose continued his litany, unshaken. "Deus, Pater omnipotens, qui omnia creasti et redemisti, auxilium tuum praesta, quaesumus."

The demon sneered, its voice dripping with scorn. "Your God is not here, priest. This is my domain!"

The air in the room grew colder. Shadows stretched reaching towards them. Father Ambrose, though, remained focused, his faith unyielding. "Your arrogance blinds you, demon. The Lord is always with us, and He will protect us."

Denis, though terrified, felt a surge of determination. "We won't let you have Tom. His soul is not yours to take!"

The demon, visibly agitated, let out a roar that echoed through the dilapidated halls of the asylum. Tom's body arched at an unnatural angle, the sound of cracking bones reverberating in the confined space. "You think you can challenge me? I am ancient, I am eternal!"

Father Ambrose, his voice unwavering, continued the exorcism, his faith a shining beacon in the darkness. "Spiritum sanctum dominum, qui te replet veritate et humilitate, precor ut hostem virtutis tuae expellas."

The demon laughed mockingly, its hold on Tom seeming to strengthen. "Prayers? You think your prayers matter to me?"

Denis, bolstered by Father Ambrose's unwavering faith, took a step closer. "Tom, if you can hear me, fight it! You're stronger than this demon. Don't let it control you, we are here for you Tom!"

The demon, through Tom's eyes, glared at Denis, it seemed to be searching for his soul. "Silence! You have no power here."

Denis, undeterred, raised his cross towards Tom, the symbol of faith glowing in the dim light. He joined Father Ambrose in the incantation. "In nomine Jesu, qui te ad judicium vivorum et mortuorum venire faciet, exi ab hoc servo Dei!"

The room trembled, a sense of dread filling the air. The demon's laughter turned into a snarl. "You cannot win this battle. I will not be cast out so easily!"

Denis watched in horror, the entity's influence seeming to grow stronger. The atmosphere thickening with its presence, the darkness pressing in, suffocating their resolve.

Father Ambrose, his resolve as strong as iron, continued his relentless assault of prayer and faith. "Vade retro, Satana! Numquam suade mihi vana! Sunt mala quae libas. Ipse venena bibas!"

The demon stopped its thrashing, a sinister smile spreading across Tom's face. "You think you can win? Foolish mortals!" it taunted, its voice a hissing whisper.

The temperature in the room was so cold, the chill gnawing at their bones. The shadows danced and twisted around them, lashing out, threatening to strike them.

Denis, feeling a surge of fear, looked at Father Ambrose, searching for a sign of what to do next. The priest, however, remained undaunted, his face a mask of divine determination.

"Your tricks will not deter us demon. I have seen them all before." Father Ambrose declared, his voice resonating with an authority that seemed to transcend this earthly realm. "Your time in this body is at an end."

The demon within Tom, let out a low, menacing chuckle. "Is it, priest? You underestimate the depths of my power. This soul is mine."

Denis, trying to keep his voice steady, addressed Tom directly. "Tom, listen to me. You are not alone in this. We are here with you. Fight it!"

The demon, wearing Tom's twisted grin, replied mockingly. "His will is my will. His flesh is my flesh. You cannot save him."

Father Ambrose stepped forward; his eyes fixed on the possessed form of Tom. "By the power of Christ, I compel thee. Leave this innocent soul!"

The demon writhed, Tom's body contorting in a disturbing display of the entity's resistance. "You think you can compel me with your Christ? I walked this earth long before your Christ was born!"

The room seemed to pulsate with an unseen force, the air thick with the entity's dark energy. Denis felt as if they were standing on the precipice of an abyss, the darkness clawing at the edges of their light trying to pull them in.

Father Ambrose spoke, his voice rising above the cacophony of the demon's laughter. "In the name of the Father, and of the Son, and of the Holy Spirit, I command you to leave this servant of God!"

Its laughter ceased, replaced by a rasping growl. Denis watched, his heart pounding in his chest, as Father Ambrose continued the rite, undeterred by the entity's threats. The priest's words were a steady drumbeat, a litany of faith against the darkness. Tom's body began to shudder, the demon's presence seeming to weaken under the relentless barrage of Father Ambrose's exorcism. But, its grip on Tom was not fully relinquished, its dark essence lingering like a poisonous vapour. The struggle continued. The demon opened Tom's mouth and let forth a swarm of flies, just as the team had experienced a few days ago. Its growling laughter tormenting them.

The room, once filled with the harsh sounds of the exorcism, now buzzed with the sudden, overwhelming presence of flies. They swarmed around Tom's convulsing body, a dark cloud of writhing, buzzing chaos. Father Ambrose, undeterred by this new development, continued his recitation, his voice steady amidst the disarray.

Denis, his face contorted in disgust and horror, swatted at the flies. But they seemed unending, pouring forth from Tom's mouth as if summoned from the very depths of Hell.

"This is a manifestation of the demon's desperation!" Father Ambrose shouted, his eyes never leaving Tom. "It's trying to distract us."

Denis still waving his hands in a futile attempt to swat at the flies, "It did this to us before."

The air was thick with flies, their incessant buzzing creating a noise that vibrated through the room. Tom's body, now barely visible under the swarm, twitched and jerked unnaturally, the demon inside him fighting against the exorcism with all its strength.

"Keep going, Father! Don't let it stop you!" Denis yelled, his determination steeling him against the nightmarish scene unfolding before them.

Father Ambrose's voice grew louder, more commanding. "I rebuke you, unclean spirit, in the name of the Lord! You have no place in this world, and no power over this soul!"

The flies seemed to pulsate with the demon's fury, the air around them vibrating with its dark energy. As Father Ambrose continued, the swarm began to diminish, flies dropping to the floor as if the demon's power was waning.

"See, Denis! The power of Christ compels it! It's losing its grip!" Father Ambrose called out, his voice filled with hope.

Denis, though exhausted and overwhelmed, found a renewed vigour. He stood beside Father Ambrose, his presence a silent support against the darkness. As the swarm of flies began to dissipate, the ominous buzzing that had filled the room gradually diminished to an eerie silence.

"This is not the end, priest. I will return." Behind Tom's form, a sinister shadow emerged, undulating eerily as if it were alive. The shadow morphed, its form shifting and twisting into a body of smoke. This dark, smoky apparition lingered for a moment, hovering with a malign presence before seeping through the nearest wall, disappearing into the unknown. Tom's body collapsed onto the floor, his form still and silent. Father

Ambrose and Denis rushed to his side, checking for signs of life. Tom lay motionless and cold on the floor. Father Ambrose looked into Denis's eyes and shook his head. Tom was dead.

The revelation hit Denis like a physical blow, a mix of shock and grief washing over him. He stared at Tom's lifeless body, his mind struggling to accept what his eyes were seeing. Father Ambrose's expression was sombre; he placed a gentle hand on Denis's shoulder. "We did all we could," he said softly. "The demon's hold was too strong. It drained him; his body could not withstand it."

Denis's eyes filled with tears as he knelt beside Tom. "He didn't deserve this. We were supposed to save him." Denis murmured, his voice breaking.

Father Ambrose knelt beside him. "Sometimes, Denis, we fight battles that have costs beyond our understanding and control. We must find solace in knowing that this man is at peace now, free from the clutches of that thing. His soul is now free, but we need to protect him. I will bless his body with Holy Water to prevent anything trying to inhabit him again, and we'll need to get him out of here."

Denis wiped away a tear, "We can't move him yet, this is still a crime scene according to the police."

The silence in the room was unbearable, the aftermath of the exorcism a stark reminder of the brutal struggle they had just endured. The air still felt heavy, a lingering reminder of the evil that had pervaded the space just moments before. Denis, his hands trembling, gently closed Tom's eyes.

The two men remained in solemn silence, a moment of respect for the innocent soul that had been tragically lost. The shadows in the room seemed to recede, the oppressive aura dissipating, leaving behind a hollow emptiness. After a few moments, Father Ambrose spoke, his tone resolute despite the grief. "We must ensure that his passing was not in vain. This entity, this demon that we've now witnessed, must be confronted and banished. We cannot allow others to suffer as he did."

Denis nodded, wiping away his tears. "You're right, Father. We have to stop this from happening again. But how? How do we fight something that powerful?"

Father Ambrose stood up, his eyes glinting with a determined flame. "We continue our work, Denis. We fortify ourselves with our faith and our knowledge. Evil like this preys on the weak and the unprepared. We must be neither."

Denis rose to his feet, a newfound determination replacing the grief in his heart. "Then we'll do it. Let's find this thing and finish it."

Emerging from the room, they were met with a stark reminder that the presence they needed to confront was still here. The corridors of the asylum were groaning with the remnants of tormented souls, amplifying the sense of dread around them.

Father Ambrose, his face drawn with apprehension, led the way. "This demon, it's not merely confined within these walls, it's interwoven itself into the very fabric of this place," he said, his voice barely rising above a whisper.

Without warning the air crackled with an unseen, sinister energy. Objects began to stir in the gloom. An old rusted wheelchair creaked as it rolled eerily across the corridor. A pile of decaying books cascaded from a shelf, their pages somehow fluttering in the deathly still air. Father Ambrose, undeterred by the chaos, began to recite a prayer, his voice a steady force against the encroaching darkness. But before he could complete his invocation, a scream filled the air. Denis was lifted off his feet, his body pinned against the wall by an unseen force. Father Ambrose, his prayers intensifying, stepped forward. "In the name of the Holy Trinity, I command you to release him!" he exclaimed.

Denis struggled against the unseen grip, terror contorting his face. Suspended off the ground, he clawed desperately at the invisible hands around his neck. The air shimmered with a dark, menacing energy, their torch lights flickering wildly as Father Ambrose's prayers grew louder. Denis tried to join in, his voice choked. Gradually, the grip on him loosened. His body released, started to drop, Father Ambrose attempting to break his fall, eased him to the floor. Denis lay there, shaking, gasping for air. His breath coming in ragged gasps.

"That... thing, it's stronger than anything I've ever encountered," Denis gasped, his eyes wide with fear and shock.

Father Ambrose, his expression etched with deep concern, knelt beside Denis. "Are you hurt, my son?"

Denis shook his head, composing himself. "I'm alright, just... shaken. We must proceed with extreme caution. That thing is dangerous and unpredictable."

They moved on, keenly aware that the entity could strike again at any moment. Their torches barely lit up their path in the suffocating darkness. Pausing, Denis strained his ears trying to decipher the whispers that filled the corridor, voices from the past speaking words of fear and despair. The sounds sent shivers down their spines time and time again. They resumed their prayers, their voice steady in the sea of haunting whispers. "Lord, shield us from the evil that lives in this place. Grant us the fortitude to confront this darkness."

Father Ambrose felt a sudden, chilling clarity. The disembodied whispers seemed to converge into a single, clear voice in his mind. He gripped his crucifix tighter, sensing the dark presence more acutely than ever before. His faith had always been his guiding light, and now it was leading him towards the heart of the darkness. "There's a room down this way. That's where we need to be." He said firmly, "We must go... now!" His was voice firm and urgent. "I can feel it. It's drawing me in there."

They moved as one, their footsteps adding to the noise of the whispers in the long, shadowy corridor. The asylum seemed to sigh around them, its tragic history emerging from its walls.

Father Ambrose beckoned to Denis, "Stay close," he urged, leading the way. "We're almost there."

The corridor seemed endless; each step forward felt as though they were heading into a horde of tormented souls. Disembodied voices echoed around them, some crying for help, others screaming in agony.

Father Ambrose stopped in front of a door. "This is it. This is where we face the entity."

Denis nodded, "Okay... We end this... here and now."

Father Ambrose pushed the door open. It groaned roughly, as if complaining at the intrusion. Inside the room, the debris of the asylum's harrowing past was chaotically strewn around the room, fragments of furniture and broken glass scattered across the floor. Faded drawings on the walls spoke of forgotten lives. At the far end of the room, they saw a figure, shrouded in darkness. Stepping inside, an overwhelming sense of dread enveloped them both. The room seemed to pulse, as if it were the very heart of the darkness that infested the asylum. The whispering intensified, now a desperate, pleading discord. Denis clutched at his head, besieged by the raw intensity of the emotions that bombarded him.

In the murkiness of the room, something stirred a presence darker than the deepest shadow. They realised then they were standing at the precipice of their greatest challenge. The struggle, not only for their souls but for all the souls bound to this place, was about to intensify.

A gust of air swept through the room, causing the scattered papers to rise in a ghostly whirlwind. A low, menacing growl emitted from the darkness, bouncing off the walls with sinister intent. Denis, even though he felt overwhelmed with fear, stood resolute. "We can't back down now. Whatever it takes, we must end this."

Father Ambrose, his faith unwavering, stepped forward, his crucifix held aloft. "In the name of all that is Holy, I challenge you to reveal yourself!"

With a chilling laugh that seemed to emanate from the walls, the demon responded to his challenge. The darkness in the room deepened even more. The meagre light from their torches struggled to shine into the blackness. They braced themselves, knowing that the demon would not give up easily. The real fight to save the asylum and its trapped souls from the clutches of this ancient monstrosity had started. The surrounding darkness closed in, as they stood side by side, united in their purpose, ready to face whatever horrors lay ahead. The room trembled, shaken by an unseen hand. Objects stirred; an old, dust-covered lamp teetered on the edge of a decrepit table before being thrown against a wall, sending shards flying across the room. A stack of rotting books flew from a shelf, their pages fluttering like the wings of a colony of bats. Denis flinched as a cold, unseen force hurled a piece of glass narrowly missing him and shattering against the wall, leaving a pinging echo in its wake.

"It's toying with us again," he muttered, his voice tinged with fear.

Father Ambrose, though startled, maintained his composure. He started to pray again, this time with a fervour that seemed to pierce the suffocating darkness. "We stand in the light. Evil cannot prevail against us! The Lord God and Jesus Christ protect us!"

The demon responded with a rage that chilled them to the core. Objects continued to be hurled through the air by invisible hands, a symphony of chaos orchestrated by an unseen conductor. The walls of the asylum groaned under the weight of the force that besieged them. gradually, the chaos eased. The swirling objects fell to the floor one by one, inanimate once again. The oppressive darkness seemed to recede, leaving them in a tense silence, the sound of their breathing loud in the sudden stillness.

Denis, his heart pounding in his chest, scanned the room, his torch trembling in his hand. "It's just playing with us," he repeated, his voice hushed, yet carrying a weight that filled the room. Father Ambrose, his eyes also scanning the shadows, nodded solemnly. "This is its cunning. It seeks to unnerve us, to break our spirit and feed of our fear."

In the eerie calm, the faint sound of sobbing echoed through the halls, a sorrowful lament that seemed to drift all around them. It was a sound that spoke of pain and suffering. Denis, his resolve hardening, spoke up. "We need to find the source of all this. We need to find and seal the portal."

As they cautiously navigated through the corridors, the air was cold. Their torch light cutting through the darkness, revealed rusted bedframes and discarded belongings. The prayers from Father Ambrose echoed in the silence, "Guide us, O Lord, in our quest to banish this darkness. Grant us the power to banish this evil."

Their journey took them deeper into the asylum, each step now made more difficult by the ghosts that protected the demon. More objects were now being thrown at them. Bed frames, chairs, and cabinets slid across the floor, blocking their passage. As they rounded a corner, they were greeted by a sight that stopped them in their tracks. The hallway stretched out before them. The walls oozing a thick black substance. Denis and Father Ambrose stood shoulder to shoulder; their resolve unwavering in the face of the sight that confronted them. They knew that the final confrontation was near.

Denis turned to Father Ambrose. "I think we need to retreat to take up our original plan. We need Julie and Fiona to help us fight this. They can use the Holy Water and burn sage as we chase the demon to its lair."

Chapter 13

The two men, their faces etched with the weariness of their ordeal, left the foreboding structure of the asylum and made their way towards the command centre. As they reached the van, the rest of the team looked up expectantly. The interior was bathed in the artificial glow of screens and monitors, a marked contrast to the dark, domineering atmosphere of the asylum. Yet, even here, the sense of unease lingered, a reminder that the entity was lurking, not far away.

Father Ambrose, his voice carrying the feelings of their grim findings, addressed the team. "That entity we faced is far more powerful than anything we expected. It's woven itself into the very fabric of the asylum, drawing strength from the suffering experience in there."

Denis, leaning heavily against a table, his exhaustion evident, added, "We're going to need more than just prayers and determination to confront this demon."

The team, their faces reflecting curiosity and fear, listened intently as Father Ambrose laid out their next course of action. "Julie, Fiona, we need your help. Holy Water and white sage can create a defence barrier to protect us and drive back any spirits the entity might hide behind or use against us."

Fiona, having some experience in spiritual defences, nodded in agreement. "We can create a perimeter around us, a barrier to keep us safe while we work."

Julie, her expression grave, spoke up. "It has shown it can manipulate the environment and attack us physically. We need to be prepared for anything. It knows I'm psychic and it doesn't not like that."

As they discussed their strategy, the only other sounds in the van were the beeping of monitors and the faint crackling of static from the screens showing disjointed images of the asylum. Father Ambrose, his voice steady, addressed the team. "We must approach this with both caution and conviction. Our faith, combined with our physical defences, will be crucial in this battle. We will start at both ends of the ground floor and work our way upwards."

Denis spoke up. "Once we are in there, we need to push it towards the mirror room. That's where we will confront it and force it back through the portal."

The team nodded in agreement, their expressions somewhere between determination and apprehension. Fiona, checking the Holy Water, added, "We've collected all we can. Let's hope it's enough. we'll need plenty to face this head-on."

Denis grabbed a vial of Holy Water and nodded. "We have each other's backs. We've come this far together, and we'll see this through to the end, together." He held up his crucifix in his other hand, "We must not let fear take hold. Remember, it feeds on fear and terror."

They re-entered the asylum; the building, as always, looming over them, its facade reminding them of the horrors that lay within. Fiona and Denis went to the right, while Father Ambrose and Julie went to the left. Their mission was clear, cleanse each room, drive out the clinging spirits with prayer, Holy Water, and the purifying smoke of white sage. It was slow, painstaking work, but necessary to corner the malevolent demon they were up against.

As they stepped into the asylum, the air seemed to grow denser and the chill more biting. Their torches flickered, casting long, twisting shadows on the walls that seemed to resemble tormented souls within. The atmosphere was filled with a sense of dread, the pain of years of suffering pressing down upon them.

Starting on the ground floor, they moved methodically, Father Ambrose leading his small team, praying, his voice steady but charged with an undercurrent of urgency. Julie followed, sprinkling Holy Water hissing as it hit the walls and the floor, as if boiling upon contact with the corrupted building They worked in unison, their rituals a barrier against the darkness.

With the ground floor cleansed, the four regrouped at the top of the stairs. With a solemn gesture, Father Ambrose moved forward and placed a crucifix at the top step, a symbol of faith to ward against the evil that existed on the upper floors. This act created a spiritual barricade, ensuring the spirits could not return to the ground level.

"We need to go to the top floor. We'll split up again to clear that floor," Father Ambrose announced, his voice echoing in the hollow space. "Our goal is to drive the remaining spirits either into the light or down to the first floor. That will be our battleground."

On reaching the top floor they split into pairs once more, continuing their sacred task. The third floor was the usual maze of hallways and abandoned rooms, each with a tale of despair. As they moved through the corridors, dark figures moved around them in the shadows, fleeting glimpses of lost souls roaming the halls. The wails of the tormented echoed through the empty rooms, a chorus of despair that chilled their very souls.

Fiona, her hand trembling slightly as she lit another bundle of sage, whispered, "These poor souls, trapped here for so long."

Denis, his face set in grim determination, replied, "We'll free them, Fiona. We'll make sure we free them all."

Entering one of the rooms, Father Ambrose halted, a sense of overwhelming sorrow washing over him. The room, once a patient's quarters, now a hollow shell, the walls stained with the passage of time. He could feel the presence of a young woman, her spirit lingering, trapped in an endless loop of her final, agonising moments.

Julie, also sensing this paused, joined him in prayer. Together, they worked to release her, to end her suffering and send her into the light. Their voices merged in a prayer for release. The air shimmered around them as the spirit of the young woman appeared, her face etched with desperation and confusion.

"Go in peace child," Father Ambrose said, his voice gentle yet commanding. "You are released from your bonds here on earth. Go now and find eternal peace." With a final, shuddering sigh, the spirit faded away, her presence leaving a profound absence in the room.

Denis and Fiona were facing their own trials. In one of the larger rooms, they encountered a group of shadowy figures huddled together, their whispers filling the air with a discord of anguish. Denis stepped forward, his voice strong as he recited a prayer of exorcism. "The Almighty God, in His supreme authority, commands you, He whom you, in your boundless arrogance, dared to consider yourself equal to. God who desires the salvation and enlightenment of all humanity. The Father commands you. The Son commands you. The Holy Spirit commands you. Christ, the Word of God incarnate, commands you; He who brought about our salvation now casts you out, wickedness vanquished by your own envy. Return to where you belong. Back to the depths of hell, I command you… be gone!"

As Denis's voice echoed through the decaying walls of the asylum, the shadowy figures recoiled as if struck by an invisible force. Their whispers turned into howls, howls of despair that chilled the very air. Then the room erupted into chaos. Broken pieces of furniture began to rise from the floor, swirling around them in a menacing vortex. Denis and Fiona dodged as a rusted piece of metal whizzed past, embedding itself into the wall behind them, with a solid thud.

Fiona, her voice trembling but resolute, joined Denis in the recitation. "By the power of Christ, we command you! Leave this place and return to the shadows whence you came!"

The figures, now writhing and twisting in the air, seemed to merge into a singular, dark mass, pulsating with a frightening energy. Father Ambrose and Julie, hearing the commotion, rushed to their aid. The four of them stood together, united against the dark force that confronted them.

"Stand firm," Father Ambrose shouted over the noise. "Our faith is our shield!"

The shadows, sensing their impending defeat, intensified their assault. The air crackled as more objects were hurled towards them with deadly intent. A heavy bookcase groaned as it began to tip, its massive frame threatening to crush them under its weight. Julie, focusing her energy shouted, "We are not afraid of you!" Her voice seemed to resonate with a power that was more than human, bolstering the group's resolve.

Now a swirling maelstrom of darkness and rage, the mass of shadows let out what seemed like a hundred piercing screams that reverberated through the room. The team continued their incantations; their voices merging into a powerful chorus of defiance, The dark mass began to dissipate, its form unravelling like smoke in the wind, the swirling objects started to lose their momentum, clattering to the ground harmlessly. Then finally the shadows vanished, sent back to the depths of Hell.

The third floor cleared. They gathered at the staircase, their faces weary but resolute. Father Ambrose placed another crucifix on the top stair, then said a blessing that sealed the stairs preventing evil from ascending them. "Let's move on," said Denis, his voice echoing through the hollow building.

They descended the stairs to the second floor, their steps heavy with the threat of what was to come. Father Ambrose and Julie, Denis and Fiona, parted again and began their methodical cleansing of the second floor. Each room was a new battle against the lingering spirits. Father Ambrose led Julie, his crucifix held high in front of him, muttering prayers under his breath. "Stay close, Julie," he urged. "This place is alive with suffering."

Julie, clutching her own crucifix, nodded. "I'm right behind you, Father," she replied, her voice steady despite the tension. As they worked their way around the second floor, they filled each room with the smoke of white sage and sprinkled Holy Water. As the liquid touched cursed surfaces it sizzled, hissing and steaming. The evil spirits, unseen but present, recoiled from the sacred rites, their anguished wails filling the air.

"Leave this place," Father Ambrose commanded, his voice strong. "In the name of God, be gone!"

The spirits, driven out by their faith and the Holy Water, fled the rooms, retreating down to the first floor.

In other rooms on the same floor, Fiona and Denis worked together, their movements synchronised by fear and determination.

"I hope this is working?" Fiona said, her voice barely above a whisper.

Denis glanced at her, his face grim. "We have to believe it is," he said. "We have no choice, there's no turning back now."

They entered a room filled with the faint scent of old paper mingled with something more sinister. Fiona stepped forward, her hands trembling as she sprinkled Holy Water on the floor, and with a large black feather, wafted white sage smoke from the back of the room towards the door.

"Spirits of this place, we command you to leave," Denis said, his voice echoing around the empty room.

A sudden gust of wind blew through the room, scattering papers and causing the door to slam shut in front them. Fiona jumped, her heart racing, but Denis remained focused.

"Don't worry," he said, "They're being driven back, we need to keep going."

Room by room, the four continued their work, the spirits either being released to pass on in peace or forced down to the first floor. Each encounter left them more drained, but also more determined. Father Ambrose and Julie reached the end of a long corridor, the final room on the floor. The door, heavy and scarred by fire, seemed to resist their approach. Father Ambrose pushed it open with effort, revealing a large, empty ward. Shadows danced on the walls, forming twisted, fleeting images.

"This is the last room," he said, his voice steady. "Let's finish this."

They entered, and began their prayers, evil spirits, cornered and desperate, lashed out, their disembodied voices rising in rage.

"Be strong, Julie," Father Ambrose urged. "We're almost done on this floor."

Julie nodded, her voice joining his in prayer. The Holy Water hissed on the floor, the spirits howled, retreating from the sacred words and the smell of the white sage, their presence thinning until, with a final wail, they were driven out of the room.

As Fiona and Denis finished their section, they felt drained. Father Ambrose and Julie met them at the top of the stairs.

"I believe everything that remains here now are all down on the first floor," Father Ambrose said, his voice filled with relief.

"We've been preparing for this. Now, we must face whatever demon is here." Denis said, taking a deep breath.

With the second floor now sanctified ground, the first floor awaited them. It would be the battleground, the place where the remaining spirits had been driven to make their last stand. With the walls closing in, they prepared for their final confrontation.

Reaching the first floor, Father Ambrose once again placed another crucifix on the bottom stair creating a spiritual barricade. An icy breeze swept through the building, rustling debris that was scattered across the floor. The crucifix at the top of the staircase leading from the ground floor began to emit a faint, eerie glow as it guarded the descent refusing any escape for the demon and any remaining spirits. Father Ambrose led them to the centre of the first floor, where the air appeared thickest, charged with malevolent energy. "This mirror room. Is it near?" he asked, his voice resounding in the corridor.

Fiona pointed to a nearby door. "It's there, it's in there."

"Then that is where we will battle the demon, were we will make our stand."

They entered the room. It was cold and foreboding. Shattered pieces of mirror lay on the floor, reminding Fiona of Janet's rescue. She quickly recounted this to Father Ambrose.

"You were lucky to get her back. She could have been lost forever. We still have three remaining mirrors we can force it into. Once the demon has been forced through one of them, we must quickly break it, then immediately break the other two. That should prevent it from coming back to this world."

They formed a circle, holding hands to draw strength from one another. Julie began to chant, her voice rising and falling in a rhythm that seemed to vibrate through their very bodies. Fiona joined in, her voice harmonising with Julie's, creating a melody of protection and power.

Denis, standing next to Father Ambrose, sensed a surge of strength coursing through him. He knew that the demon they faced was gathering itself, preparing to unleash its fury upon them.

Then it began.

The surrounding air crackled, a sense of malice filling the room. Shadows danced along the walls, twisting and writhing as if alive. A low growl echoed from the darkness, steadily growing louder and more menacing.

The demon revealed itself in a whirlwind of shadows, a formless mass of darkness that seemed to consume the light around it, circling them, like a predator eyeing its prey, its presence suffocating, overwhelming. "Welcome," it hissed, its voice a distorted mockery of a human voice, "I've been looking forward to meeting you again."

Father Ambrose, undeterred, raised his crucifix high. "In the name of the Father, the Son, and the Holy Spirit, we command you to show yourself! I demand you tell us your name!"

"You demand nothing of me!" It sneered, laughing at the group.

The demon paused, then, with a sound like the screech of a thousand lost souls, it manifested fully before them. It was a creature of nightmares, its body a writhing mass of serpents. Huge leathery wings on its back blocked out the light. Its eyes, burning like hot coals, were fixed on them with hatred and fury. The demon's laugh was cruel, a chilling sound that reverberated through the room. "You think you can challenge me, priest? You have no idea what you're dealing with."

"Then enlighten me, who am I dealing with?"

The team stood their ground, their chants and prayers shielding them against the demon. It lunged at them, a blur of shadow and hatred, but recoiled as it hit the barrier they had created. A sound that was somewhere between a hiss and a growl came from the demon, a sound that spoke of an ancient evil, that had existed long before the walls of the asylum were erected.

Julie, her face pale but resolute, stepped forward. "We are not afraid of you," she declared, her voice trembling slightly with fear. The demon laughed again; a sound that chilled them to their core, a laugh devoid of any humanity.

"You should be," it hissed, its voice a serpentine whisper that slithered through the air. "You stand in my domain, challenging powers beyond your comprehension," the demon sneered, its eyes glowing brighter. "You are all so weak, so fragile. I will break you, one by one."

"You expect us to be afraid of you, a nameless creature from Hell."

Denis, his resolve hardening, stepped beside Julie. "We've come too far to back down now." He whispered to her, then, in a more forceful voice said, "We stand united against you and all the darkness you represent."

"Be gone, foul spirit!" Father Ambrose commanded, his voice ringing with divine authority. "In the name of the Father, the Son, and the Holy Spirit, I cast you out!"

The demon's response was swift and terrifying. Its wings beat once, sending a gust of putrid air that almost knocked them off their feet. The creature leaned closer, its face a grotesque image. "You think you can defy me? I am ancient, I am as old as fear itself." It sneered. "I am Ah-Beh-Djoh!" It said raising its voice. "I AM FEAR!"

The air around them shimmered, and in a flash, they were no longer in the asylum but transported again to scenes of their own past traumas. Each member of the team ensnared in their own personal nightmares, it was feeding off their fear and sorrow. But even as they were submerged in their traumas, a part of them remained aware that this was the demon's doing, an attempt to weaken them.

Denis found himself standing beside the burning wreckage of a car, a crash in which both his parents died. He was seven years old, standing there, helpless, calling out for his mother and father. The searing heat of the flames engulfed him, the smell of burning metal, rubber and flesh assaulted his senses with ruthless intensity. He was back at that fateful, horrific night, a helpless child amidst the chaos of twisted metal and all-consuming fire. The night sky, once filled with stars, was blotted out by thick, acrid smoke.

The car, once used for joyful family outings, now a mangled wreck, the flames greedily consuming what was left of it. Denis, small and frightened, was frozen in horror. The glowing embers of the car cast an eerie, flickering light on his young face, tears cutting clean lines through the soot and grime as he called out for his parents. His voice, filled with fear and desperation, broke with each cry, "Mum!... Dad!..." But the only response was the crackling of fire and the distant wail of approaching sirens, sounds that were far too late to provide comfort.

He watched helplessly as firefighters put out the fire, their voices sounding distant and muffled, as if he were underwater. The world around him moved in a surreal, slow-motion blur, each moment etching itself indelibly into his young mind. Time seemed to stand still, each moment stretching into an eternity. Denis, trapped in this fragment of his past, sensed a familiar feeling of helplessness washing over him. Watching his world once again turning to ashes, unable to do anything.

This was the demon's doing, a cruel trick to break him, to use his deepest fears and memories against him. With this realisation, the scene before him began to waver as he concentrated on the present, the edges of that memory blurring, reality forcing its way back into his consciousness. Denis, a man again, stood with his colleagues in the room once more, his heart pounding in his ears, sweat mingling with the tears on his face. The horror of the past still echoed in his mind, but he clung desperately to the present. He was no longer that helpless child; he was a fighter, a survivor. With a deep, steadying breath, he finally pulled himself out of the grasp of his horror filled memories, and back into the reality of the asylum. The entity had failed to break him.

Father Ambrose had his own nightmare, he stood in the midst of a war-torn village, the scene unfolding around him as vivid and harrowing as it had been years ago. The smell of gunpowder filled the air, mingling with the metallic scent of blood. Buildings, once homes, reduced to rubble, walls scarred by the violence of war. As a young priest, he had arrived in the village, filled with a sense of purpose and faith, only to be confronted with the harsh reality of human suffering and cruelty. His white robes, a symbol of peace and hope, were now stained with the blood of those he had tried to comfort in their final moments.

Cries for help echoed in his ears, each plea a sharp reminder of his failure. He moved among the wounded, offering prayers and last rites, the haunting knowledge that he could not save them weighing heavily on his heart. Children, their faces etched with fear and confusion, clung to their fallen parents, their innocent eyes searching for help and soldiers, some mere boys, lay gasping their last breaths, dreams and hopes fading.

Father Ambrose, overwhelmed by his visions, fell to his knees, his hands trembling. He prayed fervently, not just for the souls around him but for some semblance of understanding, for some sign that their suffering was not in vain. The sense of helplessness and the guilt of being unable to offer more than prayers in the face of such overwhelming pain, enveloped him. The memory was a relentless tide, threatening to drown him in sorrow and despair.

But amidst the pain of his past, Father Ambrose fought hard to regain control. He reminded himself that this was not real, it was the demon's doing, a cruel illusion meant to weaken him. Relying on his faith and life experiences, he could overcome the painful memories and focus on the satisfaction he gained from aiding others.

Slowly, the sounds of war faded, the visions of the blood-soaked village dissipated. Father Ambrose was once again back in the asylum, his heart still racing, but his resolve stronger than ever.

Julie found herself in an ominous room that she remembered well, the memory so vivid it was as if no time had passed. The walls closing in around her, the shadows cast by flickering candles stretched and twisted casting eerie patterns on the walls. Her mentor, the woman who had introduced her to realms beyond the ordinary, lay lifeless on the floor. Her eyes, once bright with knowledge and wisdom, now dull and vacant, staring into nothingness. Julie remembered the shock that had gripped her. The paralysing realisation that the world of spirits and entities was far more dangerous and unpredictable than she had ever imagined. Julie could sense the entity they had accidentally summoned, a force that had lashed out with deadly consequences. She could hear her own breath, quick and shallow. The sense of isolation was overwhelming; she was alone, without her mentor's guidance, facing an unknown and terrifying power.

Julie's younger self was frozen with fear, kneeling beside her mentor, desperately hoping for some sign of life. But there was none. Overwhelmed by despair, she was hit with the bitter realisation that she was now alone, no guidance or protection. The room grew colder. The darkness pressed in on her. She could feel the entity moving around her, an unseen predator toying with its prey. The air, charged with its dark energy, sent shivers down her spine.

It was then that she experienced a touch, cold and spectral, against her cheek. A whisper, not in words but in sensations, slithered into her mind, a message of darkness and despair that sought to overwhelm her. But now, as she relived this memory, Julie understood now, what she had not back then. She felt the power held within herself growing with the knowledge and strength she had gained since that fateful night. Tapping into this newfound strength, Julie stood tall in the memory, confronting the unseen entity with a boldness she had not exhibited before. She spoke the banishment incantation with confidence and power in her voice.

The demon in her past recoiled, its presence diminishing as she continued to chant. The oppressive atmosphere of the room lifted, the shadows retreating from the candlelight. And then the vision shattered, the memory dissolved around her. She was back with her friends, her heart still racing, but her spirit emboldened. Knowing now that the demon had tried to use her past fears against her and feed off her past sorrows, and that she had confronted those fears and emerged stronger.

Fiona had returned to her childhood home, where her psychic abilities had caused her family to distance themselves from her. She was hiding in her room, her young ears straining to hear the words of her parents as they argued about her in hushed, fearful tones. The loneliness and confusion of those years weighed heavily on her, dragging her back into the isolation she had once felt so deeply. Fiona, in the solitude of her childhood room, surrounded by the echoes of her parents' fears, took a deep breath. She had long since come to terms with her abilities, embracing them as a part of who she was. As she accepted this once again, and drew strength from it, the walls of her childhood home faded, and she was brought back to the present.

As each of the four emerged from their own personal nightmares, they found themselves back in the asylum, united, together, unbroken. Having failed to break their spirits, the demon let out a frustrated howl that threatened to bring down the walls of the building.

Galvanised by their shared success, the team rallied to confront it again. knowing the battle would be difficult, but they had each other, together they stepped forward.

Father Ambrose, chanted in Latin, his words a shield against the darkness. "Exorciso te, omnis spiritus immunde, in nomine Dei Patris omnipotentis, et in nomine Jesu Christi Filii eius, Domini et Judicis nostri."

The demon spoke in a rasping, guttural tone. "Do you think your words can harm me? I reign supreme here! Your god is powerless in my realm." The demon laughed, it was a chilling sound that reverberated around the room, "You think your faith can banish me, priest? You are nothing against my darkness."

Denis raised his crucifix. "The Almighty God, in His supreme authority, commands you. He whom you, in your boundless arrogance, dared to consider yourself equal to. The God who desires the salvation and enlightenment of all humanity. The Father commands you. The Son commands you. The Holy Spirit commands you. Christ, the Word of God incarnate, commands you; He who brought about our salvation now casts you out, wickedness vanquished by your own envy. Return to where you belong. Back to the depths of Hell, I command you... be gone!"

The demon let out a rasping laugh. "You are pathetic. You cannot banish Ah-Beh-Djoh."

Fiona and Julie splashed Holy Water towards it and wafted the white sage smoke in its direction. The demon opened its mouth and spewed forth a torrent of shadows, a black mist that absorb the light. The Holy Water sizzled as it contacted the shadows, evaporating into hissing steam. The sage smoke twisted and recoiled, as if repulsed by the shadows emitting from the demon. Julie, her face a mask of determination, chanted more incantations, her voice rising above the chaos. "Lux Christi te imperat! Fugere ad infernum!" Her words imbued with power and confidence cut through the darkness like a beacon of hope.

The demon, its form flickering and warping under the assault of their faith, sneered. "You cannot defeat me. I have dwelt in the shadows from the start of time, I feed on the fears and despair of mere mortals. I am fear itself!"

Father Ambrose, undaunted by the demon's words, continued his chant, his voice unwavering. "In the name of the Holy Trinity, I command you, Ah-Beh-Djoh, leave this place!"

Denis, his arms aching from holding the crucifix aloft, could feel a surge of fresh energy being emitted by the symbol of his faith. The air was crackling with an unseen battle of wills, the forces of light clashing against the darkness.

Fiona, moving forward, continued to sprinkle Holy Water, each droplet shining like a star against the encroaching shadows. "By the power of the Holy Spirit, be gone, demon!"

The demon's laugh turned into a roar of rage. The room trembled, the walls seeming to buckle under the violence of its anger. Objects were lifted and hurled towards them by the demon's unseen force. Julie was caught by a flying book, but her determination was unbroken as she continued her incantations. "Tibi imperamus, virtute Dei, daemon, hinc abire.!"

The demon's head reared back, eyes clenched shut, gathering the very essence of malice and darkness within itself. Opening its mouth wide, it threatened to unleash untold horrors upon them. At that moment, in an act of sheer audacity and bravery, Fiona dashed forward. Her movements were swift and decisive, her face was set with a determination that belied her fear. In her hand, a vial of Holy Water glistened, a small yet potent weapon against the darkness that loomed before them.

The demon, sensing her approach, snapped its eyes open. Its gaze, swirling flames of hatred, fixed upon her. But Fiona did not falter, with a cry that echoed the depth of her resolve, she thrust the vial into the demon's gaping mouth, pouring the Holy Water into the very heart of the beast.

The effect was instantaneous and dramatic. A savage howl burst from the demon, a sound drenched in pain and rage, reverberating through the asylum and shaking its very foundations. The Holy Water, imbued with the purity and power of faith, hit the demon, a light piercing through the darkness. The room shook, the walls themselves cried out as the demon convulsed. Its form flickering, warping, shadows and light clashing within it in a tumultuous battle. The Holy Water sizzled within the demon, emitting steam that filled the air with a sound like a thousand serpents recoiling in agony.

Denis and Father Ambrose in unison recited the exorcism prayer. "Exorciso te, omnis spiritus immunde, in nomine Dei Patris omnipotentis, et in nomine Jesu Christi Filii eius, Domini et Judicis nostri."

"Again." said Father Ambrose.

"Exorciso te, omnis spiritus immunde, in nomine Dei Patris omnipotentis, et in nomine Jesu Christi Filii eius, Domini et Judicis nostri."

"AGAIN!" He shouted.

They both stepped forward, taking a deep breath, and with all the strength they could muster loudly recited, "EXORCISO TE, OMNIS SPIRITUS IMMUNDE, IN NOMINE DEI PATRIS OMNIPOTENTIS, ET IN NOMINE JESU CHRISTI FILII EIUS, DOMINI ET JUDICIS NOSTRI."

Julie watched in stunned silence, her own fears momentarily forgotten in the face of Fiona's courageous act. The demon, its body contorting in unnatural ways, lost its form, dissolving into a shapeless, twisting cloud of darkness.

Energy filled the air, creating a storm of conflicting forces. The room darkened even more as the demon fought against their prayers. Its roars becoming desperate, pained, no longer the confident taunts of a superior being but the agonised cries of a creature facing its demise.

Fiona, standing her ground, shouted over the evil screams, her voice resolute and clear. "In the name of all that is Holy, we banish you!"

Father Ambrose joined in, "Be gone, Ah-Beh-Djoh, creature of darkness! You are not welcome in this world! We banish you to the depths of hell!"

Denis, moved by their display of bravery and faith, stepped forward, and thrust his crucifix deep into the swirling mass that was the demon. "By the light that vanquishes all shadows, we command you to return to the depths whence you came!"

Julie, her hands clasped tightly together, added her voice to the chorus, "We stand united against you, demon. Your reign here is over!" she said as she stepped forward and threw the rest of her Holy Water at the demon.

Now just a vortex of shadows, it let out one final, ear-piercing screech. which reverberated through the room so loudly, plaster fell from the walls. The demon then vanished into the closest mirror. Denis and Father Ambrose smashed that mirror and moving swiftly around the room broke the remaining two mirrors using their crucifixes. Instantly the chaos ceased, the darkness lifted, dissipating like mist under the morning sun.

The four of them stood there, lungs aching, hearts racing, adrenaline from the sheer intensity of the battle they had just fought overwhelming them. The room, once a stronghold of evil and fear, now felt like any other, free of the oppressive presence that had once controlled it.

Julie closed her eyes, inhaling deeply, "There is one more spirit we need to rid this place of. It is weak, but the other spirits here fear it. It is the doctor, the one who used to experiment on the bodies and minds of the innocents that were housed here."

Once more they prayed together, demanding that he leave this building, to walk into the light and receive judgement for his past. After a time Fiona, her chest heaving with exertion, looked at her companions, a mixture of disbelief and triumph in her eyes. "We did it. He's gone. They are both gone. All the other spirits in this place are now free to leave."

Father Ambrose, his usual composed self, allowed the beginnings of a smile to grace his features. He bowed his head slightly, "Through faith and unity, we have prevailed."

Denis let his gaze wander around the now peaceful room, he felt a sense of awe at what they had achieved. "We faced our fears, our darkest moments, yet here we are, victorious."

Julie, her eyes moist with unshed tears, whispered, "Yes, we've freed this place, and ourselves, from a darkness that had lingered here too long."

As they stepped out of the room, they knew their lives would never be the same. They had come face to face with something that defied understanding, a darkness that sought to consume not just the asylum but their very souls. And yet they had emerged alive, not just individuals, but a united force. The asylum, once a symbol of despair and horror, now stood silent, its corridors no longer echoing with the cries of tormented spirits. The team walked through its halls, their steps confident in the newfound stillness. Each footfall a testament to their triumph over the evil that had been there.

Outside, the dawn was breaking, casting its light upon the old building. The morning sun cleansing the last vestiges of the night's terror, bathing the asylum in a warm, golden glow. The air was fresh, free of the overwhelming heaviness that had once hung over the place. As they stood outside, looking back at the building that had been the stage for their battle against the darkness, they felt a sense of relief.

Reaching the command centre, the rest of team welcomed them with applause, praising their courageous efforts. I turned to Fiona. "What about your three friends? Are they safe?"

Fiona, her eyes brimming with tears, shook her head. "We found no trace of them, and I couldn't sense their presence, not even after the demon was defeated. I fear they might be lost." Overcome with emotion, she buried her face in her hands, her shoulders shaking with sobs.

At that moment Alex, who had been methodically shutting down the equipment, suddenly froze. Pointing at one of the monitors, he exclaimed, "Look! What's that?"

Everyone's attention snapped to the screen, fearful of what they might see. On it, three figures could be seen staggering out of the building, looking confused. A wave of excitement washed over the team as they left the van, rushing towards them.

It was, Carl, Mark, and Janet, the missing members of the team. Relief and joy erupted in a chorus of cheers and hugs. "We're so relieved you're safe," they echoed, their voices a mixture of joy and disbelief.

The reunion was emotional, tears and laughter mingling in the cool morning air. The ordeal was over, and against all odds, they had emerged safe and sound.

Fiona wiped away her tears. "What happened? Where were you?"

Carl shook his head. "I don't know; we had some help. A spirit or ghost maybe? I don't know what it was, it kept us hidden. I don't know where, but we felt safe."

Julie nodded, a gentle smile on her face. "It was Emily, Steve's sister." Julie turned to me with a soft smile. "Emily is here, Steve. She's been waiting for this moment. Would you like to speak with her?"

My eyes filled with tears. "Yes, yes, please. Can she hear me?"

Julie, with unshed tears, smiled and nodded again.

My heart pounded in my chest, a mix of grief and disbelief swirling within me. "Emily... is it really you? Are you here?"

The air seemed to hum with a gentle energy, before manifesting into a gentle golden glow, and there, amid the glow, Emily's form appeared. Her expression was one of peace and love, a sharp contrast to the chaotic memories I held of the last time I saw her.

"Steve," her voice, soft and ethereal, filled my heart. Her words carrying the power of their enduring bond, unbroken by time or distance.

Tears rolled down my cheeks as I gazed at the shimmering form of my little sister. "Emily, I've missed you so much. I'm sorry, I'm so sorry I wasn't there for you. I couldn't save you. Please forgive me."

Emily's smile was tender and forgiving. "It's okay. You were always there for me, in ways you never knew. I've been watching over you. Hoping one day you would believe."

I felt overwhelmed by emotion, struggling to find the words. "I didn't believe... I couldn't... until now."

"I know, and it's alright. Coming to believe was your journey to make, and you've made it. I've always been proud of you, big brother."

"Can you stay? Please, don't go," my voice braking, the child within me reaching out for the sister I lost.

Emily's face took on a bittersweet expression. "I'm sorry Steve, I can't stay. It's my time to move on, but I needed to see you one last time. To tell you I love you, that everything is alright and I'm at peace."

The Emily's form started to fade, the moment slipping away like grains of sand through open fingers.

"Emily! Wait! I love you little sis."

"And I love you Steve. I always will," Emily's voice echoed, as her image vanished, leaving behind a lingering warmth in the air.

I stood there, tears streaming down my face, my heart filled with a mix of sorrow and gratitude. Julie placed a comforting hand on my shoulder, silent support in this moment of grief and closure.

I took a deep breath, a sense of peace settled over me. "Goodbye, Emily," I whispered, a last farewell to a beloved sister who would forever live in my heart.

The whole team, not a dry eye among them, shared a silent, respectful moment, honouring the poignant farewell between siblings, a testament to the unbreakable bonds of love that transcends even death. In that moment, among the tears and soft whispers, came a profound understanding that while some goodbyes were forever, the memories and love they carried would always remain.

Back in my flat, after everyone had left I sought refuge in a long, steaming shower, desperate to wash away the harrowing events that clung to my thoughts. I tried to push the grim memories aside, focusing instead on my sister's image and her parting words. After the shower, I prepared for bed, my mind a turbulent sea of thoughts. Staring into the mirror, toothbrush in hand, I scrutinised my reflection with an intensity that bordered on madness. "It's going to take ages to process everything that's happened," I thought, my inner voice a whisper of exhaustion.

I rinsed my mouth, switched off the light, and got into bed, hoping that sleep would come easily, and without the nightmares of the last few days. A wave of tiredness swept over me; I fell instantly to sleep.

In the night's silence, a faint cracking sound whispered from the mirror in the bathroom. Behind the glass, a shadowy cloud swirled, a barely perceptible face appeared at its heart, its red glowing eyes looking out into the room. The glass quivered and through the thin crack in its surface, a single fly slowly emerged. It buzzed around the room for a while before coming to land on the closed bathroom door.